Praise for Liz J. Andersen & *Some of My Best Friends Are Human*

"Excellent . . . . But you'll probably have to shorten it to sell it."

—Andre Norton (Okay, it took a while. RIP, dear friend)

"*Some of My Best Friends Are Human* is adventure with heart! A ripping good yarn told with grit and grace by a professional cat wrangler. Who says SF can't be fun and scientifically accurate?"

—Erika, Cat Lady and Professional Nit-Picker

"Liz never would have made it through the Sierra Nevada without me, but she sure can ride a runaway horse."

—Carla, Backpacking Buddy

"I haven't read the book but I love the cover!"

—Kathy, Artistic Consultant

"Which character am I?"

—Brian, Liz's Musician Husband, and, eerily, not present for the first drafts of this novel

"Don't forget, I gave Liz the title. But I thought this book was supposed to be funny. All of the stories I helped Liz write for Analog were funny. Instead this is just one fur-raising adventure after another."

—Tommy, Liz's Cat

Some of My Best Friends Are Human

Some of My Best Friends Are Human

Liz J. Andersen

Labbwerk Publishing
Eugene

Labbwerk Publishing, Eugene 97404

Printed in the United States of America
ISBN 978-0-9988448-0-0 (paperback)

Labbwerk Publishing gratefully acknowledges the generous support of:
Kathy Baron: Cover Design
Anders Andersen: Front Cover Painting
Søren Østergaard: Front Cover Painting Photo
(Front Cover Painting Color Adjustments by Labbwerk Publishing)
T.J.: Front Cover Silhouette Drawings
Carla Salido: Spine Photograph
Terry Whittaker: Back Cover Caracal Photo
(Caracal Photo Color Adjustments by Labbwerk Publishing and Kathy Baron)

Names: Andersen, Liz J., author.
Titles: Some of my best friends are human / Liz J. Andersen
Identifiers: ISBN 9780998844800 (softcover)
ISBN 9780998844817 (electronic book)
Subjects: LCSH: Bildungsromans. | Coming of age—Fiction. | Ecology—Fiction. | Extraterrestrial beings—Fiction. | Friendship—Fiction. | Multiculturalism—Fiction. | Transgenic organisms—Fiction.
GSAFD: Science fiction. | Adventure fiction.
Classification: DDC 813/.6—dc23
OCLC Record: 1013677229

For My Friends,

Past, Present, and Future

PART 1

INSIDE

JOURNAL ENTRY 1

The very first multiple choice question fused me: "How do plant pigments relate to the color of the sky?" Correct answer: hardly at all—and even less to my own life. That was the problem. That was always the problem, since I was shipped to the Center.

So I ejected from an exploding space ship into hard vac, when I discovered I couldn't bring myself to answer a single question on Naemar's science exam. The last question had the nerve to ask how to age an old-growth tree without damaging it. At that point I gave up. How I hated it here!

The end-of-class bell rang after an agonizing eon. Branem, the stocky, handsome human who sat next to me in the last row, slotted his stylus and stood up with a sigh.

Branem had smooth very milky brown skin and a typical hint of an epicanthic fold, so his brown eyes narrowed as he peeked at my screen. He tossed his curly black bangs as he grinned at the red STAY warning flashing on my screen. "Good luck!" he said. At least he never treated me like a human freak.

"I'm out of luck."

"No you're not." And with that ridiculously optimistic remark, he pushed his way through the noisy rush to evacuate our science classroom.

I laid my head down on my arms. Last class of the day, and I had to pull this stunt. Pulse pounding, I peeked at my teacher.

Naemar stood over her deskcom. She must already know. Sweat ran down my sides and steamed from my collar. Naemar stared at our test results on her screen and squinted up at me. She strode down the aisle that led between our crowded desk rows, turned left at the last row, and halted in front of me.

Here comes the big lecture about studying, which I thought I'd never have to hear—

"What's the matter, Tajen?" Naemar folded her tan arms and loomed over me, despite being the shortest adult human I'd ever met. Yet she sounded surprisingly calm.

I rubbed my eyes. What *wasn't* the matter, being stuck in a Federation of Intelligent Life Orphan Center on Arrainius? "Where are the stars?" I whispered, barely holding back tears.

I hadn't meant to say such nova nonsense loudly enough to hear, but she took it seriously. "This test covered our plant module. We'll get to astronomy—"

"There are too many lights on Arrainius to view any stars without going to sea, so why bother? For that matter, why talk about old-growth trees when they no longer exist on this world?"

"Oh, so this isn't just about my subject material?"

"Your subject matter?" I exploded from my seat, launched by rage I'd kept locked up for far too long—

over half a dozen standard years since my mother had disappeared, ruining everything. “Why don’t you shove all this vac-brained garbage up your right nostril?” I said. “It should fit perfectly!”

I knocked over my multi-species chair in my rush to escape the classroom, so I wouldn’t break down in front of her.

If I could have broken out of the Center in that micro, I would have. Even with nowhere to go. Instead all I could do was lose myself in the end-of-school-day crowds.

JOURNAL ENTRY 2

I wiped unshed tears out of my eyes as students wound through a maze of light green walls below a pale blue ceiling, both of course completely graffiti-proof.

Rumor had it that authorities designed the Center maze to keep us from feeling too shut in, and selected wall and ceiling colors from our commonest planets to keep us calmer, as if we lived among meadows under tranquil skies. But the walls had developed an unfortunate muddy sheen, and beyond a certain point, the baby-blue ceilings simply annoyed most of us. In other words, they only seemed to soothe babies.

I suspected the Federation of Intelligent Life had given up long ago on trying to help us, after getting the brilliant idea of efficiently housing planetary overflow orphans with similar environmental needs in various galactic sector facilities. Where of course hardly anyone wanted to make the effort to travel, only to risk an adoption that might not work out. Fertility treatments and local orphans made us nearly useless anyway.

Maybe that's also why FIL hardly ever put any credits into expanding the original Orphan Centers.

I squeezed into one of a row of stuffy translifts and punched a manual control panel, since it was still too noisy for voice command.

At last I noticed other students' alarmed stares, and worked at releasing my fists and ungritting my teeth, while we spilled into an unfamiliar hall. Blue carpet—Five. Space, I'd missed my whole Level!

I bumped my way back against traffic into the lift.

"Taje is a GMO with kluormahx hair-color genes!" Cam shouted out his dangerous joke to Trist in my green-carpeted Level Six hallway, as soon as I arrived.

I should have immediately zapped the coppery-scaled young Lorratian. But instead I froze a micro out of range of my door's sensor.

Shandy would know.

Blast it all, why hadn't I remained the shy, quiet student in the back of the classroom? The one who always made obediently good marks and never complained what a nova waste of time it all was? Who even told Aerrem she should pay more attention to her grades, if she ever wanted to do anything important with her life.

I shuddered. As one of my best teachers, Naemar hadn't even deserved my outburst. But somehow my roommate, Shanden Fehrokc, always seemed to know when I felt fused—no matter what it was about or how I acted—and he'd want to know why.

Aerrem has warned me repeatedly that I'm a vacfully poor liar. And maybe that included my emotions, which had reached terminal velocity today.

Or maybe Shandy had simply learned the hard way to notice problems fast. He hadn't ever told me why, but he'd already failed with several roommates before he got me, on my first try out of a dorm family.

So it was too bad I'd rather plummet into a black hole.

Someone in the hall traffic bumped me from behind, I stumbled forward, and my door noticed me and slid open. So I had to vector inside. The Center lay almost entirely underground, but it was hardly ever dark or private enough to hide in.

JOURNAL ENTRY 3

A micro later I remembered to breathe, and I let out a muffled sigh of relief.

Nova homework had already consumed Shandy. Chin in hand, he sat bent over his deskcom so his thin yellow-orange shirt, layered over another thin long-sleeved pale blue shirt, outlined his knobby spine. (It was another source of teasing, and I used to wonder why he wore so much orange, until he told me it reminded him of his homeworld.)

Shandy prodded his blond bangs out of his eyes with his stylus, but he didn't even glance at us when Max squealed and ambushed me at the front door.

I picked up my squirming young kluormahx before he used his horns to playfully poke another hole in the cuffs of my baggy, ill-fitting pants from Central Supply. (Our choices were simple. Shorts or pants or skirts. T-shirts or blouses or tunics or robes. Pocket belts and sashes for kids with scales or fur or feathers. You could choose any color, but it was all made from the same cheap, thin synthetic. Like we'd outgrow it all before it wore out. Sure. It was more like we weren't worth anything better.)

Most kids who wore clothes chose T-shirts with shorts, blouses and skirts, or tunics for our controlled environment, so I looked odd enough without sporting unexplained rips around my semi-protected ankles. I needed to get around to filing Max's horns, now that I was through uselessly cramming for my science test.

I hugged Max, and hurried through Shandy's small, narrow, but neat front section of our room to my own little cluttered refuge in back. (Rumor had it these used to be undivided single rooms.)

Sheefharn, Shandy's vlordabird, zapped me with her usual glare, and snapped her crest at me from the top of our grilled divider. Vac-headed, ugly bird. I stuck out my tongue at her.

I tried to ignore her as I faced the chaos threatening to overwhelm my section. Like my whole day today, some late-night snack trays had begun to stink. I set Max down so I could shove the trays back into my food dispenser.

I should have sorted most of the clothes on the floor and my bed for the cleanser chute, but an even bigger mess distracted me. My normally fascinating colony of tiny hairless ubucs had pitched food pellets everywhere, from their terrarium on my dresser. I'd forgotten to put the top back on after feeding them this morning. Shame on me. They came from an offworld desert environment and needed to stay warm.

I shoved the cover back on and increased the heat setting on a timer, so I wouldn't forget again and roast the poor critters.

Next I quickly turned to my desktop aquarium, where Stripes and Ribbon, two electric-blue and red fringed glippers, undulated hungrily, too distracted by my arrival to take advantage of the ubuc pellets that had landed in their tank. Thank the Galaxy, because these fish were native to this planet, and had entirely different nutritional needs. Who knew what ubuc pellets would do to them.

Fortunately my glippers also ignored the blue and orange feathers which must have floated out from the queet cage on the shelf over my bed. Molting Squeaker waddled out of her feather-lined nest and quivered her antennae nervously at me, while Max circled my ankles and cried for attention.

Max was a young rescue from a terrible import store, and I had bought him with my silence. I felt guilty about that every time I looked at him. But we had fallen instantly in love, his price was otherwise out of my league, and I couldn't leave him in his cramped, filthy cage, or keep my big mouth shut in the shop.

I plucked soft clumps of Max-hairs off the mahogany shirt I'd picked to hide his shedding fur. (Fortunately the Center com runs Central Supply, and it's too stupid to wonder why I never order more than one color for my shirts and pants now.) I gazed dazedly at the whole stupefying, claustrophobic mess. How could I possibly hide all of this in time, if honor guards ever came to search my room for any reason?

Fortunately I'd greatly lowered that risk by leaving the pet-smuggling business, and I couldn't think of any other reason for a search, unless I got very careless with my pets. But how had I managed to let myself get this tied down?

"I fed Max for you." Shandy's gaze remained locked on his comscreen. "He was getting rather impatient."

"He already seems to know exactly when I'm due back. I wasn't all that late, was I?" I bit my trembling lip and my hands shook as I measured out proper glipper food.

Stripes and Ribbon went for the bait, while I fished out waterlogged queet feathers, ubuc pellets, and clogged filter packs, and hauled the whole mess into our bathroom. Max whined at my heels, and I lowered our universal toilet for him.

I made it through the rest of my pet chores on automatic pilot. Next I collapsed cross-legged on the floor, with my deskcom screen in my lap and my back against my bed.

Alongside me, Max flopped down with a frustrated moan, his short legs splayed and fuzzy chin on the carpet. I absentmindedly petted his plush mahogany coat. Unfortunately his fur was too dark and richly colored to look anything like my weird light red hair, which I kept hacked short.

And Cam shouldn't even joke about a pet in Center hallways. Or make fun of transgenic people, especially in front of Trist. It's rude to call anyone a GMO, even when it's scientifically accurate. Cam's joke still irritated me. I should have zapped him back.

Instead I tried to shut the whole day out as I checked for messages from friends. Branem's grinning face appeared. "Trust me. You don't need to worry about what happened today." That was all, and I didn't know him well enough to believe him.

So instead I scanned through some of my stored artwork, mostly drawings of animals and friends, or dorm-clutter still lifes. But today all their flaws launched straight at me.

I could never get Aerrem's amazing fluffy brown hair or Cam's intricate copper scale patterns quite right. And one might guess Max was never conscious, because he only held still long enough to draw when he was asleep.

Shandy steadfastly refused to pose for me, so my sketches of him were the worst—done quickly on the sly, with him napping or his back turned; or from memory, which must be stunningly bad, considering we shared the same room.

It was a shame, because Shandy had an interesting face, obviously very smart, a bit exotic in an elfish sort of way, and not as bony as the rest of him.

I never drew Shandy as short or skinny as he really was, because to me he was a big friend. But I couldn't com why every portrait I attempted made him look like some pasty inhabitant from a zombie holo, instead of a human roomie—

Truthfully, I had lost most of my youthful interest in art, although I had friends and teachers who wanted me to keep at it. Now I saved all my work from reckless deletion by quickly switching to a scene from my holo collection of Smooth Worlds.

A great scaly rolling length broke through the churning surf near the base of a dark, jagged cliff. The emerald-green serpent stared at me with golden eyes, while two blue-grey fisher hawks soared free overhead.

Suddenly I felt so jealous I ached—

"What's the matter, Taje?"

I looked up, and swallowed hard along with Shandy.

He stood now in the open doorway to the right of our divider, which he gripped white-knuckled as he swayed slightly. I normally took it for granted that my roommate appeared even paler and thinner than I did.

So I guess I only managed to notice he seemed slightly dizzy because I scanned for it on autopilot, ever since I'd found him passed out on our carpet near the end of first quarter.

"Did you have trouble with your science exam? Is that why you got out late?"

Zap! Just like that, Shandy had read me like a first grader's edprogram. Even then I wondered how deeply his intuition had led him—to the deepest, most nova secret I wasn't ready to share with anyone?

I switched to another holo, a riding trail in the woods on Donshore, my homeworld. But all the colors washed together, and I squeezed my eyes shut.

Shandy returned to his deskcom, and I slipped into our bathroom to have my cry in the privacy of our shower.

JOURNAL ENTRY 4

The day slid further into a trash cycler as I started to undress and discovered my belt pouch was missing.

I'd spent part of my science test silently inventing a new theory for the beginning of our universe. Why use a vacful old term like the Big Bang, when—unlike the results of a normal explosion—everything in our universe is flying apart faster and faster? Why not call it the Big Suck?

Obviously that didn't take me the whole hour to com. So I spent the rest of my time looking up my credit status on my ID and reviewing the contents of my belt pouch (an extra comscreen, stylus, hairbrush, pet treats, etc.). Great Galaxy, I must have left my pouch behind. So much for my already nearly hopeless idea of simply never returning to class.

I ducked into the shower so Shandy couldn't hear me weeping. But the progress of my gradually enlarging nipples fused my mood further, and I covered them up with my wash cloth. I was human, so next came breasts, but why should I ever want to grow up? Human adults seemed far more alien than any Center resident, but now even my own body was changing on me.

I rubbed the recent injection site on my left hip, while tears streamed down my face. Other kids celebrated their microchip injections, and I got mine late, but I wouldn't have minded being even more late. The chip, a tiny artificial birth control gland slipped under my skin, was also supposed to suppress mood swings along with some messy discharge, but I wouldn't be the first human girl to question its complete effectiveness.

I dried off and dressed only after my fingertips began to shrivel up. Then I faced my roommate in his half of our room. Shandy looked up, startled.

"How did you guess?" I quickly demanded, trying to override a quiver in my voice.

"What?"

Sometimes Shandy also acted surprisingly vac-headed!

"You're right," I said, "I crashed my science test. In fact, I left it totally blank, and finished it off by telling my teacher she could stuff it all up her right nostril." The memory burned on my face.

Sheefharn squawked, flapped around the room twice, shedding some of her human puke-colored feathers, and landed on Shandy's desk. The nova Istrannian bird captured Shandy's brown-eyed gaze—the only part of him that proved he wasn't an albino. People like Shandy and I weren't in most stories, except as rare bad guys in thrillers, because we didn't look like most humans. We were living proof that pale-skinned humans weren't quite extinct.

Shandy stroked Sheefharn's soft chest feathers with his long, gentle fingers. Long thin fingers that added to his cruel skeletal reputation. But even in my fused despair and anger, I couldn't help admiring the bond between my roommate and his bird. Jealous Max butted my ankles, and I scooped him back up into my arms.

Shandy coughed and his bangs curtained back over his eyes. "You've only complained about all your classes, especially science, for as long as I've known you. I thought I'd never hear the end of it last night. Besides . . ."

"Besides what?" I backed up against the opposite wall, as if there wasn't room for what he'd say next.

"Uh, well, I happened to notice—when I fed Max—that Squeaker is pregnant."

"Again?" Gravity suddenly won. I slid down the wall and landed in a puddled heap on the floor. I let go of Max so I could sob into my hands.

Queets come from a fiercely competitive jungle ecosystem, and they're perfectly capable of parthenogenic reproduction at the first hint of environmental stress. It's their only defense.

I'd tried so hard not to trigger mine again, after I'd learned the first time. Squeaker, like most of us here, was a throwaway. The Center queet market was already flooded—hardly anyone lives stress-free here. Aerrem would zap me!

Our door buzzed, and Shandy got up to tell our hall servocleaner to come back some other time. Our door slid closed as the cleaner rolled away. Shandy sat back down at his desk, and waited respectfully for me to finish crying. "Are you in a lot of trouble?" he asked at last, very quietly.

"I don't know. I've at least flunked the test. Oh, blast it all, I must be. But the worst part is facing Naemar again, after what I said to her." My stomach opened up a deep cold bottomless pit, and I toppled into it. Not exactly the escape of my dreams.

JOURNAL ENTRY 5

I woke up in a cold queasy sweat well before my alarm went off the next morning. And I couldn't even pretend to sleep any longer when Shandy threw my clothes at me.

"Hurry up," he said, "or I won't have time to walk with you to Naemar's office before breakfast."

Max and I both groaned, but the bribe got me up. Last night Shandy had suggested I see my teacher privately during her office hours, before I had to confront her again in front of the whole class.

Maybe he came along now to make sure I didn't back out at the last micro, or crash my time on wrong turns. But having a loyal roomie at my side still felt good on that vacful walk to the teachers' offices.

I stopped a little beyond range of Naemar's door sensor to thank Shandy. "I hope you weren't serious about that breakfast," I added, heart pounding. I wasn't sure which of us looked sicker this morning.

Shandy shrugged and smiled and looked down, so his hair fell back over his eyes. He scuffed the carpet with a sneaker—a rare choice in this temperate building. Most of us wore sandals. But maybe his obviously long feet embarrassed him. I never saw him barefoot.

I commed his illness also embarrassed him. I'd noticed human males don't seem to like to admit to any weakness. Even if it's beyond anyone's control, and even if it means nearly dropping dead without warning.

I expected it then, but Shandy didn't leave. He stood stubbornly waiting for me to enter the office. "Never prolong the inevitable," he'd reminded me of one of Aerrem's favorite sayings last night. So I nodded.

"Naemar's a decent teacher," I reminded myself, but all it did was make me feel guiltier. This wasn't her fault. I took a deep breath and plunged in alone.

"Ah, Tajen Jesmuhr." Naemar glanced up from her deskcom as her door slid shut behind me. "Take a seat."

Good teacher or not, I suddenly felt so trapped I needed all my willpower to keep from jettisoning again. But if she hadn't already, I couldn't let Naemar look inside my belt pouch and see those pet treats.

I hunkered down in the human-style seat, one of several chairs parked in front of my teacher's desk. I sat there sweating while Naemar rushed to finish some notes, probably for another vacful lecture. At least her smooth face still revealed no anger, oddly enough—

"So. My quietest student has come to talk to me at last," she said.

I'd scanned how vac-brained rebellion landed kids in the nasty section of Level Two. So why on Arrainius had I done this to myself? Because I couldn't stand to waste any more of my time. I stared at the grey carpet in mute terror.

"I doubt all my exam questions completely stumped you yesterday. Are you this frustrated with all your classes, or is science a special case?"

Sadly, science was my favorite subject. "It's all so useless," I muttered softly.

"What?"

"I'm not learning anything I want to know!" it suddenly blasted out of me. "GIP is a filthy lying cheat!"

"I realize the General Instruction Program is a name ripe for ridicule, but I wish you students wouldn't call it that." Yet a baffling hint of a smile now twitched at the corners of Naemar's wide lips. "I've reviewed your records, Taje. Why in space aren't you in the Honors Program?"

Because I'd become an expert at losing myself in the protective cover of the crowds here, and teachers had discovered me too late. Because it had intimidated my brain waves into random white noise when I sat in on some of the Honors classes. And because even if I black-holed it to catch up, the Honors Program still offered nothing I needed. I bit my lip, determined not to cry in front of her.

"Taje, this Center is far too big for us to sort you all out the way we should," Naemar broke the silence at last. "You have to talk to somebody if your edprogram isn't right. What do you want to learn?"

I gulped at her, stunned. No one had ever bothered to ask me that before. No one. The question zapped me so hard I wanted to tell her the truth.

Sure, admit I needed wilderness skills, deep animal and plant biology, planetary science, and first aid. Oh—and by the way—let's throw in a way to leave the

Center on more than a fused day pass, before I rotted to death in here.

"Forget it," I said to her caramel-colored face, framed by her perfectly braided hair. She'd probably grown up in a real family. "You can't help me."

"How can you be so sure? The Center offers a variety of special edprograms—"

"No." I knew all about the special programs, and I didn't care about any of them. Aerrem's younger sister, Trist, having apparently inherited all the Nathegorn family ambition, had already gotten into the engineering program. Hurray. "There's nothing for me."

"You're that sure? How about one of these?" Naemar tapped her deskscreen, and a short list appeared on my side.

I skimmed a list of programs I'd never seen before, but it was the very first entry that kept catching my eye. "Planetary ecology? With field trips?" I coughed. "The Center has a whole offworld ecology program?" It seemed too close to be true.

Naemar grinned as she leaned back in her black padded chair. "Of course you picked an especially challenging one. You'd have to pass an essay question to get in. Think you can handle it?"

Shandy and I—even Aerrem for that matter, and a close circle of friends—studied wilderness ecologies despite the torment involved, in what little free time our vac-brained homework allowed us. Who wouldn't, having to live on totally overbuilt Arrainius, especially after coming from planets with real wildernesses? All of us knew what it was like to hike or ride where there was no sign of civilization, not that far from home. So we gobbled up holos of natural ecosystems like candy.

"Can I see the question?" I said, actually eager.

"Certainly." She tapped her screen again at the listing, and the essay question appeared: "Why is planetary ecology important to the Federation of Intelligent Life? Be detailed and specific."

My heart plummeted and crashed into deep rage as I stood up. I should have remembered I'd had to check hope in at the door when I was shipped here. "This is completely fused!"

"What do you mean?"

"Why, I'd have to cover the entire history of FIL, right back to the discovery of paraspace, the Great Colony Rushes, and even earlier. Historians have recorded whole series on this subject. This is totally nova—"

"Taje—"

"You might as well shove this—"

"Sit down, Taje, before you say something we'll both regret. I should have warned you I'm recording this session, but I was up late last night preparing for classes, and I forgot. I have to record all meetings with students." She saw the look of disgust on my face. "It's actually for your protection," she added hurriedly. "And you've already passed this test."

My jaw dropped as I crash-landed back in my seat. "I what?"

"You passed. You clearly possess a more than sufficient idea of what you're getting yourself into, which is all this test is really designed to determine. Congratulations!"

"I already—passed? Oh. Uh, smooth. I mean, thanks." My face flared hotly and no doubt very visibly, since only freckles kept me from scanning almost as inhumanly pale as Shandy.

"You can thank me by passing my final with your usual high marks, so our ed committee won't ask why I'm suddenly flunking one of my best students. Or why I'm transferring you to an advanced program after end-of-school-year break."

"Uh," I said again, "okay." I felt so stunned I had trouble making words.

"In fact, why don't you retake yesterday's test today, and pass it with flying colors?"

"Um, sure."

"And you can thank me by keeping this transfer to yourself," Naemar said. "We have good reasons why some Center programs aren't common knowledge, so you should not feel free to discuss this with anyone else. Is that clear?"

"Yeah, I guess," I said, startled, though it really wasn't any clearer than a glipper tank with a broken filter.

"Good. Now we have that on record as well. Meanwhile, have you had any breakfast this morning?"

"No. Why?"

"Better hurry. Classes start soon." She turned back to her own work, a harried look on her face.

"Oh. Right." I got up, choking on questions, and almost made it to the door.

"Taje!"

"What?" I spun around, hoping against hope for some micro crumb of extra explanation.

"You shouldn't leave this lying around." Naemar smiled as she handed over my belt pouch. Had she looked inside it? "And I'm very sorry," she said, "but

I'm stretched way too thin to tell you more. Just please promise me you'll talk to someone if this new program still isn't right for you."

"Well, okay. Uh, thanks." I smiled back at her. I sprinted to the nearest translift, after only a couple of wrong turns. I didn't make it to breakfast, and I didn't care. I did make it to class on time, and I tried hard to pay attention, for all the good it did me that day.

And that's how this whole mess began.

JOURNAL ENTRY 6

Of course that evening I told Shandy all about my nova talk with Naemar. Except how to pass the test, since we're not cheaters. But how could I keep the rest a secret?

Shandy wasn't "anyone else"—he was my loyal roomie. We both ran late in class that day, so we met for dinner at our usual back corner table, in one of the smaller snack bars. It felt less claustrophobic to escape our room for meals, but neither of us liked the big noisy dining halls that dorm families used for younger kids.

"So maybe you can get into this special edprogram too," I said at the end of my story.

Shandy shook his head. "I already tried, and failed. I get to be your T.A. instead."

"You—what?" My fork dropped with a clatter. "Shandy, you have a lot of explaining to do. Why didn't you tell me about this sooner?" He didn't even look happy!

"None of us is supposed to know anything about these special programs until we're secretly chosen," he said. "So I was afraid I'd spoil your chances if I told you anything. And if you don't want to ruin it for anyone else, you should probably keep your promise of silence in the future. Besides, I just found out about my teaching assistant position today too."

"But this is totally nova," I insisted. "Did you know about these secret programs already? Is that why you weren't allowed in? Or if you flunked the test, how come you get to be a T.A. instead?"

"What test?" Shandy asked angrily.

I gulped. "I scan it—but I don't com it!" If anything, Shandy was a much more serious student than I was. He never talked about his grades, so I never asked. But I commed that all his hard work must earn scores even higher than mine. "Why wouldn't anyone test you, Shandy? Did you—uh, draw any special attention to yourself, the way I did yesterday?"

He simply nodded. Great Galaxy, what that must have cost him! Shandy guarded his privacy even more than I did.

I shook my head as I tried to fit the pieces together. "Shandy, you're even smarter than me. So maybe they used a different scheme, to test you for the T.A. position."

"And maybe I did know too much," he retorted. "Some kids can't help bragging, if you know when to listen—kids who tend to move on to the gold carpets of Level Eight."

"I thought that was for stuff like engineering, and the Honors program."

"The Center would certainly like all students to remain in a similar state of ignorance—" he caught the insulted look on my face, and quickly apologized. "But it's tough to hide certain edprograms completely. And merely knowing about them seems like an overly petty reason to shut me out."

"But then why?"

"I wasn't told—and maybe I shouldn't tell you any of my suspicions."

"How could it matter, if I don't tell anyone else?" I was humoring him now—I simply couldn't believe how bitter he sounded.

Shandy nodded. "Programs that require special training—including offworld field trips—must cost a lot, so the Center has to be highly selective. And that's much easier if hordes of students aren't clamoring to get in only for the fun of leaving vacful Arrainius."

My face reddened. Guilty as charged. "But why offer anything that selective at a FIL Orphan Center?" I quickly changed the subject. "We're all dumps of one sort or another."

"Did you get a good look at that program list?"

I shook my head, now sorry I hadn't read it more carefully. What if I'd missed an even better choice?

Shandy saw the look on my face. "Naemar probably put their best guess at the top. But it's for some of FIL's most isolated and hazardous careers. So maybe I was merely considered . . . unfit. With no families to leave behind or worry about us, we're actually ideal students. We're, what would they call us? Expendable."

Wow, what rank paranoia! That's what I foolishly thought at the time. As I watched my roomie nurse along a thin soup, crackers, and fruit for dinner, I couldn't help wondering if he was indeed not healthy enough for the training. Maybe a T.A. position would lead him into a more studious—and safer—career.

I chowed down the rest of my dinner. I was really starting to grow, and found it almost impossible to eat enough. So I said no more, until Shandy apologized near the end of our meal.

"I'm sorry, Taje. Instead of complaining, I should be feeling grateful that neither of us has to spend another year in GIP. And now they don't have to split us up either."

"Why would they do that?"

"To keep their vacful secrets."

"Oh," I said, rather than argue with his conspiracy theories. Instead I thought about the rest of this year. "But how am I supposed to survive year-end break?" I sighed.

I'd been looking forward to simply wasting time. Staring at the walls if I felt like it. Not having homework, watching adventure holos, ice skating, visiting and playing games with friends also made my list. "I couldn't wait! But now, between the suspense of whatever it is we've gotten ourselves into, and the challenge of not telling anyone else about it, I don't know how I'll endure our vacation. How am I ever going to keep this a secret from Aerrem?"

"Good question." Shandy studied his unfinished soup. "I'd stay away from her as much as possible."

"Oh, sure, with another queet litter on the way, and Aerrem's big business bash coming up." My old dorm sister would fuse if I didn't show up for her party.

Shandy shrugged helplessly over that one. He was smart, but few people were smart enough to outwit Aerrem.

JOURNAL ENTRY 7

"When in the next millennium do you plan on completing that banner and joining my party?"

My hand jerked, and I had to repaint some cat whiskers. Fuse it all, this party decoration was my best evasion, and Aerrem Nathegorn, my favorite dorm sib, had already commed me.

"Go ahead, Taje. I can finish it up," Cam volunteered from the other end of the wallscreen, before I could stop him or distract Aerrem.

"And what is that pup-squeak doing in here?"

He's trying to earn enough trust for a pet, I couldn't tell her, as I shut off my spectrabrush and jumped down from a chair to face my sib.

"How'd he slip past my door guards?" Aerrem's tail whipped behind her as she planted her fists on her fanciest scarlet hip boots, a homage to one of her favorite old SF authors. The boots must have cost her a fortune Outside. Along with the rest of her party outfit, a silky maroon tunic with intricate embroidery around the border, over matching pants tucked into her boots.

No doubt the tail hole was custom-made, and I think she'd spent weeks making the beaded belt for her tunic. She topped it all off by tucking into her hair a large dark brown clickbird feather, which occasionally shimmered bright red when the light struck it at the right angle.

Aerrem and her younger sister were among the Center's rare and most obvious transgenic residents—unusually healthy and mostly clones of their human mother.

However, a few spliced genes from their Kralvin father gave them each their smooth, furry brown tails, and wildly fluffy brown hair. However, no one got away with calling Aerrem a GMO or mocking her, like they did with Shandy and me.

Kids also called the two of us earthworms, skeletons, or ghosts, when they weren't busy mistaking us for something not human. Shandy turned to littler kids, raised his hands, spread out and wiggled his long thin fingers, and growled, and I learned to follow suit, so they ran away from us. We had to ignore or run away from bigger kids, and we'd learned many escape routes.

Maybe that's why Shandy and I were roomies—even though the Center rarely puts a boy and a girl in the same room—because together we could deflect or evade all the taunts—

"Arrainius to Taje. Come in, Taje! Are you even listening to me?" Aerrem waved a hand in my face. "Your little partner here will brag about this party to all his little friends. Which means news about our supposedly secret business will transmit everywhere," she said, while Cam's coppery shoulder spikes trembled into view.

"When I quit helping you with the business I didn't forget how to swear someone to secrecy," I said, stung. "And I swore for him at the door. Besides, I should think this whole party already breaks all our security rules."

"Oh, quit fusing over it. I've reserved the snack room, and my head of security has all the doorways covered. And I see you've used your usual discretion with your banners.

"Even if you're too much of a loner to enjoy the party, I thought you'd at least like painting them—so why are you sharing the glory?"

"Just because I'm good at something doesn't mean I enjoy it!" I surprised both of us with that outburst.

I must not tell her, I must not tell her about my new edprogram. It ran like a feedback loop through my head, until I couldn't focus on anything else, much less enjoy our last night of break. Space, when could I politely jettison?

Aerrem was momentarily taken aback, until underlings distracted her with packages of smooth food from Outside, and questions about utensils and music. When she finished her orders, she found me slumped in my chair, and Cam struggling with a painting of a bright red, lop-sided kluormahx.

Cam was obviously working hard to tease me, but my mood had crashed so badly that I couldn't even crack a smile over the joke or his technique. It wasn't fair, having to keep my new edprogram a secret from Aerrem.

"What is it, Taje? You could challenge your transfer out of our math class, if it's fusing you this badly."

Was I an open com for everyone now? At the beginning of break, when I'd turned my latest queet litter over to Aerrem, I'd at least had to tell her I couldn't go to math with her anymore. My pulse began to race.

"A transfer isn't worth fighting," was all I could honestly say. I dared not try to lie. We'd grown up in a Center dorm family together, and now Aerrem was also the extremely crafty leader of our highly successful pet smuggling business—with a very effective spy network.

Aerrem sighed and nodded. "I suppose no GIP move is worth disputing. But that's no excuse for making yourself scarce around me. If we can't see each other in class, we have to get together more outside of it.

"I live right around the corner from you, Taje, but I've only seen you twice since break began, and the first time was for business. I understand why you haven't dressed up—" Aerrem smirked at my mahogany shirt and pants—"but where's your roommate? I realize Shandy owns one of the few legal pets in the Center, but I still invited him, for quietly putting up with all your animals."

"He's not feeling very well," I said, not adding that Shandy hated parties even more than I did. Aerrem lived by her own rules, and they didn't include respecting the privacy most Center residents crave.

"Nobody can com how to fix him?" Aerrem beat the air with her tail, and Dojan nimbly dodged it on his way around her. "I hope those putrid bio-terrorists got sucked into the nearest event horizon!

I nodded numbly. I found it difficult to understand why Shandy longed more than anything to return to plague-devastated Istrann, where his father had worked as a human ambassador—until his parents and almost everyone else on the planet had died.

I could barely stand the idea of living on what was almost a cemetery world. But worst of all was the thought of living with the remaining native telepaths. The Fehrokc family must have been stuffed with purely virtuous thoughts, which I'm not. I liked what privacy I could get.

But I still didn't believe that fear of mind reading FIL members—even if they looked like giant pale spiders—justified mass murder. Aerrem and I both guessed the Center let Shandy keep Sheefharn because the nova bird was his only surviving Istrannian friend.

"So where's your younger sister?" Dojan asked Aerrem as he joined us. He couldn't afford party clothes, but he wore a fancy tooled leather belt from his homeworld, with a fake dagger, over leather-brown clothes with a forest green vest and cap. "Trist's done such great work on our door sensors—"

"She's partying with her fellow dorm family grads, and she's too full of herself and her new engineering skills to risk here—"

"And when do I get to meet your new roommate, Aerrem?" I eagerly added to the change in subjects. It was a good one. Aerrem's previous roommate had developed mysterious allergies, and had tactfully requested a transfer before her doctor ran incriminating tests. And now Aerrem was getting a guy too!

"Visit us!" Aerrem slapped her boots with her tail. "My new roomie couldn't come tonight. He'd already signed up for a pass for an Outside party, which I bet you and Shandy haven't bothered to do in way too long. You probably haven't even stepped Outside—"

"There's nothing out there." Nothing but malls, government buildings, piles of housing, and miniature artificial parks—civilization, smothering all the tiny continents of Arrainius. Fortunately ocean life made our oxygen, so we didn't all choke to death. But I still felt like I was suffocating.

"I checked. You and Shandy still don't even have personal sites on the Center's com. If you also avoid parties, how do you expect to make more friends?"

"Aerrem, look at me. I'm ugly! And those sites all ask for a personal holo. Not to mention all the teasing Shandy gets."

"So you two have a lot less pigment than most humans. That doesn't make you ugly. Just a little unusual."

"A little unusual! You only say that because you grew up with me and you understand being different."

"You've sure got a lot of excuses," Aerrem said. "But I suspect both you and Shandy simply spend way too much time on your vacful homework—"

"And how are you going to get anywhere, if you don't study harder?" I said, with more despair than ever.

"I'm not going anywhere anyway, so why worry about school?"

"It may feel that way, but someday the Center will declare us adults, and release us—"

"Oh, that's too nova, coming from you, Taje." Aerrem gazed at me cannily. "We both know you and your roommate would jettison in a micro, if you could find any way to bypass Center security. And life's too short to worry about some vacful future—my parents certainly proved that."

"You don't even know if they're dead!" I blurted out, and my face reddened. Unlike Aerrem, I do try to respect the privacy of my friends.

"They might as well be!" Aerrem retorted, completely unembarrassed, although Dojan, Aerrem's head of imports, was now twitching his sensitive, furry Tliesjian ears. He looked as if he'd rather disappear into a black hole than listen to this.

"So why don't you try to enjoy life a little more?" Aerrem persisted. "Go with Dojan on his next buying expedition this weekend. If you put in for a day pass right away, you might find another smooth pet for yourself."

Now I wanted to throw myself beyond an event horizon. "Uh, I'm rather full up at this point, and Max is such a jealous pet, I don't think I should get any more." Did Aerrem notice how weak that sounded? But how could I tell her I'd soon need a heroic pet-sitter, if I was truly going on offworld field trips?

Aerrem blinked at me, and turned to Dojan. "Didn't you also say you got transferred out of our math class? Did you know that happened to Taje too? Will the Center at least dump you both into the same class?"

Dojan zapped me a horrified micro-scan while my pulse soared to light speed, and we both tried to cover with shrugs.

"Who knows what the Center has done to us?" Dojan said carefully. He was using one of Aerrem's favorite techniques—answering one question with another, to avoid lying. Luckily the music began to blast next. "Ouch!" Dojan clapped his clawed hands over his ears.

"I have to manage everything!" Aerrem stomped off, and a micro later the music level grew slightly more tolerable.

"Planetary ecology?" Dojan quickly whispered.

"Yes. You too?" But of course, Dojan was another friend who missed his homeworld's great forests.

"How are we ever going to keep this a secret from her?"

"I have no idea—shhh, here she comes again."

"I almost forgot to tell you some smooth news." Aerrem swished her tail happily.

"What?" We both focused on her with too much hope. Had she actually commed the game, gotten into the program, and put us to the test?

"We found new homes for all your queet pups!"

"Oh—that is—smooth—Aerrem," I said, very unsmoothly. "How did you—manage it?"

"I finally thought to ask an interplanetary veterinarian for help, and she gave them all neuter vaccines. With endless litters no longer a problem, they sold like nova. You should look into it for Squeaker."

"A vet—she won't tell on us?"

"Nah—she says we have client privacy rights."

"Space, why didn't I think of calling a vet?"

"Admit it, I've always been the brains of the business!" Aerrem grinned.

I howled and Aerrem shrieked with laughter as I chased her around the tables. At last the food distracted us. I carted off a tray for Cam and me, and we munched away as we put finishing touches on the banners.

Afterwards, we snuck out, and got caught up in a duckball game in our hall. At the end of it I returned to my room. In honor of Aerrem, I'd worn my only boots—simple ankle-length hiking/riding boots—instead of my normal sandals.

I slipped them off and held Max's muzzle shut to tiptoe past Shandy, now sound asleep in his bed. We made it to my back area without waking him up.

In bed I quietly watched a favorite holo adventure about Scout Ship explorers accidentally stranded on a strange new world. Survival adventures on exotic planets were my favorite stories, especially ones that emphasized smarts over violence. Of course, I had to ignore the fact that none of these stories had pale-skinned or redheaded characters, except for a few villains.

At any rate, these particular explorers encountered all sorts of interesting lifeforms both good and dangerous on my screen. I knew only the foolish characters would die before the rest were rescued. It was a vac-headed way to try to fall asleep. I drifted off at a very nova hour.

JOURNAL ENTRY 8

The next day I found out Shandy's guesses about our new edprogram were amazingly correct, and he didn't even get to hear the news. At least live and in person.

Our new class met Shandy during a tour of a whole series of classrooms off an unusually quiet, gold-carpeted Level Eight hallway. Drehx Tarnek, our new lead instructor, proudly showed off a lecture room, two labs, a workshop, a student lounge and several study rooms, a locker room, and even a small gym. All for eighteen of us (not counting Shandy)—less than half our normal class size.

I wandered through it like a stunned zombie. Well, a guilty stunned zombie. I wasn't too tired to feel slightly bad about using an expensive ecology class with little intention of becoming an ecologist. And I was already wondering if I could escape during one of the field trips (probably not), or just use them to get a little fresh air.

Tarnek introduced "Shanden Fehrokc, our class T.A." in the life sciences lab, where Shandy was unpacking all sorts of intriguing samples. I grinned at him and he smiled back. Next we returned to the lecture room, where Tarnek told us about our new program.

Yawning, I took a seat in the front row, a bold new move for me, especially since I commed I'd have to fight off sleep. But Tarnek thrilled us with his enthusiasm, starting with his announcement that he was a real planetary ecologist from a FIL SEAR Ship.

"A what ship?" a copper-scaled, male Lorratian named Dainer asked.

"A FIL Survey, Education, Assistance, and Research Ship," Tarnek said. "Most of us work for FIL SEAR or Scout Ships."

"Smooth!"

Tarnek explained each FIL ecologist had to take at least one leave from the field for teaching. So he'd requested this Center because he'd also grown up here.

Like Naemar, he was another short human. And like most humans, he had golden skin, deep brown almond eyes, and thick, dark, wavy hair. He was also muscular and agile. So he was beautiful to watch, as he paced like a panther in front of us.

He reviewed how much we'd already messed up our home planets, when the Kralvins released their discovery of paraspace, and we all flung ourselves into the galaxy. Soon we'd found ourselves too busy handling multiple First Contacts to notice how many more worlds we'd already crashed. To help fix those messes, and to prevent more from happening—that was what we'd learn about here.

"I believe it's the most important profession in the Federation of Intelligent Life," he stated boldly. "Sometimes it's remote, dangerous, and isolated work, but it's also tremendously rewarding, and absolutely vital."

He told us we'd still have to take our core courses in math, communications, physical education, and in social, physical, and life sciences, but in here all subjects would blend in with planetary ecology, so we might not even notice. For instance, we'd learn advanced math from all the eco-calculations we'd need to run, and communications from the reports we'd have to review and generate.

We'd start with several weeks of planetary sciences (physical sciences), and then tackle a series of environmental case studies (life sciences plus more physical sciences). Some examples would be occupied by intelligent life (social sciences), and some not. All would involve oxygen-carbon dioxide cycling planets, where we could work without atmosphere suits. "We'll leave the rest for other intelligent species—"

"How on Arrainius are you going to relate phys ed to ecology?" a human girl named Crell interrupted, and the students around her laughed with her.

Tarnek came to a halt before us, with a surprisingly serious expression on his handsome face. "Look at all of you. Most of you haven't walked—much less run—on an uneven surface for years, or spent more than a few minutes in a storm. If you didn't scan the controls in our gym, you're in for a few surprises."

Everyone's faces lit up. We became even more excited when he showed us a holo of our very own little class spaceship, which would ferry us to wilderness experiences not possible in any of Arrainius's pathetic little parks. And we actually cheered when we heard we'd use our next end-of-school-year break to help with a real FIL fringe world eco-survey, for our final exam.

But that led to the subject of the nova expense for our training—FIL's excuse for exclusiveness and secrecy—all that space junk Shandy had already suspected or commed. So anyone who did hear about this program from friends might gain an unfair advantage over more qualified students. And of course anyone caught cheating on the entrance exam would be disqualified.

Tarnek talked next about teams. "I've divided you up into pairs for lab work. We'll encourage a lot of teamwork, because that's how FIL normally works, but we also hope you'll find it very rewarding. However, if you find yourself in an awkward team, don't complain to any of your teachers about it. Work it out. FIL won't give you choices in the field, where the real action happens."

I was paired with Branem, who'd sat next to me in the back of Naemar's class. As far as I knew, he was a decent guy. We'd helped each other whenever either of us was late for science, but we'd never bothered to become close friends. Maybe no one knew that.

The two Lorratians in the class, Nikk and Dainer, were put together, and Dojan was teamed with Kijan, the only other Tliesjian. But the Tliesjians scanned like they knew and liked each other, and the Lorratians may have already been a couple, as one was a coppery male and the other a golden female. I found it hard to miss the delight on their faces, knowing Cam's expressions as well as I did.

This Center mainly housed humans, so we had only two other aliens in the class, a short blue Telmid with feathery antennae named Piel, and a horned, olive-skinned, stocky Altruskan named Gkorjneil. Piel was paired with Jael, who was almost as short as Shandy, but more solid. Gkorjneil was paired with a stout human named Errek. I couldn't tell if any of them cared.

But I couldn't help feeling jealous as I finally realized what it meant to have Shandy as a T.A. Branem was okay, but why was Shandy even made a T.A., when our records must show what a smooth team we'd make?

While that zapped home, Tarnek told us about the general immunity boosters we'd need for our offworld passports, as well as some surprising comwork awaiting us in Admin.

"You must all realize by now that at your age, being adopted is extremely unlikely. Nevertheless, to ensure we don't lose you from this program, you must agree to let me become your official guardian for the next year—what, Kijan?"

I believe Dojan's partner was the only one among us to attempt a serious question in all the excitement that morning. "What happens next year?" he said. "Surely you can't teach us everything in one year?"

Tarnek gave us his first sneaky smile. "That's true . . . but it also depends on what happens this year. I can't say more for now, except I hope you all feel fired up by this program description! Your previous teachers have placed each of you here because of your intelligence and hard work, and it's an honor to serve you.

"Nevertheless, I don't want anyone feeling obligated to stay in this program. You have earned your positions in here, and other options are always available for any student who has made it this far, and discovers a need to change directions. That is my policy, and I will stand by it through the very end of our year together.

"Now go get your errands done, so we can start."

JOURNAL ENTRY 9

"Which section of Level Two did Tarnek say we should head for?" Kijan asked in the nearest translift.

"I've already forgotten." Dojan's furry ears drooped. How long had he lingered at Aerrem's party? "Just stay away from that one." He pointed a claw at a manual button for Discipline.

"It can't be In-patient," I whispered and cringed, remembering how sick Shandy had looked in there. Aerrem had cried.

"I think Tarnek said Environmental Health," Taemar said, ordering the lift, and indeed we found we were expected there for our immunity boosters.

We rubbed our sore arms as we rode another lift to Level One, and got into the always ridiculously long slow lines of red-carpeted Admin, the only Center Level above ground.

I glanced through the only real windows of the Center, and felt no jealousy here. Multiple layers of streets and buildings blocked all views of ground and sky. FIL laws prevented this from happening to more newly discovered worlds, but it was far too late for Arrainius.

Some of my new classmates balked a bit over their sudden "adoption." But I suffered no second thoughts when it came time to ID my forms, which involved my signature, a fingerprint, a retinal scan, and a holo of my sleepy face.

"Why do you need all of this?" Sheejar asked angrily.

"You already have it in your files," her partner Crell added.

"For permission," the Admin com replied tonelessly. "Now please place one of your fingers on the reader."

We stopped at a snack bar and brought food back to our class lounge for a quiet lunch, before moving on to our lecture room for our first planetary science lesson. Shandy sat to one side at the recorder for our room coms.

Time zapped past as we greedily soaked up information we actually wanted to learn, but it dragged to a halt as I waited outside our main door for Shandy. The hall had emptied of all other school traffic by the time he exited.

"Well, what do you think?" he asked as we strode together to the nearest lift.

"It's fantastic. I can hardly believe it." I could say it was a fun subject, even if I felt like an imposter. But I couldn't tell Shandy all of that, at least not yet, and I doubted I sounded very enthusiastic.

"But I do think all that vacful secrecy belongs in a garbage cycler," I said instead. "And why weren't we made teammates, when we'd be so perfect together?"

Shandy smiled and shrugged. “I guess we should just be glad we got in.”

“Aerrem will find out about this—you know she will. Then what?”

Shandy couldn’t come up with any new answers for that either. And neither of us guessed what a vacful mess lay ahead, which was mostly my fault.

JOURNAL ENTRY 10

I wish I could delete this part from my memory and from this journal. But it would leave too big of a hole in my conscience and in what actually happened.

I have to admit I treated Branem badly. Like a lab fixture, not a real partner. At least I know that now. But at that time I focused a lot more on trying to find a few micros to spend with Shandy during school. The class's early fumbles in labs and the light speed intensity of our courses made that goal vacfully difficult.

Shandy also had to work doubly hard to stay a step ahead, so he could help everyone. That meant long hours of work outside of class as well as inside. And he became a very good T.A.—so good the respect he earned actually put more distance between him and our classmates.

I should have felt proud of him, but instead the set-up fused me. I didn't have many friends, but Shandy possessed even fewer, and in Tarnek's program my roomie became a lonely assistant for everyone, instead of a buddy for anyone. Most teams quickly became chums, if they weren't already.

So I suspect I took out my frustrations on my quiet lab partner. Any little lab error and I went nova on him. Otherwise I tried to act polite, but that was it—I was acting, and probably not very well.

And at some vacful point I crossed the line beyond politeness. When I wasn't berating Branem, I was only pretending to listen to him, or even worse, ignoring him altogether.

Although Aerrem thinks I ought to tell my whole story, I doubt I have time to recite every fused incident. Nor do I want to die from embarrassment over my long list of wrongs.

I'll get by with the most nova examples that have stabbed themselves into my memory, because I ended up hurting other people too. That's bad enough.

Early in our first quarter, Tarnek introduced our most important FIL instrument. Shandy handed out tough FIL field model wristcoms, with memory, calculation, and scan functions far beyond anyone's expectations. We couldn't wait to try them out, while Tarnek made us promise not to misuse them. Instead he loaded specs and exercises on the board which kept us busy.

"You'll spend all year learning how to run complex scans and analyses with these wristcoms. But this morning we'll start with two simpler functions—recording and location techniques."

Simple? Right. Holo adventures had apparently left out all the hard parts, and our teacher and T.A. stayed busy helping out as our noise level intensified. I couldn't record anything, despite what seemed like easy instructions on my deskcom.

"Taje, could you please have a look at my wristcom?" Branem said. Thinking back about it, I wondered how he could still act so polite towards me. In retrospect, I think he was a nice guy I ended up pushing too hard.

"Why?" I stared at my own nova wristcom's fuzzy holo.

"Arrainius has macro numbers of them, but I can't pick up any clear Arrainian satellite signals."

"Try following your deskcom directions."

"I did. It's still not working—"

"Sorry, but I'm working on recording right now," I said, not hiding my irritation. I almost got to the point of unscientifically crashing the fused piece of space trash into my desk, when I glanced up and discovered Shandy had landed at last on a nearby counter.

"Shandy, I could use some help."

Shandy glanced around, with an oddly nervous look on his face. "Sorry, but I think Nikk and Dainer put their hands up first." He vectored to the Lorratian pair, leaving me a bit puzzled and upset.

But I knew Shandy had to be careful to not even scan like he was playing favorites. How many classmates already knew we were roommates? We didn't talk about it, but in such a small class it was hard to hide anything. So I shrugged and struggled on alone, until Branem docked Tarnek at our table.

"Have you calibrated for local conditions?" Tarnek asked Branem. My ears would have perked if I'd been a Tliesjian, and Piel's feathery antennae actually did quiver, all the way across the room.

"Oh," said Branem, "no, I haven't done a baseline calibration."

Neither had I.

"You can't expect equipment to be field-ready, straight out of a SEAR or Scout Ship's hold."

"Oh yeah," Branem said.

We immediately turned to our deskcoms for relevant calibration data. And we finally noticed everyone around us doing the same.

"You're welcome to work together on this," Tarnek said, sounding surprised.

"She doesn't want to," Branem muttered.

"Taje," Tarnek said before I could object, "perhaps you don't understand. This isn't like your old classes. We encourage teamwork in here, and we'll tell you when we won't allow it for tests."

"Okay." I already knew the rules, but I'd found the info I needed, and my wristcom began to behave. Tarnek shrugged and moved on, and Branem slowly tackled a methodical checklist.

I tried to wait for him after I finished most of the board problems, but he kept getting sidetracked. So instead of fusing over it, I joined other teams vectoring throughout all our classrooms for location exercises. We could use Arrainian satellites, but it was a lot more fun trying to com each other's coordinates without, like we'd have to do on more newly discovered planets.

At last Tarnek's face took over our wristcom screens to call us back to our lecture room, and now the day turned truly strange. Tarnek pointed out some controls we hadn't covered yet, while Shandy stood at his side, looking unbelievably paler by the micro.

"Everyone made it through the first two sets of exercises faster than I anticipated," Tarnek announced. "So let's cover one more function today. What have I left out?"

"Translation," Hannen, a human I remembered from Honors classes, guessed correctly, first try, and our class cheered.

Even though this Center received biped, air-breathing orphans from all over our sector of FIL, it didn't mean we all knew how to communicate with each other. Everyone received a cheap (and almost useless) wrist translator on arrival, but we were also stuck in an intensive FIL Universal Communication class, and we didn't get to learn anything else until we passed it.

(Meanwhile if you owned a real wristcom, you had to turn it in, ostensibly so you couldn't distract or be distracted by talking with friends or playing games during class. You could use your deskcom in your room, but you'd get caught if you tried to use a class deskcom for personal purposes. The same explanation was given to each outraged new orphan. As if we hadn't lost enough already. Some had spent big on multi-function wristcoms. No worries. Everyone would get their wristcoms back during adoption or graduation. When they'd most likely be totally outdated.)

We did come out of UC class with different accents. Tliesjians lisped from mild muzzles. Lorratians had a bell-like ring to their voices. Little Telmids sounded slightly squeaky. Horned Altruskans had rougher voices. But even humans, who came from many places on many worlds, had accents, like v's for w's, h's for j's, or rolling l-like r's.

Some kids complained about difficult accents, but I thought all the variety was fun. Until one sad day I realized I'd quit hearing any of it. It all simply sounded normal.

So UC was why hardly anyone in the Center bothered to learn serious translator controls. But we'd be fairly lost if we ever needed to work with anyone unfamiliar with FIL's common language. Now we knew the Center was serious about training us for offworld work.

"Right," Tarnek said to Hannen. "I must admit I can only review translator basics, since I'm not an expert linguistic technician. But briefly, this wristcom function scans and translates electromagnetic brain emissions, and transmits conscious communication efforts into the receiver's central nervous system language and emotion centers—question, Taemar?"

"If that's how it works," Taemar, Hannen's human partner and probably also an Honors class student, said, "Could it be used to translate between us and nonintelligent animals?"

"Good question. It has been tried, with some interesting if rather mystifying results. Perhaps you'd like to research this subject further, and give us a report?"

"Sure!"

It was a good question—so good I almost didn't ask mine. What if I could talk with my queet, to get her to calm down? A neuter vaccine had ended her parade of pregnancies, but not her hair-trigger nerves.

"Anybody else?" Tarnek asked. "Okay, so let's—oh, Taje—you had a question?"

I lowered my wavering hand. "Am I to understand," I finally choked out, "that this thing reads minds to work?" I still had too many secrets to take any chances—

"Hmm, not exactly—well, perhaps, in a sense, it does. But unless your brain works very differently from the rest of us, a translator won't broadcast your private thoughts, if that's what concerns you."

Tarnek chuckled nervously, and I returned his smile uneasily as he continued. "It only transmits your spoken words, and some of the feeling behind them. And sometimes it won't even get that right. Generally the less you have in common with the species you're trying to communicate with, the less successful the process.

"But the less we have in common with another species, the less likely we are to even recognize each other as intelligent beings, much less attempt to communicate. Would you even consider stopping to talk to a crystalline asteroid colony living in a space vacuum, and if so, what would you try to say to it?"

That sounded like an interesting challenge, but now I watched Shandy turn almost green, and I fell silent.

"I won't pretend it's not a complex process," Tarnek continued, "and if this answer doesn't satisfy you, I could invite a translator technician to cover it in more depth—"

"Uh, no, that's okay," I said. It sounded safe, but once again I commed I could never stand to live on a planet full of true mind readers, like Istrann.

Meanwhile, I still scanned Shandy, and hoped for his sake he wouldn't throw up or collapse in front of everyone. He brushed beads of sweat from his forehead as he wavered on his feet.

"Very well," Tarnek said. "I'd like to start with a fluent demonstration from someone who can actually think in another language. Since our T.A. grew up on Istrann, I'll ask Fehrokc to speak a few sentences—"

Shandy turned to Tarnek now, and spoke in such a low voice no one else could tell what he said.

But Tarnek answered so everyone could hear. "I'm sorry, Shanden. I'll enter an excuse from class for a checkup in your new wristcom. You'll need to take it with you, in case you can't return today. I hope you feel better soon."

I quit holding my breath. Thankfully Shandy hadn't held out too long this time, trying to hide how he felt. I couldn't even imagine the added stress of using a language he'd shared with so many people now dead. And I still couldn't fully relax until he made it out the door without puking.

Tarnek turned back to the rest of us. "Can I have another volunteer?"

"You should know who can do it," Kijan dared him, "since you have access to all our records!"

The class laughed and booed, but Tarnek met Kijan's challenge. "Very well, you'll do nicely. Come on up and share a bit of a Tliesjian language, please!"

Kijan jumped up to cheerfully comply, and burned our ears with some elaborate Tliesjian curses. Or should I say our brains? We tried plugging our ears, and we could still "hear" him, and even detect his enthusiasm. So it still felt a bit like mind invasion, no matter what Tarnek said.

JOURNAL ENTRY 11

As I exited a lift to my hallway that afternoon, I couldn't help admiring my new wristcom. I'd already sent new data from it to my deskcom—but now someone grabbed my arm from behind and spun me around.

"Oh, it's you!" I hadn't expected my roommate to be the source of such sudden strength, especially today. "How are you—"

"What on Arrainius do you think you're doing?"

"Huh?" What had gotten into Shandy today? "What are you talking about?"

Shandy released my arm, and I rubbed it crossly while he took a deep breath. "You'd better try to treat your teammate a lot better, if you want any of your plans to succeed."

"Plans?" I gulped. "What plans?" Had he somehow guessed that I'd started trying to com an escape from here for real, now that I was getting the training I needed? But how did he suspect it?

"I just meant that if you want to stay out of trouble with Tarnek, you'd better start acting nicer to Branem."

Shandy rubbed his temples as he turned away, and stumbled towards the lifts without looking back.

I stood there, trembling. What did Shandy know, and what had he truly meant? And, for that matter, where was he going on the lifts? Certainly not back to our room. At last I shrugged and turned towards our door. I was too puzzled and vexed to remember any of his advice. Instead, I actually began to question our friendship.

JOURNAL ENTRY 12

"Hey, Taje, want to get together on our homework this evening?" Branem caught me in the lift, although I'd tried to avoid him. I knew this was coming. Tarnek had put him up to it this morning.

"Maybe some other time." I yawned. "I'm too tired tonight." Our already long school days had grown even longer with the addition of a "basic" first-aid class that felt more like a crash med school program. I was also cold and sore from our end-of-the-day gym workout—today a duckball game on a simulated hillside in the middle of a windy rainstorm. Fun times!

We exited at the same stop, which meant Branem must live nearby. Lovely. I wasn't much of a social studier, especially when I knew it would slow me down. I might not be doing quite as well as when I first launched into the class, but Branem was in real trouble now that we were well into our first case study. While we learned in social studies about a human colony that had made some typical mistakes, Branem added his own.

This morning in life sciences I'd recorded plant growth results while he supposedly calibrated his wristcom for soil analysis. But halfway into our first specimen scan I realized his readings didn't make any sense. I had to run the whole baseline procedure again on my own wristcom, before we could start over.

A soil specialist supervised this lab, but Tarnek wandered over and pulled Branem aside for a talk. I thought it was about time, and I couldn't help overhearing most of it while I worked furiously to catch up.

"Branem, I've noticed you seem to be having some trouble with the material in here lately. Are you dealing with any special problem I should know about? Is there any way I can help you?"

Branem answered inaudibly.

"What?"

"No." Branem scuffed a sandal.

"Are you sure? I know you have the ability to handle this program. Have you joined a homework group? Many teams find it helpful to get together outside of class, and do remember your wristcom will let you in here any time after-hours."

No reply.

"Okay?" Tarnek pressed.

"Okay," Branem muttered as he returned to our experiment, scratching at his dark curly hair and nervously shifting our samples around. So I was supposed to rescue him? Well, Tarnek would probably at least keep after him if he didn't improve. It wasn't fair that my partner was also slowing me down. It simply didn't occur to me that his bad attitude, which affected his work, had anything to do with my bad attitude towards him.

So of course Branem became worse, not better, as we neared the day of our first midterms. And the more patiently I tried to correct his work, the angrier he got. So I became fused too. The last afternoon before our tests I frantically scanned our pooled wristcom data for our physical science atmospheric analyses.

"Where are our atmosphere test results, Branem?"

"I erased them. You said I crashed the whole experiment, remember?"

"So where are our samples?"

"How should I know? I'm not the only member of this team making mistakes—right, Sheejar? Crell?"

Sheejar and Crell were two human teammates with long dark glossy hair who worked at the lab bench opposite ours. Sheejar shrugged. "None of us is perfect."

I stared back at them. "Did either of you scan who dumped our samples?"

The two girls simply shook their beautiful hair as they returned to their own work. Gkorjneil, teamed with Errek at the table to my left, silently scratched the base of one of his neatly trimmed horns when I asked him.

"Branem, we're running out of time!" I had to face my teammate alone. "Now we'll have to ask for new samples. Our results are due today!"

"No, really? So go ask!" Branem retorted, as Shandy walked right past us to help another team.

Ever since his odd outburst the day he left class sick, Shandy had said not a word more about Branem and me. In fact, he said very little to me, when he saw me at all. Usually he left for class before I woke up, and often he stayed late too. But in class he acted as if my problem with Branem no longer existed, although by now everyone else had scanned some clue about it.

I kept telling myself Shandy must feel caught in the middle, but it hurt. Avoiding Aerrem, quarreling with my teammate, and getting no support from my roommate—I hadn't felt this alone since my mom disappeared and our animals were removed from our farm on Donshore. Now I had to go ask Tarnek for new samples, and he was so gruff about it that I felt doubly humiliated.

The timing was totally fused. I tend to be a crammer, but I finished class late and I was too tired, angry, and upset to study as much as I'd planned that night. Out of spite I tried loading my favorite game from my personal deskcom onto my wristcom, a set of exotic wilderness survival challenges, and was unsurprised to find the game blocked. Now it was so late that I had to go to bed and simply hope for the best.

But getting to sleep was a pitched battle, and I suffered school nightmares the rest of the night. They felt so bad that brief relief zapped me when I finally woke up the next morning. Then I remembered the tests ahead of me, and my heart sank.

JOURNAL ENTRY 13

I struggled as hard to fully wake up as I had to get to sleep. So that left me only a miserable micro to get dressed and launch from my room. I thrust my way single-mindedly through hall traffic to the nearest bank of lifts, which is how I mindlessly crashed into Branem.

But my teammate was headed the wrong way. And across his handsome milky-chocolate face an evil grin now spread, which exaggerated the skin folds surrounding his dark eyes, turning them into angry slits.

"Running late, Taje?" He poked me hard in the chest, which was currently a tender area. I backed up on autopilot as my jaw dropped. Sheejar and Crell and some Lorratian sidekick with a coppery male scale pattern I didn't recognize flanked Branem. They stepped forward together, prodding and shoving me and invading my space as quickly as I abandoned it.

"You have more to worry about this morning than getting to your midterms on time," Branem said as I crashed into the wall behind me, between two water fountains.

I tried not to shake as I stood trapped there. Branem looked like he was scanning for blood. I happened to be taller than him, but I was skinny and he was solid. Like many human males, he had an unfair set of built-in muscles.

I scanned frantically for the nearest security cam, and discovered Branem had already arranged one of the oldest tricks in the Center. Another human kid I didn't recognize held a screen in front of the lens of the only cam within range, no doubt showing it a harmless hall recording. With our cheap system, that's all it took to fool it.

"What's the matter, Branem," I tried to boost my fading courage, "is this the best excuse you can come up with, to put off flunking your tests?"

"You'd love it if I flunked out, wouldn't you? Great Galaxy, you hate me for simply docking in your way. Well, let's see how far we can vector you from class—"

Our class hadn't started self-defense lessons yet, so I quickly commed I stood only one chance. I had to act first and fast. I pushed off the wall and buried my fist in Branem's stomach, in an attempt to break free from the ring he and his friends had locked around me.

Branem doubled over, and his light brown skin actually turned a bit pale against his red T-shirt and black shorts. But in the next micro the Lorratian slammed me back into the wall so hard I learned how bad it really felt to have one's breath knocked out. I gasped for air like a glipper in an empty tank, and would have slid to the floor except Branem's bodyguards held me pinned to the wall. The Lorratian's scales dug into my wrist.

"We have her now, Branem," he said, digging his scales in even deeper. "What do you want us to do with her?"

My stomach churned and I almost screamed. "Coward," I choked out instead, trembling uncontrollably now. "You can't even fight your own fight!"

Branem straightened up, and took a deep breath as he brushed sweat-shiny dark curls from his face. "Let her go."

"But Branem!"

"I said, let her go. It'll take me about a micro to dump her into vac!"

His friends backed off, but only enough to block a growing crowd gathering around our ring. As soon as Branem's helpers let go of me, I had to launch at Branem again, before he zapped me. I used my new height to throw him to the floor, but unfortunately I clumsily let him yank me down with him.

We rolled on the carpet, exchanging vicious punches, while our audience provided a loud jeering soundtrack. Cam and Trist's frightened faces appeared for a micro in the background, and moments later the first honor guard arrived.

JOURNAL ENTRY 14

The Center enlists honor guards from senior Center residents, but the first guard had to call for backups. Branem and I didn't stop fighting until they pulled us apart and cuffed our wrists behind our backs with orange spider-stick. Amazingly, Tarnek arrived next, but already almost everyone else had bolted.

"Any of you kids who saw what happened had better stay right here," he said to the rest, in that awful teacher's voice that demanded obedience.

I finally quit glaring at Branem long enough to notice all his "buddies" had vanished. Good—they weren't here to distort the story. Now I also scanned Aerrem, ginger-colored arms folded in front of her. She leaned against the wall as if she always docked here.

My face burned, but she couldn't have stood there long, or surely she would have leaped in to help me. So had she scanned enough to help defend me? I zapped her a quick secret smile, and she smoothly pretended not to notice.

"Tell me what happened." Tarnek faced down our greatly dwindled audience, and received headshakes interrupted by nervous glances at wristcom time meters. Everyone was already late for their first class.

Tarnek turned to Aerrem. "Do you have any idea how this began?"

The hackle on Aerrem's brown furry tail stood up, and she nodded mutely.

"So who started it?"

"Well," Aerrem said, "I think Branem and several other kids backed Taje against a wall. Taje hit Branem to break free, and then—"

"So Taje threw the first punch?"

"Well, I guess, but—"

"That's enough for now. What's your name?"

"Aerrem—Aerrem Nathegorn."

"Okay, I'll com your teacher a tardy excuse for your first class. In return I'll expect to interview you in my office during lunch—I'll include the room number in my message to your teacher. The rest of you can leave now, but I will not issue any other excuses."

Students ran in the otherwise empty corridor, while Branem and I still worked on catching our breaths. Branem had a black eye, which was already swelling closed, while my sore nose began to drip.

Aerrem gave us one last uneasy glance while Tarnek looked up her teacher on his wristcom. Her tail drooped as she walked away. Tarnek sent a message and then turned to our guards.

"Remove Branem's restraint and accompany him to class. He knows where to go, but keep it quiet—I have a test going on in there. My T.A. can help him get started. I'll take the other one with me."

Branem grinned as one of his guards used an enzyme patch to melt his cuffs, and then he sauntered to the lift between his guards.

Tarnek took hold of my arm behind me, marched me into another empty lift, and said one horrible word. The worst button lit up.

JOURNAL ENTRY 15

I sat frozen on the cot against the back wall, while the clear doors that formed the front of my small cell locked behind Tarnek. He strode away without looking back.

A servocleaner rolled through a moment later, and sucked up bright red droplets from the white carpet of the otherwise silent Level Two hall.

My brown shirt soaked up more blood dripping from my nose. It began to show. My hands were still trapped behind my back—Tarnek hadn't even bothered to melt my rubbery cuffs before he left me in here.

I tugged and wriggled my wrists uselessly, and tried equally uselessly to stop my nosebleed with my shoulder. The taste of iron and salt ran down the back of my throat.

"Life isn't fair," was all one of our dorm parents had ever said about any of our complaints. It took me years to realize that might be true, but why did people have to voluntarily add to the unfairness?

So now I wondered why I'd landed in here, while Branem got to return to class. Like all of FIL, the Center forbids violence, but it takes more than one person to cause a fight.

And if Aerrem had witnessed it, why didn't she jump in immediately, to help defend me? Years of handling the nastiest parts of pet-smuggling—like fused animal owners or kids threatening to turn us in—gave Aerrem lots of experience protecting herself and others. She even had a whole on-call emergency team—a team I'd refused to serve on. Aerrem knew I'd never gotten into a fight this serious before, so why hadn't she given me any backup?

Okay, so maybe she'd lied about scanning the whole fight in person—maybe to protect both her younger sister and me. But if so, she'd failed miserably. Now I was in Discipline lockup for the sake of a first punch—for defending myself against four attackers! Where was the justice in that?

Caught up in his T.A. job, Shandy had abandoned me weeks ago, and now Tarnek had fused. Maybe his lunch interview with Aerrem would straighten out the story, but I didn't feel that hopeful—

An older girl beat on my clear cell front before her Altruskan guardian could stop her. I jumped up to my feet as my heart tried to launch from my throat. I could scan the girl's laughter as her horned guard dragged her on past, and she was so thin and lacking in human pigment that for one fused micro I thought I was viewing some bleached evil twin.

They walked on by and I was left standing there, gagging on my own blood. I spun around and stumbled through a small doorway in the rear wall. Thank the Universe it led to a tiny bathroom, where I kneeled over the toilet and retched and retched, until the water turned nearly as red as Branem's shirt.

I dared not cry—it might worsen my nosebleed, which I couldn't control. I'd lost control of everything.

JOURNAL ENTRY 16

"Great Galaxy, what happened to you?"

I blinked awake, startled by the Lorratian honor guard leaning over me. My cheek felt tight from streaks of dried blood. A clot blocked that side of my nose, and breathing through my mouth had made my throat raw. I swallowed painfully.

The gold-scaled guard reached over me to a wall-com I hadn't even thought to scan for, and aimed for the emergency button. "Don't bother," I croaked. "The bleeding has stopped."

She frowned at me, uncertain, and her shivering shoulder spines retracted. "Your teacher will arrive soon. He can decide. I'm here to melt your cuffs. Roll over."

I sat up instead, turned around, and yawned. "Finally. What time is it?"

"My dinner time. Hold still."

I felt her scaly hands fumbling. At last I could pull my wrists apart, and peel off the last soft bits of melting orange goo. But that's when I also noticed the slim metallic bracelet locked on my right wrist.

"What in space is this for?"

"Ask your teacher." The doors opened for Tarnek and the guard jettisoned.

I turned cold and dizzy, and hastily lay back down with my back to Tarnek. I knew what the thing on my wrist was, and I had nothing to say to my teacher, and no desire to faint in front of him either. I heard the doors slide closed behind him, and for a moment there was silence.

"Tajen, it's late, and I want to go home."

"So go," I muttered.

"What? You're in a lot of trouble. You'd better sit up and talk to me."

He used that awful voice again, and I found myself obeying, although the room spun a few times. I hadn't had anything to eat or drink all day, and thinking about it now made my sore stomach clench. Sitting on the edge of the cot, I tried to focus on a rusty spot between my teacher's sandaled feet. My dried blood. Concentrating on it helped hold my tears in check. "Have I done my time in here?" I asked softly.

"Do you have any idea what you've done?"

"Do you care?"

"I don't have time for this." Tarnek shoved a screen and stylus at me. "Sign that, please, unless you want to consult with an advisor first, so you can waste some more of my time!"

"What is it?" I could scan words on the screen, but suddenly I couldn't read any of them.

"The terms of your punishment, for committing violence in the Center. It's standard. Four weeks in here. After the first week you can go back to regular classes, but you'll return here when you're not in class. Then you'll move to a new room on Level Five—I don't think you should be allowed to live with any of my students.

"Meanwhile, I'll be working to get you off my guardianship as quickly as possible. How did you ever get into my program in the first place?"

By being vac-brained enough to believe someone in the Center actually cared what happened to me. But I kept my mouth shut as I signed, just to get rid of him. I didn't want an audience for my next round of puking.

JOURNAL ENTRY 17

My wallcom buzzer went off in the middle of the night, setting off my pounding pulse before I fully awakened.

"Who is it?"

The screen lit up with Trist and Cam's grinning faces. They pushed and shoved each other in and out of view.

"Let me tell her—I did it," Trist crowed. "Aerrem said it wasn't even possible!"

It shouldn't have been. I'd tried with the wallcom and my wristcom to contact every friend I had left, but all my personal calls were blocked. I had access to medical departments, Admin, the library, GIP, and the Discipline office, period.

"But I need to tell her I'm taking care of all her pets," Cam said, "and they're all okay—"

"You both need to get off my com right now—before you end up in here too!" And with that, I switched off their shocked faces, and cried myself to sleep. So ended my first and easiest week in Discipline.

JOURNAL ENTRY 18

The next morning my wallcom woke me up, gave me a new schedule, and announced I'd have to return to GIP, or my bracelet would locate and tell on me. In FIL, putting any sort of GPS signal in or on citizens is illegal, as it makes spying far too easy, but law-breakers lose their right to privacy.

By now I felt utterly stir-crazy, but of course the deliberately visible tracer also branded me in front of everyone. As I entered new classes mid-term, students stared and snickered at me. And I didn't get back into the same math class with Aerrem, which spared me immense embarrassment, but also deprived me of any support.

I returned to back row seats out of self-defense, and that's where Naemar found me at the end of the school day, with my science deskcom untouched. Too bad I was stuck in my old science class. But I discovered I couldn't look up from my blank comscreen into Naemar's face.

"What happened, Taje?"

"No one wants to hear my side of the story." I tugged my silver bracelet in an orbit around my wrist. I had a skinny hand, but I couldn't pull the fused device off. It fit me too well.

"I'm listening."

"I was a bad girl." At last I shot a nasty look at Naemar, who was standing once more with her arms folded over me. "Now can I please leave, before I get into trouble for not returning to my cage on time?"

She snorted and turned away, allowing me to jettison. So why did I feel more rotten than ever?

JOURNAL ENTRY 19

I'd taken a couple of eon-long days to discover I didn't have to return to Discipline for lunch. So I picked a cavernous dining hall packed with various cliques and noisy dorm kids, because I knew none of my friends would dock near it. I hadn't the courage to face anyone I knew yet.

I sat by myself, ordered a tray of food at a small back table, and kept my head down as I ate. That usually discouraged potential tablemates.

"You look familiar." An unusually scarred, thin-faced, blue-eyed human sat down with her tray across from mine. Had she actually gotten all those scars in fights, and did she really refuse any medical repair? Her scars showed despite skin less pallid than Shandy's but more so than mine, and her blond hair looked more golden and disarrayed than Shandy's.

I quickly scrunched up my screen around my stylus and sealed both in a pants pocket.

I'd started my journal in my cell. I'd found nothing to draw in there, and I needed to rail about what had happened to me. I could sort of understand now why

Aerrem spent so much time on her SF stories, although why she didn't think they were good enough for anyone to see them baffled me.

Unlike Aerrem, I might even try to post my rant on the Center com, where every smart kid here could find it. But I'd mainly recorded it for myself, and I'd gotten so caught up in it that I'd lowered my guard.

I shook my head at the girl. "I don't know you."

Now I stared at the telltale bracelet on the girl's pale wrist, and noticed a whole pack of JD's at the next table over. Shouldn't our tracers set off some sort of proximity alarm against this? Was this another flaw in the Center's security system? Or did security simply not care?

"Ah-hah, I remember." My uninvited tablemate pointed her salad fork at me. "You're the new girl in Discipline. Remember? I said 'Hi' on my way out!"

Oh, smooth. I picked up my spoon and blew on my steaming vegetable soup. Like Shandy, I couldn't seem to eat much else lately. Nor did I have any idea how to handle a whole new set of treacherous friends. My hand shook.

"My name's Chark. What's yours?"

My face burned, but I refused to look up again. I had a hard enough time guiding my spoon to my mouth.

"Have you suddenly gone deaf? I asked for your name!"

I swallowed hard. "It's none of your business," I said at last. "And if you don't mind, I'd rather eat by myself."

"What's the matter, flame-head!" She slammed her fork down hard enough to slosh the milk in our glasses. "Think you're too good for me?"

I shook my red hair, focused on my lunch, and refused to be drawn further into another game I couldn't win.

At last Chark stood up with her tray, but as she sauntered around the table, she suddenly dumped the contents of her glass over my head. Cold milk soaked through my hair to my scalp, ran down my face and neck, and splattered all over the grey shirt from my unimaginative cell.

"That should put out your fire!" Chark joined the shrieks of laughter from her gang at the next table, while something in me finally snapped and launched into high orbit.

I stood up, sputtering and shaking milk out of my hair, and hurled my hot soup bowl at her back. It created a unique multi-colored abstract on her pink blouse, expressing all my pent-up feelings perfectly.

"Ouch!" she screamed.

Then she joined the JD's at the next table as they all grabbed food and drinks and hurled them at me and anyone else in the way.

JOURNAL ENTRY 20

When the tables couldn't resupply them fast enough, Chark's gang stole ammunition from other lunchers' trays. So the food fight swept swiftly around the cafeteria, and I quickly gained allies, or at least diversions.

We ducked behind tables and chairs, and launched utensils, dishes, and trays when the food ran out. Tables contained food-delivery chutes so they were bolted down, but we even hurled chairs at each other, before launching into shouting, pummeling clumps on the floor.

Astonished sightseers replaced frightened evacuees at the large open doorways, but I was scanning only for Chark.

The first honor guards, responding no doubt to the security cams, tried to keep us from adding more blows to insults. They received misfired hits for their trouble, and quickly retreated to call for more help.

It took four guards to haul Chark and me apart for spider-stick and to drag us off in the howling parade to the lifts. Discipline quickly overflowed and more fights broke out in the holding cells, forcing multiple reshuffling.

Teachers and dorm parents arrived next and various groups disappeared into conference rooms, but at last some dorp commed where I belonged, and I was dumped back in my private little room after I refused to talk.

Gradually the muffled yelling died down, and most of the kids got to leave with their guardians.

Instead of hopping over to my cot, I'd knelt on the floor first. I foolishly tried to yank the stickum off my ankles from behind. The goo around my wrists melded to it, and I fell on my side.

This was a ridiculous complication I'd never seen in any action holo. So I was still lying curled and tangled on the carpet, my hair spiked and shirt stiff and stinking from dried milk, when Tarnek arrived hours later.

"I should leave you there." He scanned as if I was puke rotting at his feet.

"Why not?" My rage ignited. "I haven't got anything else to lose." With a tracer on my wrist until I grew too old for the Center, I'd never even get out on a day pass. I didn't know if I'd ever see my pets again, and he'd flushed my education and friends down a toilet along with my blood. What was left? "Did you come here just to gloat?"

"No, as your soon-to-be ex-guardian, I am supposed to inform you that after reviewing security footage, you've been charged with starting a riot and will be locked up for the rest of your four weeks. Or you'll wear restraints if you manage to come up with any excuse good enough to let you out of here meanwhile.

One more misstep and the Center will transfer you to a juvenile rehab facility."

The only place worse than a Center. I blinked, suddenly remembered the incriminating journal squashed in my pocket, and said nothing more.

"Now, maybe you could try a little harder to verify that you at least understand why you're here," Tarnek said grimly.

"Why I'm here?" I sputtered. "Because—because I broke Center rules, trying to defend myself in an unfair fight against four other students. And refused to join a gang of JD's. Now, maybe you can tell me why Branem and Chark's gang aren't rotting in here with me!" I refused to cry in front of him, but it took all I had.

"Well, I guess I'll have to do a better job of explaining." Tarnek folded his muscular arms over me. "A punishment serves no purpose if you don't understand why you're receiving it. But hasn't it occurred to you even once in here how lonely it feels to have no one on your side? You turned Branem into an outcast in my class, and he already faces more than enough challenges. Chark actually tried to make friends with you. So she's not very good at it. Did you have to burn her back?

"And was it really necessary to damage an entire cafeteria—scaring a lot of younger kids in the process—to avoid one pitiful group of kids?

"So don't go blaming me for your predicament. After our first midterms, I kept the class late, and asked everyone to help me decide whether to keep you in our program. The decision was too serious to make by myself, but apparently you disrupted the learning environment for nearly everyone. The class voted to expel you."

"So Branem turned everybody against me!"

"Branem? Aside from Shanden Fehrokc, Branem Fordem was the only student who voted to offer you a second chance."

And with that strange and deadly blow Tarnek left my room. Once again he'd forgotten to melt my bonds, abandoning me on the floor like the fused piece of garbage I was.

JOURNAL ENTRY 21

I couldn't sleep until the spider-stick finally melted on its own, sometime near dawn. Meanwhile, suffice it to say the Guilt Party began at last, and I was the Guest of Honor. I'd treated Branem very badly, not as a possible friend but as an obstacle, and now I deserved to suffer the loneliness I'm made him feel in class. I still didn't like how Shandy got treated in there, but that wasn't Branem's fault.

And I had quickly done the same thing to Chark.

I started crying, and couldn't stop. All Center residents carry pain in their hearts, and no one has the right to add to it.

So why had Branem voted to keep me in the class? The question zapped me as I paced and cried over the next couple days. Had he actually forgiven me first? How shameful. I didn't com how I could ever make it up to him. In here I couldn't even apologize—

I sat down on my cot and tried to make another comcall, to save one last shred of my self-respect. I was allowed to get through for this one, but I wasn't answered, so I had to leave a message requesting a return call.

Through the next week I left the same request over and over. I was polite, and refused to beg, explain, or hope. But I began to despair—apparently I was so worthless he would never talk to me again—until Tarnek finally called me back.

"What is it? I'm not your guardian anymore, so if you need advice, ask Admin for the Legal Aid Office—"

"I just want to apologize," I quickly launched, before he could disconnect.

"Is that all?"

"Yeah—yes." My heart pounded in my chest. "I'm very sorry. I shouldn't have treated Branem so badly. If you could give him my apology," I choked back tears, "and let the whole class know how sorry I am, I'd really appreciate it."

"If you think this will get you out—"

"No. That's all I want." And to prove it, I shut off my com. And cried some more. But I felt a micro better.

JOURNAL ENTRY 22

I commed that was the end of it. I'd said my piece, and I'd keep my story to myself, but I could never undo what I'd done. So I'd finish my time in Discipline. Then I'd go on with my lonely, claustrophobic life, until I got out of the Center some eon from now, with a fused education that would never let me leave Arrainius.

But two days later Tarnek let himself back into my cell, at lunch time. Fortunately I wasn't eating. I set aside my screen, which I was now using to catch up with GIP, to prevent further mortification when I returned. I sat up on my cot. What now? Had the Center decided to ship me off to rehab after all? I was afraid to ask, and began to tremble.

"Did you really mean it?" he said at last.

"Mean what? My apology? Of course. Did you tell Branem and the rest of the class for me?"

"No."

"Ohhh." I looked down and bit my lip, bracing myself for whatever he'd come here to say.

"I thought maybe you'd prefer to tell everyone yourself."

I stared wide-eyed up at him. "But I'm not allowed to leave here for another ten days—oh, you mean, after that? Maybe you could give my wristcom and my bracelet a pass so I could come during school hours—"

"We could do it that way. Or I could take you right now, in cuffs."

I gulped while my blood morphed into ice water. I suspected Tarnek was testing me. I had no idea why he'd bother, but as Aerrem says, never prolong the inevitable.

I'd already made up my mind to apologize to everyone possible in person, as soon as I was allowed out. So the time had arrived a little sooner than expected. I braced myself and stood up. "Okay. Now would be fine."

I enjoyed a micro of surprise on Tarnek's face, before he called in a guard to squirt fresh spider-stick around my wrists, behind my back.

Tarnek guided me to a lift that soon filled with gawking, giggling noontime crowds. I had to wait in front of the lecture room for everyone to return from lunch, and the looks on their faces ranged from astonishment to disgust.

The room blurred as I personally apologized to Branem for my meanness, and to everyone for any disruptions I'd caused. When I finished, Tarnek walked me back out, so everyone could see why I'd kept my hands behind my back. I wiped my eyes on my shoulders in the lift back up to Discipline.

Tarnek applied the release patch back in my cell. "Feel any better?"

"Yes. Thank you." Now please leave me alone. And even though Tarnek possessed no obvious esper genes, he quickly left, thank the Universe.

And after ten more tedious, lonely days filled with embarrassment and regret, something must have changed. My cell opened for me and told me I could return to my old room on Level Six. I thought about deleting my crimes from my screen, but it would take too much time and work. I needed my homework on it, so instead I snagged the screen and walked out of my cell.

JOURNAL ENTRY 23

In a translift, both elation and terror zapped me. I had received an unexpected reprieve, but once again I had only a micro to prepare another apology. Totally distracted, I exited into the wrong Level Six hall, and got so lost I had to find another lift and start over. But I still hesitated outside my door's sensor range.

What did Shandy think of me now? He had warned me about trouble from the outset. But I'd dumped his advice into vac, and fused any chance of staying in the same classroom with him. Would he forgive me? And how could I ever face Branem in this hallway again? Maybe I would have done better in Level Five, the other residential Level.

I don't know how long I stood there, my brain churning uselessly, before I took a deep breath and a step forward to meet my fate. I'd already dumped my life into vac—how could I make it any worse?

Max immediately ambushed me inside, hysterically happy to leap back into my arms. He poked his damp nose in my face. His coat looked recently groomed, and I buried my nose in his warm, clean-smelling fur. Then

I looked up, and realized two people were waiting for me in my roomie's front section—Shandy and Branem.

I'd expected to face Shandy right away. But Branem too? Were they actually friends now? Where did I fit in? And how would I ever find the right words for Branem? Ridiculously, I wanted to flee back to my cell, where the doors were clear, but hardly anyone ever looked at me.

"Hello, Taje." Shandy swiveled around on his desk chair. His smile clashed with a miserable look on his face. "My com said to expect you back tonight."

Sheefharn squawked angrily, and flapped from the divider down to Shandy's shoulder. Well, at least that was one individual who always made it quite clear where I stood.

"Hi, Shandy. Uh, Branem?" My brain flooded with white noise and I stood there like a vac-head, my mouth open but no words ready to launch.

"Hi, Taje," Branem said from his seat on Shandy's bed. "I've come to apologize to you, for myself, and for the whole class."

Astonished, I nearly dropped Max, and he whined until I got a better grip on him. "Branem, you've commed it all backwards! I'm the one who's supposed to apologize, to you and the class—"

"You already did. That was the bravest apology I ever scanned. And when the class still refused to let you back in—"

"Back in?"

"Tarnek asked for a second vote, wanting to be sure, right after he returned—from Level Two. And I'd already told everyone how I forced you into that vacful fight in the first place—"

"Tarnek didn't tell you?" Shandy's look of misery turned to shock, and his long hands knotted and turned white on his knees.

I shook my head, while a surprisingly vast disappointment crashed down on me. I'd had weeks to get over losing the class, aimed at a career I'd told myself I didn't even care that much about. I couldn't imagine returning to face everyone in there. But I still ached all over again.

"Blast!" Branem punched the bed. "Tarnek probably didn't want to disappoint you, in case they voted no again. And now I've gone and told you—"

"It's not your fault!" I told both of them. I would not let my mistakes zap anyone else again, if I could help it. "If Tarnek didn't warn you, how could you possibly know not to tell me?"

They both nodded reluctantly, and I sighed with relief. "Look, I never expected a reprieve. I only asked for permission to apologize. I knew I'd have to go back to GIP, but I won't have to work very hard at it. Instead I'd like to share your homework, if you're willing to risk it."

I was proud of this plan I'd just invented. I hoped it would make us all feel better. But Shandy and Branem both froze, before giving each other guilty looks, which sank my stomach. I set Max down and got him to chase one of his balls in Shandy's room, while I waited for the rest of the bad news.

"You tell her." Branem stood up to help kick the ball.

Shandy stared off into outer space, before returning to Arrainius and nodding. "We're quitting the class."

"You're what?" I halted in my tracks.

"We're leaving the class," Branem confirmed, focusing on the game with Max rather than meeting my eyes.

"We can no longer tolerate how Tarnek treated you," Shandy said. "It was bad enough when he began to complain about you behind your back, and I wasn't supposed to say anything. I can't stand it in there anymore."

"We can't learn in that kind of atmosphere, so we thought it best to submit our resignations," Branem said, nodding. "The class needn't waste its precious time on us either."

"Have you both gone nova?" I frantically scanned the determination locked into both their faces. They didn't even know I'd joined the class for my own selfish reasons. "I was thoughtless and cruel," I said instead. "I had plenty of warning, and I still crashed my place in the class. You two don't deserve any punishment for my vac-headedness!"

"We aren't being punished," Branem insisted.

"We are merely preserving our self-respect," Shandy said.

"This is your education, your futures you're dumping into vac—" for a career I'd chosen merely so I could leave Arrainius. I should have told them the truth long ago. I should tell them now.

But my deskcom chose this moment to buzz. I growled with inarticulate fury as I stomped past the grilled divider into my section to answer it. Max abandoned his ball to race after me.

"Hello?" I stared at my aquarium, which was crystal clean, and my glippers undulated over to eye me back. Not a speck of food or litter lay outside my neatly maintained ubuc terrarium, and Squeaker was sleeping peacefully in a fresh nest. But now I suddenly wondered why I kept any pet that had to live in a cage—

"Taje?"

I finally glanced at my comscreen. "Oh, Aerrem! Great Galaxy, it's so wonderful to see your face!"

"You're really not mad at me?"

"Why on Arrainius would I be mad at you?" Had everyone gone nova tonight?

"For telling on you, and taking your place in the class."

JOURNAL ENTRY 24

"Why didn't you tell me about Aerrem?" I demanded a moment later, back in Shandy's section.

Shandy stared down at our green carpet, so I turned to Branem.

"We were afraid," he said, also glancing away. "Afraid you'd get angry. When Tarnek made Aerrem tell him about the fight, he discovered she was eligible for the class, and he didn't want to waste your place."

"Misplaced grudges zapped me into Discipline in the first place," I said. "I really meant it when I apologized to everyone, because I did learn my lesson. If Aerrem can take the place I crashed and make a good launch from it, that's more than smooth with me. What I want to know now is whether you've told Aerrem about your plans to jettison."

Neither of them launched a reply, which answered my question anyway. The door buzzed, Aerrem asked to come in, and I told it to open.

"Taje, I can explain everything—" Aerrem rushed in, and Max rushed to greet her, butting her ankles until she picked him up to rub his soft chin.

"Aerrem, I am so glad to see you!" With no more secrecy! I could really talk with her again!

"You're truly not angry?"

"Truly. But I'm afraid you will be."

Puzzled and worried again, Aerrem scanned us all. "What's wrong now?"

I folded my arms. "Go on, tell her what you two plan to do." But Shandy and Branem remained silent. "Okay, you shameless cowards, I will. They're dropping out of the ecology program."

"What?" Aerrem's tail drooped. "But I've got so much catching-up to do, I'll need all the help I can get! I promoted a whole new pet-smuggling leader, so I could quit the business and make enough time for this program! You can't jettison on me now!"

I leaned against the wall, and watched an expert go to work. But she couldn't win. Shandy and Branem simply refused to answer Aerrem's objections.

"We're just banging our heads against a bulkhead!" Aerrem said at last. "Come on, Taje, let's blast out of here."

My brain was too tired to spend the rest of the evening scheming, but I followed her as far as the lifts. I stopped there. "Where are we going?"

"Ready for some exercise?"

I lit up. "How'd you guess?"

"Oh, I've heard the—accommodations—on Level Two are a bit cramped. But don't ask me to ice skate. I'm not feeling *that* generous."

We changed into bright yellow gym clothes and gloves during a short wait for a maze court to open up. It was Aerrem's favorite game, not mine, and I played badly, but with relish. It felt wonderful to have room to run and jump, and smash away at the small but very bouncy ball Aerrem chose, whenever I managed to hit it at all.

However, halfway through the second maze I crashed. I was out of shape and came to a gasping halt. I eyed Aerrem warily. But even she was breathing hard. "Had enough?" she asked, grinning.

"Yeah—"

"Great! Take a seat! I reserved for three rounds."

Great Universe, leave it to Aerrem to find some privacy at the Center! We dropped our rackets on the rubbery green floor, and sat down against the nearest similarly soft, low green barrier.

For a while we leaned back and breathed hard. At last I eyed my unusually quiet friend. She cocked a dark eyebrow back at me, and nervously tossed the bright orange ball from hand to hand.

"I couldn't call you, Taje, or I would have explained a lot sooner—"

"I know, Aerrem. It's okay. The better person earned my place. But I don't understand why Shandy and Branem would dump their futures into the same vac with me!"

"Well, Shandy's a rather protective roomie—"

"He tried. But I didn't listen. And Branem—I treated him so badly—"

"He wasn't the only one treated badly!"

I stared at my amazing dorm sib. "How much do you know, Aerrem?"

Now her ginger-colored face flushed, and she scanned her lap. "More than you probably realize."

"How much—" I gulped, wanting to know but afraid of the answer, "how much did you actually see of the fight I had with Branem?"

"Enough."

"So you really scanned the beginning of it?"

"No. Trist and Cam found out about that part and told me."

"Oh," I said, as I remembered to breathe. "So you didn't have time to help defend me—"

"I couldn't help you, Taje. I'm sorry—"

"It's okay! I know you tried to explain what happened to Tarnek—"

"He used me to jettison you, Taje. I still don't understand why Tarnek was out to zap you so badly. I called him because I thought he'd settle you and Branem down fast enough to prevent serious injury. But that's not what I was trying to tell you. Are you still sure you want to know all of it?"

"All of it?" My voice faded to a squeak. Somehow, I suddenly realized, she'd already known which teacher to call!

Aerrem shook her head. "I should get this over with. Never prolong the inevitable. And you'll find out soon enough. I couldn't jump in, because you were fighting with my new roommate."

"Ohhh," I groaned, bending over my lap to plant my elbows, and covering my frying face with my hands. "This just gets better and better! But I heard classmates are made roommates, to protect class secrecy. You weren't in the class when they moved Branem to your room. Why did you get him as your new roomie?"

"Branem needed to room with me. And even that's more than I should say about him." Yes, Aerrem said that. Aerrem saw my look of shock, sighed, and stood up. "Enough. It's getting late. Have you had any dinner?"

"No thanks." Food was the last thing I wanted after all this vacful news.

"Nonsense." Aerrem led us to the showers, we toweled off, and changed back into our regular clothes. Next she insisted that I join her in ordering dinner at a nearby snack bar. I nibbled, pretending to eat.

JOURNAL ENTRY 25

Despite Aerrem's best efforts, I didn't eat much that night, or even the next day. I dragged through my classes, did my schoolwork, and was polite to Naemar, despite classmates' stares and nasty whispers.

After classes I rushed back to my room, as if I wanted to jump from a burning space ship into cold vac. But I wasn't expecting to find Shandy, Branem, and Aerrem all waiting for me there with galaxy-spanning grins.

Even Max did an extra energetic dance at my feet. I picked him up and gently hugged him to my chest.

"We thought you'd never get back—"

"We did it!" Branem interrupted Aerrem. "We got our validated transfers this morning—"

"Smooth," I said. "Now you've ruined your futures too. Remind me how this is supposed to make me feel better—Aerrem, I thought you at least were on my side!"

"I am! And I think congratulations are in order."

"What?"

"We got you reinstated!" Branem burst out.

Aerrem scanned the fear of hope on my face. "It's true!" she tried to reassure me. "Check your com."

"When the class understood how serious and upset we felt about it, they voted one more time—in your favor," Branem said.

"Fortunately, or I'd have threatened them next!" Aerrem added.

"With what?" I imagined Aerrem's emergency pet defense team tracking down and tormenting every classmate, and I laughed. "No, don't tell me." I shook my head. "But Tarnek didn't object?"

"I think he was actually pleased and relieved," Shandy said.

"Great Galaxy! So I'm really back in."

"You're back, on probation." Aerrem snickered. "But the work of catching up should keep you out of any more trouble—you're now at least as far behind as I am."

"Thanks for reminding me. But wait—don't tell me you guys plotted this all along?"

"That's our secret," Branem gloated.

"Shandy?"

"Uh, maybe it crossed our minds, once or twice."

"Great Universe, what a nova risk you took!" I coughed, and turned away.

"Taje, don't disappear!" Aerrem jumped up. "We've planned a celebration in our snack bar—"

"Can you dock here first, for a few minutes, please? I think—I need a quick shower first."

Anyone else would have left me alone then, but Aerrem followed me right into the bathroom.

"You have one last duty," she said, hands on hips, as I lowered the toilet for Max.

"What?" Her face blurred. Whom had I forgotten to thank or apologize to? I wiped my eyes and quickly stripped.

"Invite Trist and Cam."

"What?" I vac-headedly repeated.

"Invite them to our dinner party. Cam worked so hard taking great care of your pets—"

"I thought Shandy must have helped with that—"

"He would have, but Cam volunteered and stuck it out faithfully. I don't know how much guilt had to do with it, since he and Trist reported the fight to me. That's probably why they also persisted in trying to call you, despite dire threats on my part—"

"Oh, their comcall! I'm sorry I crashed down on them so hard, but I was so afraid for both of them—"

"Oh, believe me, they got it worse from me, when they had the nerve to brag about it the next day. Trist should have to stay behind in her room tonight for her trouble! But she did help us find out where you were, and how long you'd be stuck there."

"I'm really sorry," I said again as I stepped into the shower, and the curtain closed. "You can invite them. You all risked so much—"

"Taje, you've already said it. That's enough. But I should say I'm sorry I didn't have the courage to face your personal apology in class. I'm ashamed now to admit I hid in the bathroom, as soon as I heard the rumor that you were coming. But it must have been hugely smooth—"

"It will never be enough," I muttered.

"What?"

No answer.

"Taje? You still in there? Are you crying?"

What did she think I was doing? Escaping out through the drain?

"Okay, whatever. Just hurry up. I'm starving!"

I wasn't the slightest bit hungry, but I'd do anything for these friends. Anything.

JOURNAL ENTRY 26

"A party-sized pan-galactic pizza," Branem said as we sat down at a round table in the snack bar. "Nothing less will do!"

"With krazzle claws?" Cam chimed in bravely. "This is Taje's party!"

"Oh, not krazzle claws!" Trist and Aerrem's tails lashed in unison as they wrinkled their noses.

"A pan-galactic pizza has everything!" Cam insisted. "Right, Taje?"

I swallowed. "Right. I'll take them on the side—"

"Not tonight," Aerrem said stoically. "We'll order claws on a third of it."

"No, really—a third?"

"Cam deserves a fair portion of them too." Aerrem grinned savagely, yet Cam nodded proudly. "But remember, no meat on Shandy's section. Tofu will probably work." Shandy also nodded. Istrannians were vegetarians, so that was how he was raised, and he still didn't even like the taste of most meat cell cultures.

"Okay. Everyone stick in their ID's," Branem said. We slotted our cards, Branem gave the menu our complicated order, and the steaming platter emerged from the center of our table a moment later, while plates popped out at our places.

Aerrem snagged Trist's card. "It's not even the right color." She stared at both sides suspiciously.

Trist grabbed it back from her. "It worked, didn't it? And why does the Center care how much pizza I've eaten this month? It has all the major nutrients—"

"Whew!" Aerrem changed her focus to the pizza, and quickly shoved the krazzle claw slices onto the plates in front of Cam and me. "Eat fast!" She was a lot more relaxed about serving Shandy. But I wondered if the smell of Naridian sausage on the rest of the pizza bothered him. If so, he was too polite to say anything about it.

While the pizza consumed my friends' attention, I ate the smallest claw off my piece. I still wasn't hungry, but I always did like the crunchiness of the purple shells, and the squiggly blue part inside. I peeked at Shandy, caught him nibbling the vegetables off his slice, and we exchanged smiles.

I cleared my throat and snatched up my milk glass. "Thanks, everybody, for docking with me, even when I didn't deserve it!" We clashed our glasses together, and next I toasted each friend in turn.

"Thank you, Shandy, for being my faithful roomie, now and always."

He nodded, his cheeks turning red.

"Thank you, Branem, for finding some way to forgive me."

"It takes at least two to make a fight. And it wasn't a fair fight or a fair punishment."

I shook my head at him, and turned to Cam. "Thanks for the best care my pets have ever had!"

Cam's shoulder spikes had erected as he poked the claws on his pizza with his fork, but now his iridescent spines retracted and he gave me a beautiful coppery human-style smile.

"Thank you, Aerrem, for being my dorm sister, and for always doing what's right, no matter how difficult."

She nodded proudly.

"And Trist," I grinned, "thanks for finding me for my friends."

"You told her!" Trist turned to Aerrem. "I thought we weren't going to tell her about that—"

"Shhh! Never mind!"

My grin disappeared. "Never mind?"

"It's nothing—"

"It was too something!" Trist interrupted Aerrem. "I had to learn how your wristcoms worked, sort out the correct tracer signal, and teach everyone how to triangulate quickly. So we could locate you outside of Level Two, during lunch—"

"Trist!" Aerrem roared.

"Well, it wasn't that easy, that's all." Trist took a bite, a strand of cheese stretching between her mouth and her pizza. "My sister really wanted to consult with you over the choice of a new leader for the business—"

"Shut up, Trist—"

"Aerrem!" I loudly interrupted. "I wasn't out of Discipline for very long—and if you found me, how come I didn't see you?"

Aerrem looked down at her plate, picked up her edge crust—which she normally hates—took a big bite out of it, and worked at chewing on it.

I glanced around the table, and suddenly everyone stuffed their mouths too full to talk. Even Cam finally tried a claw, and slowly swallowed with a spike-rattling shudder.

"Ohhh," I suddenly commed it. "Not *that* lunch. Please tell me it wasn't that lunch!"

Now Aerrem met my scan with an irritated look. "How could we have possibly missed it? With Trist shouting directions over our wristcoms, and all the yelling coming from that cafeteria—well, it's no wonder you never scanned us. But please don't try to claim you want to avoid conflicts, ever again, because I won't believe you."

JOURNAL ENTRY 27

Late that night, after we'd gone to bed on opposite sides of our divider and told our lights to go out, I could thank Shandy one more time. In private.

This was where we normally talked about the hard stuff. In the dark, where neither of us had to expose our red faces or our tears. I realized I'd missed this time together most of all, even though I never liked reliving bad experiences, like not knowing what had happened to my mom.

But I'd also never scanned the positive side of that, until Shandy had broken down one night and told me everyone he'd grown up with had emptied their guts out both ends and died.

Shandy was my first and only roommate since I graduated from my Center dorm family. But he finally admitted serious problems with more than one roommate, before the Center placed us together. At the time, I couldn't imagine anyone having trouble getting along with Shandy, but his confession still made me proud.

The best part, however, was gradually discovering how much we had in common. I missed riding my yusahmbul, and Shandy missed his rides on Istrannian skauls. We both missed dirt, grass, trees, streams, ponds, lakes, and open skies—clear, cloudy, or star-filled. And we'd both run away countless times on our homeworlds, trying hopelessly to stay where we belonged.

So tonight I couldn't stop myself from asking my roomie one last question. "Shandy, what in the Universe would you and Branem have done, if the class refused to change its vote? Were you really ready to quit?"

I heard him roll over, and emit a loud fake snore.

I snorted, rolled over myself, and tried to fall asleep. Tomorrow I'd face the rest of our class, and my future, which my friends had yanked back barehanded from a black hole.

JOURNAL ENTRY 28

"Hey, Taje, we've docked in here!"

I had almost walked zombie-fashioned right past our student lounge. Shandy lay in there, draped like a limp and nearly lifeless glipper across the couch, while Branem paced restlessly around him.

"Where's Aerrem?" Branem demanded as soon as I crash-landed in an armchair.

"Still working on her last test." I blinked blearily, trying to focus farther than a comscreen's distance away. I'd done it. I'd finished my first-quarter finals for planetary ecology. Whether I'd passed was another question—for tomorrow. I worriedly scanned Shandy, and Branem shrugged.

"He says it's just a headache. That last essay question was a stunner, don't you think? Three native intelligent species, living in the most intricate ecosystems—how did it all work without falling apart? Your guess is as good as mine! Do you think you passed?"

"Maybe." Even Shandy had fallen behind while plotting with Branem for my reinstatement, but not nearly as much as Aerrem and I. Branem had worked heroically to get both of us caught up in our awkward new trio team, and in the process had surprised everybody with his own progress. But some of the most basic camping gear questions had still fused me—

"Aerrem!"

Aerrem halted outside the doorway and turned groggily towards Branem's voice. We all lurched to our feet to follow her out.

"I don't know if I passed," she said, in answer to our anxious questions.

"Tarnek says you can always join one of next year's classes, if you don't make it this year—"

"But we want Aerrem with us!" Branem interrupted my feeble attempt at consolation. "Let's go ask Tarnek if she passed!"

"Right now?" Aerrem stopped in her tracks and her tail froze.

"Never prolong the inevitable!" I laughed at her.

"We haven't seen him leave," Branem said.

"Well, only if the rest of you ask for your scores too!"

We ended up pushing and shoving each other down the long hallway to the teacher's small office in back. Tarnek's door opened when we stepped within range, and he looked up at us with surprise.

"We can't let Aerrem suffer in suspense, all night long!" Branem said.

"Nor could I allow any of my friends to suffer the same fate—" Aerrem said.

"Even Branem and Shandy had to work extra hard—" I said.

"Enough, already!" Tarnek interrupted us. "I can't take any more of this frenzy myself. But one at a time, please. Aside from Center privacy rules, I don't think I can handle more than one of you in this state."

We immediately ganged up on Aerrem, before she could whip us all with her tail, and thrust her into the office. The door slid shut behind her, and we waited in long, breathless suspense.

At last she burst out shrieking, nearly stopping my heart, until she yelled, "I passed! I passed! I got C's! Tarnek says he's totally amazed!

"Now it's your turn, Taje!" She said, and I was thrown into the little room, with the door closing at my back. I gulped. Tarnek and I had treated each other with extreme politeness since my return, and I'd had to work so hard I'd had little time to wonder how he truly felt about me. Until now.

He grimly studied his deskcom screen. "Well, I've seen better."

Uh oh, here it comes. Well, it was at least worth a try—

"And I hope by our next set of tests, you'll understand more, and memorize less—"

"I passed?" How could I take more tests if I'd failed? I peered over his shoulder, and scanned grades similar to Aerrem's. My worst ever, but smooth under the circumstances, and good enough.

"Barely," Tarnek said. But now his golden face hinted at a smile. "Since you were absent for an entire month, I must assume Branem put in a lot of hard work to get you this far."

"Yessir. He did, sir. He should get extra credit—"

"Enough." Tarnek's smile grew full-force. "Send him in."

Branem came out looking very pleased and reported mostly B's. But we had to wait an extra long time for Shandy, and we all grew worried again.

Finally he exited, and strode calmly on down the hall towards our main exit. We rushed to catch up with him.

"What did you get?" Aerrem asked him.

"I passed," Shandy said.

"He never talks about his grades," I explained.

"But something's up," Aerrem said. "I can smell it."

"What?" Branem demanded.

"Did Tarnek dump more homework on you?" I asked, more concerned than ever. Was Tarnek trying to break Shandy?

Shandy smiled, and said nothing.

"You should have told us back there, when we could have fought back for you!" Aerrem said.

Shandy shrugged as he vectored out our main door to the nearest lifts. "I don't mind this homework. You won't either."

"What!" we exploded, but he refused to say more. We had to follow him back to our room to view the message waiting on his deskcom—in fact, on all our deskcoms. Then we crammed like black holes for our next pop quiz—our first practical exam.

JOURNAL ENTRY 29

Early the next morning we dumped our backpacks in a sloppy line in the hallway, outside our main classroom door. Shandy and Aerrem ran through our packing list aloud one last time for everyone.

Tarnek hadn't told us where we were going, or what to bring, aside from leaving room in our packs for food from ship stores. He'd just ordered us to get ready for a spaceflight of several days and a five-day ecosystem analysis at the end of it.

So the whole class had spent the night using our deskcoms to organize a list, and packing and repacking as our list evolved. Would the ship have laundry facilities? I decided not to chance it. If I needed more room in my pack, I'd leave some of my clothes in the ship. But it was still going to be tight, with all the gear we had to pack.

I finished closing a bulging seal on my pack, and yawned as a confused servocleaner bumped past us.

Kijan and Dojan, our two Tliesjians, coaxed us into lining up space cadet fashion, to salute Our Great Leader on arrival. Tarnek nodded at us, pleased, and introduced a new sidekick, an unusually dark tall human.

"This is Lokki Kem, our assistant trip leader, so please treat her with at least as much respect as you do me!"

Kem wrinkled her wide, dark coffee-colored nose as we all groaned cheerfully, before gearing up and followed our pack-laden teachers into the nearest lifts. We exited into the lobby of red-carpeted Level One, the only Center Level with access to tube lifts.

Tarnek deliberately inserted himself right behind me in the security gate line, and a shiver crawled up my back. But he quietly explained that he'd already arranged for the gate sensors to pass my tracer, and he promptly cut to the front.

I'd almost forgotten the bracelet on my wrist, so it was smooth that he'd remembered it. None of us had slept much last night, but it was our teachers who fell asleep in the underground tube car.

Aerrem turned around in her seat next to Branem to face Shandy and me. "What did you do with your pets?" she whispered. "I thought you would bring them over to my room for Dojan's older brother to look after, along with my zoo."

"Oh, sorry! In the Big Rush I forgot to let you know that Cam agreed to take care of them again, along with Sheefharn," I whispered back.

"Think we forgot anything?" Gkorjneil's yawn revealed wide yellow teeth, as he leaned forward in the seat behind Shandy.

"I hope not." Krorn blinked sleepy orange eyes across the aisle from me. Was he a transgenic, or a human with a mutant gene? Did his golden skin and smooth dark hair protect him, or did he get teased too? Well, it wouldn't be from me. Or Shandy.

"Think it's a test?" his very human partner Tarknes wondered. She too had golden skin, and, to go with her almond eyes, beautiful glossy dark hair, but for some reason she kept it short like mine.

"Of course it's a test!" Kijan waggled his furry ears in the seat behind Krorn.

"And if we've forgotten something important?" Piel was too short for me to see his face a couple rows up, but the tips of his blue antennae trembled above his seat.

"You can all return to the ship for the duration! Now hush!" Tarnek said with his eyes closed a couple rows back, and we all jolted even more awake.

But I fell asleep on the windowless, grav-controlled shuttle ride up to the orbital station, and Shandy had to shake me awake when we docked. We made our way to baggage claims and found our packs.

Our leaders rushed us through more wide, echoing hallways too quickly to appreciate the full range of FIL travelers on the go. I thought I might have scanned a Big Orange Cube sliding down a cross-corridor among the crowds, but I blinked and it was gone.

"When do we stop for breakfast?" Branem complained.

Shandy and I turned paler at the thought of food, and Aerrem scanned us.

"Don't you love the nauseating excitement of it all?" She grinned evilly, but she was looking a bit green herself.

At last we made it to our ship's dock. Tarnek stuck his ID in the wallcom to open the loading hatch, and the screen next to it showed our ship. It looked like a strange, glossy, bright yellow-green insect.

"Why does it look so weird?" Crell asked.

"Because it's built for atmospheric, space, and paraspace flight," Tarnek said, revealing how expensive this little transport must be. We'd seen a holo of it our first day of class, but we'd been too excited to question it. "Now get onboard and stash your packs!"

We peeked into the small engine room in back as we filed in. We strapped our packs down in the hold after removing our sleeping bags, which we used to stake out our territories on the brown carpeted floor of a large, stripped cabin. Two bathrooms separated it from the captain and pilot's cabins, set aside for our teachers.

Forward, from either side of the cabins, we entered a table-crammed lounge, which also contained a med-niche with a hospital bunk bed, a sophisticated bioscanner, a drug synthesizer, and well-stocked clear cabinets in one corner. From the lounge we took turns touring a pilot room so tiny it looked like it couldn't hold four seats, but it did.

"Okay, who's awake enough to launch us?" Tarnek asked after everyone returned to the lounge. "You'll all have to take a turn at launching or landing sometime. Meanwhile, you'll study onboard lessons and run sims, so you'll all earn Class Ten pilot licenses before the end of this year."

We would have cheered more loudly if we'd felt more awake. Tarknes, Taemar, and Hannen boldly volunteered to fill the three student pilot seats, so the rest of us could sit back and dazedly watch cloudy blue Arrainius shrink away on a wallcom screen. I nearly wept with relief as distant stars popped out around it and classmates cheered again.

Kem had warned us not to fall asleep before we launched into paraspace—apparently the transition could cause very disturbing dreams—but I don't think any of us would have missed scanning our full departure. Another cheer arose as the screen finally went blank, unable to depict paraspace in any meaningful way for us. Most of our class vectored next to the bunkroom.

Later we discovered we were simply earning very limited flight licenses for minors, which mostly involved learning how to tell the ship's com what to do, and making sure that's what it did. So our piloting lessons weren't that difficult or time-consuming. Others complained, but I was pleased with how easy I found it. That meant I had a decent chance of flying this thing all by myself, if I ever got the chance.

Kem also ran short fun classes in stuff like knot tying, wristcom map and compass reading, tracking, and camp cooking. However, by the end of the trip it felt like a big sleepover party, with classmates playing games and talking vac in groups or through their wristcoms, all over the ship at any hour.

The last night of our outbound trip, I churned restlessly in my bag. I knew I'd need all the sleep I could get for this next test. However, between all the noisy chattering, and worrying whether I could meet the challenge of this field trip, I despaired of ever getting to sleep.

As conversations faded at last to low murmurs, the bags Taemar and Hannen had sealed together began to emit callisthenic noises.

I moaned. "Doesn't anybody realize we're landing tomorrow? What in paraspace are they doing over there?"

The low night-light glinted in Aerrem's widened brown eyes. "You don't know?" she whispered beside me. "I realize you're growing a little slower than average, but you've got your implant." She patted my sleeping bag over my left hip. She must have noticed the tiny scar sometime when I stripped in front of her for showering.

"Stop it!" I shoved her hand away, glad it was too dark for her to see my red face.

"So you're still a virgin?" Aerrem persisted.

I rolled over, away from her.

"I'll assume that's a 'yes,'" she said. "But if that's the case—no, I really shouldn't ask."

"Ask what?" I rolled back.

"Never mind—"

"What?"

"No—"

"I'll tickle you and wake up everybody!" I grabbed Aerrem's bag around her waist. I knew Aerrem was quite ticklish.

"Okay, okay, I just wondered if you haven't done anything, what about Shandy?"

"Oh, Aerrem!"

"See, I told you I shouldn't ask."

JOURNAL ENTRY 30

The fresh breeze smelled so alive! Gravity felt a bit lighter here, and I stood on the toes of my new boots to peek out the hatch, before my line of classmates let me off the ship. The hatch outlined a wonderfully clear blue sky.

We all wore our new camping clothes from Central Supply. They were tougher, warmer, came in more subtle colors, and had more pockets than our usual Center clothes—and they made us feel the part more. Our scaly Lorratians carried packs that included slings and belts with extra compartments, to make up for not needing clothing, and we had all finished stuffing our pockets and packs right before landing.

I eagerly strapped into my pack in our line and climbed down the ship rungs, only to find myself on a concrete landing pad across from a civilized maroon ranger station with lavender trim and flower boxes. A neatly planted red and violet botanical garden stood to one side, and a nova pink manicured lawn stretched down to meet us. The only promising sight was a dark rose-colored forest towering beyond the station.

I scanned my pants and shirt ruefully. I'd made my first change of clothing in our class locker room, so Max couldn't jump all over me, because I'd chosen grey-green hiking clothes. They complemented my green eyes and didn't clash with my red hair. But I'd stick out here like a pet turtle running loose on Admin's red carpet.

Aerrem and Branem had done better with pale maroon and tan, respectively, but Shandy's pale orange clothes made him glow like dawn.

An olive-skinned ranger strode down a gravel path across the lawn towards us, and I felt instantly jealous of her multi-pocketed maroon uniform and smooth brimmed hat. Her pockets out-numbered ours, and our visored caps simply didn't measure up to her official ranger hat, even if it had makeshift holes for her horns.

The Altruskan embraced our two leaders and laughed at the disgusted look we gave the local scenery. "Welcome to Planet Darwin! May all of you be fit enough to survive it!" The ranger chuckled at her own obviously well used joke, and we snorted.

Tarnek turned to face us. "I know what you're all thinking! So this isn't a real wilderness? Well, what made you think ecologists only work on pure ecosystems? And how many years have most of you been stuck Inside? Show us what you can do here, before we'll consider wilder challenges!"

So we kept our comments mostly to ourselves as we tightened our pack straps and followed our leaders to a signed trailhead at the edge of the forest.

We stared up and up, now remembering or realizing how tall trees could really grow. Something chittered back down at us, and we exchanged our first smiles.

Those smiles faded fast as we stumbled our way down a duff trail for a couple of hot, sweaty hours, pursued by an annoying cloud of reddish-orange insects whenever we slowed down. They tickled, but at least they couldn't quite bring themselves to bite into our alien flesh, and we arrived breathless at a campsite in a clearing.

Trampled spaces on the ground awaited our flexitents, and our campground came complete with tables, benches, latrines, and faucets with sterilized hot and cold running water. More signs of civilization. I didn't know whether to feel disappointment or relief.

As teams selected tent sites, I spotted Shandy looking more lonely and lost than ever. I looked at Aerrem, and she and even Branem eagerly waved me over to Shandy. So I joined him on the perimeter to set up a two-person tent. Which meant we could finally release our hot, sore bodies from our packs and rejoin as roomies.

Our teachers and the ranger stood inside a central log-bench ring and gossiped, while we changed into cooler shorts and struggled to set up camp. At last we sat on the ring of logs while our leaders reviewed the boundaries of the sector they wanted us to analyze, so they could set us loose for the rest of the morning in Byrne Park.

We nervously gathered our gear and marched down the main trail just far enough for a private class meeting in a small clearing.

"Shandy, you're our class T.A. Tell us what we're supposed to do!" Jael said, and other classmates pleaded with him.

"I don't know any more about this game than you do," Shandy retorted.

Surprised, I glanced at him, and discovered he was still breathing hard from this short hike. I suddenly realized he'd only gotten to referee our exercise sessions, not join in. I'd be angry too.

"We should divide up the work," Hannen hastily suggested. "This territory is too big for any one team, and our teachers constantly emphasize teamwork. So let's use it. We have to record our own reports, but doesn't mean we can't pool our data."

"We'll need to identify as many species as possible in each micro-environment, and sort out their resources—who depends on what, where, and when," Taemar added. "But forget about anything beyond daily cycles—our teachers can't possibly expect more in five days. Which also means tagging any wildlife is pointless. We can only put together a quick and dirty holo of what's here right now."

"Shandy, didn't Tarnek give you any special assignment here?" Hannen asked, also shocked.

Shandy shook his head, looking down at his boots, which hid his eyes behind his bangs. I'd have thought Tarnek would have told him to take charge, or at least be available for team questions, but I'd given up on understanding our teacher.

"Well, why don't you pair up with Taje?" Aerrem said. "You don't mind, do you, Branem?"

Of course he didn't. We'd made up, but we'd never be best friends. And Aerrem, used to being a leader, took charge of assignments, to keep any team from repeating the work of another.

So Shandy and I, being so happy to team up, agreed to spend—or should I say waste?—our first morning on Darwin setting traps. We could scan for wildlife, but we'd need some individuals for closer study.

But I quickly became as cranky as my teammate while we tried to com what baits to use and what might be useful animal trails. Setting traps was really a wild guessing-game this early on, especially since we were also just learning how to do real field scans. But somebody had to try first, and Aerrem elected us.

Meanwhile Aerrem and Branem ran various soil, water, and air analyses, and later said they encountered more glitches than any lab test could possibly throw at them. And I don't think they were only trying to make us feel better. Despite numerous questions from every team, Tarnek and Kem mostly replied with more questions, forcing us to turn to each other for help.

All Shandy and I caught that first morning was a pathetic mass of red bugs coating a half-rotten cluster of orange berries. And I topped that off by leading us on one blind trail after another in search of our last trap. I'd forgotten to turn on its location signal.

Finally we had to call Aerrem and Branem, admit our mistake, endure their teasing, and get them to help us triangulate on the trap. We had to use a wristcom inanimate object scanner mode we'd never tried before. That took even more time to figure out, before we suffered an uphill hike back to camp for lunch.

We arrived none too soon. Furry little pinkish-grey critters our teachers called whifflegiks had invaded our camp and our backpacks and stolen some of our food, despite scent-proof packaging. Had our teachers done anything to stop the thieves or called us back in time to stop them? Of course not.

We had to use up the second half of our lunch break tying our packs in trees, after spending the first half fusing Kem's cooking lessons. I used too much water to reconstitute the chocolate pudding, much to the disgust of my classmates, but I was so hungry I drank my share of it. And I gobbled up Shandy's leftovers, while he pulled his boot off just far enough to doctor a big blister on his ankle.

"Shandy, you should have stopped right away to apply some synderm, before that got so bad!" Aerrem said.

"I didn't notice it until we were almost back here."

Aerrem and I exchanged shocked looks. Another cruel side effect from the Istrannian plague? Neither of us dared ask.

Then, after a tedious afternoon spent trying to make sense of wristcom scanner readings on a Real World, I burnt a fingertip while helping with dinner. And that was from working in the dark by belt and stove lights, because we'd returned at dusk to discover further 'gik predations on our packs.

At least Tarnek and Kem now got serious about our food storage problems, and taught us how to counter-balance our packs, hanging them from slender tree limbs far from the ground or climbable tree trunks. But it was too late to save my smooth new Central Supply pack from chew-holes, spilled food powders and crumbs, and some small but stinky gifts.

"Should we start rationing?" Taemar asked, but apparently our noble teachers had accounted for this annoying lesson. They simply shook their heads. Next Tarnek caught Piel's human partner, Jael, marching into camp with a cup instead of a water bottle hanging from his utility belt.

"Okay, listen up! How many of you didn't bother to use your bottle filters for drinking stream water today?"

Luckily Shandy and I weren't among the sheepish vac-heads who had to raise their hands. We were both too paranoid, for Shandy's sake at least.

Jael gulped. "What—what's going to happen to me? I thought we learned in first aid that unadapted native microbes can't usually infect alien visitors?"

"That's true," Kem said. "But look at this place—how many people have camped here before you? Did you think the whifflegiks only learned how to rip into packaging and eat alien food today?

"The micro-organisms on Darwin are no longer all native, and the native microbes have had time to partially adjust to us—which can be worse than full adaptation. You'll need medication from my kit, or your digestive tract will endure an uncomfortable battle tonight."

I don't know about Jael, but I endured an uncomfortable battle that night. I kept hearing strange rustlings in the bushes right outside our tent, the environmental temperature plummeted, and my blistered finger now throbbed so badly my whole hand felt like it was on fire. Meanwhile the rest of me shivered uncontrollably.

I felt crushed. I had longed forever to escape into a wilderness, even if only for a short field trip, and now I felt miserable.

I was so tired I hadn't even remembered to gaze up at real stars before I ditched into our tent and scrunched into my sleeping bag. Now I thrashed around in it, struggling to get the padded part back under me so the cold bumpy ground couldn't add to my torment.

"Taje?"

Oh, smooth! Had I kept my roomie awake too? "What?"

"Don't forget the temp controls on your bag. It's cold tonight, isn't it?"

"Oh, yeah."

"Did you do anything for that burn?"

"No. I left my first-aid kit in my pack—hanging in a tree."

"Here, use mine." Shandy told the tent light to turn on, which he'd turned off for us to undress for bed. We respected each other's naked privacy out of long habit, although I guessed his curiosity was growing along with mine. Even a quick glimpse of his long feet . . . oh well. Our friendship was too important to risk. Shandy handed me a tube from his kit. "This synderm really helped my blister."

"Thanks, Shandy."

"Any time."

JOURNAL ENTRY 31

"It's just a park!" Branem tried to rush Shandy and me, while we tried to verify we weren't merely duplicating Aerrem and Branem's recent efforts. "None of our data is going to make complete sense!"

"We'll do our best with what we have," Aerrem agreed, but her tail sagged. This was our last day on Darwin, and between having spent too much time grumbling about how artificial this whole assignment seemed, and too much of the rest of our time working out wristcom bugs we'd never experienced in class, the whole class felt anxious.

"We're almost done," Shandy said.

"I'm still not sure whether this is simply a larval phase of the same insect species you two recently analyzed," I warned Branem and Aerrem.

"Pooling our class data should clarify a lot of our questions," Aerrem tried to reassure me.

"I wish I could feel that hopeful," I retorted, wincing as I wiped sweat from my stinging face. I felt hot and irritated, and the call to lunch didn't help any, for now we discovered we were completely out of food.

"I thought you said we'd have enough without rationing!" Lowwind, another heavily tanned, brown-haired human classmate complained to our teachers. I thought of her as one of the class whiners, although I never said it aloud.

"We do have enough." Tarnek strode to the middle of our log circle. "Sit down for a moment, think about what's happened here, and check your analyses. Is the native biochemistry compatible with ours? It's the same question potential colonists will ask you, and the 'giks have already given you a strong hint."

"You want us to eat our plant specimens?" Nessel, Lowwind's very similar-looking but somewhat brighter teammate asked anxiously. Kijan and Dojan, Tliesjian carnivores, wrinkled their noses. An omnivore, I still sympathized, along with many of my nervous classmates.

Not only did a lot of our collection suddenly appear rather unappetizing, especially for those of us who couldn't digest tougher plant structures. But also most of us had counted on using our final samples for more scientific purposes this afternoon.

"Don't worry. If anything, you'll have to perform your most exacting analyses before you attempt to eat any of your samples," Tarnek said. "If we share right-handed sugars and left-handed amino acids, we're also more likely to share negative reactions to protective bio-toxins.

"And don't neglect your animal specimens. I know you weren't as successful collecting mobile species—" and here some classmates chuckled nervously, but Tarnek didn't crack a smile—"but it looks like you have enough for each of you to humanely kill and dissect one animal, before cooking any edible remains. Although our wristcoms can supply detailed scans, there are a few facts you'll only learn from necropsy, and it's time you all faced up to it.

"Now I also know some of you are vegetarians, and the rest of you are used to meat cultures," Tarnek hastily added. "But anyone who can digest animal proteins should give them a try. Some day you may welcome options, when the Federation of so-called Intelligent Life accidentally dumps you at a remote outpost with twenty crates full of the same entrée!"

"But what if—someone—refuses to kill?" Aerrem bravely asked.

"Was that person planning on passing?" Tarnek gently asked, but it was such a chilling question that Aerrem shuddered and said no more.

"And how will we do it?" Sheejar blurted out the question I was wondering. Surely we couldn't drug our victims, or we wouldn't be able to eat them. "Do we stun the animals so they can't walk off the dissection table while we take them apart?"

I figured she was being sarcastic, but Tarnek's golden face turned livid with anger—worse than I'd ever seen before. "You ever pull a stunt like that, Sheejar, and you'll flunk out of this program so fast you won't know what zapped you! Who here remembers how stunners work?"

A weapons specialist had taught us stunner theory and practice, but our teacher's ire erased all meaningful memories from most of our brains. Aerrem raised a shaky hand.

"Yes, Aerrem?"

"Stunners cause—temporary paralysis. They're a poorly named weapon, because they leave all feeling and consciousness intact. Unless they're set too high—which can stop muscles for breathing and pumping blood."

"Exactly, and therein lies our solution. Although you must aim carefully—we don't want a CPR lesson in the middle of this! And you should set your stunners for only short-range power to stop the circulation of your small specimens.

"We'll use wristcom scans to verify loss of conscious brain activity, and to guide rapidly fatal incisions. That's when you can begin dissection."

"So in a way, I was right," I heard Shee mutter, too softly for our teachers to hear, but Kijan rolled his eyes and I grinned at him.

Kem supervised this exercise while Tarnek unpacked dissection equipment and Shandy carefully set up the cooking tables.

Aerrem for once forgot her slogan and moved to the back of the killing line. I joined her there, and didn't have the heart to tease her about it. But it did mean we had to scan everyone ahead of us.

Kem provided very kind assistance when Aerrem finally stunned and pithed a big lizardy creature. It was an unfortunate choice, because the animal had such a primitive brain, and such a slow metabolism, that they had to work extra hard to be sure it was first unconscious, and then dead. Tears streamed down Aerrem's face as she finally hauled the limp body over to one of Tarnek's tables.

I had to zap a whifflegik—so scared it sat frozen in one corner of a specimen box. It was the right size for a cute little dorm pet, but I felt neither tearful, nor avenged for our lost food. My scientific curiosity took over.

The only other emotions I felt as I sliced the 'gik open in my dissection pan were shame and anger. Shame that I couldn't feel the sorrow that came so easily to Aerrem, and anger that Tarnek made her do this.

If I'd had Max pinned out before me like this, I'd have puked. I didn't understand why this was different, but it was, and the anatomy was fascinating. Gkorjneil set a panful of orange berries on the table after screening for plant poisons, and those of us with strong stomachs nibbled while we worked.

"What's this?" Jael nearly jumped off the bench as something wriggled under his forceps.

"Didn't you kill it?" Crell asked disdainfully. "Tarnek will flunk you—"

"It's totally dead! Kem verified it!"

Several of us walked around the table to stare at the opened bowel of his shovel-footed, burrowing mammalian specimen.

"I saw those structures on anatomical scans, and assumed they increased surface area for nutrient absorption," Piel said. "Papillae. Maybe you're only seeing some reflex movement—"

"No," I said, shivering, "they look like worms. "Nematodes—that's it, I bet—internal parasites! Poor critter."

"Oh, smooth." Jael moaned. "I've just discovered a whole new environmental niche, on our very last day!"

JOURNAL ENTRY 32

"Okay, who's opening digestive tracts before removing them from your specimens?" Tarnek stomped over to our table, and we all fled back to our places. "That's the dirtiest part, and it multiplies all the cleaning we'll have to do before cooking! Immunity boosters aren't perfect—and who's eating at this table? Don't you realize how unsanitary that is—Taje, what's wrong with your face?"

I swallowed my last berry stealthily. I'd thought Jael suffered the reddest face, but come to think of it, my face felt hot even in the shade today.

Kem scanned me. "She's sunburned! I did think both Tajen and Shanden looked rather odd this morning. It's quite shady here, but we forgot how little skin pigment you both have. You should wear your hats—they're not as hot as they look, and they'll shade your faces.

"When we get back I'll ask Medicine to dispense a systemic UV blocker for both of you, but meanwhile you should also use some fast-heal cream—where's your medkit?

"I know we're in camp, but by now it should be habit to carry it on your utility belt, along with your stunner and water bottle."

Later a few of my tablemates thanked me for the diversion, even if it was involuntary and excruciating. Some of the food we cooked up—and watched some of our classmates eat—was also excruciating, despite passing toxin screening.

Dojan and Kijan crunched down little roasted rodent carcasses, bones and all, and declared this the best meal they'd eaten since entering the Center.

Gkorjneil steadily munched on uncooked larvae-infested plant bulbs. "You get this smooth little pop every so often." Crell and Shee made faces, while Nikk bravely tried and decided she liked stir-fried parasites. And Crell got caught and severely reprimanded for actually trying to hand some of her less desirable samples to a begging whifflegik.

Shandy and Aerrem nibbled at their food, while Branem and I picked our cooked critters clean, wandered the tables, and hungrily sampled anything anyone would let us try. Last of all, Kem served up a great berry and nut dessert, after which Tarnek made his next scary announcement.

"It looks like you'll have enough food left for dinner tonight—" we moaned but he persisted—"and we trust you now know proper storage. So after you stash your leftovers, you have one final assignment."

Now the moans turned into loud groans and anxious glances at the time on wristcoms.

"Not finished with the rest of your work here? Too bad. Because I think you've completely forgotten one vital goal."

"What?" cried out the boldest among us.

"Enjoy being here! I know some of you brought along art and musical instruments you haven't touched. As ecologists, we should make a deeper connection with the environments we study. How can you effectively describe a world you have no feeling for?"

"Awesome," Aerrem whispered while we re-hung our packs.

"I never expected an assignment like this from any teacher," I said softly, feeling once again a nudge of guilt. "Think Tarnek will grade this one?" We wrapped our screens around our styluses, and stuffed them into cargo pockets.

Aerrem snickered, thought about it some more, and looked worried.

I scanned around our campground, but Shandy had already disappeared. So I headed off along a musical stream I'd wanted to explore, but hadn't found time for.

Around one bend in the woods I stumbled across Tarnek and Kem, necking away. I blushed, stuttered out an apology, and hurried onward.

At last I found a cool, smooth boulder to sit down against, and I attempted a sketch of the woodland stream. But I'd never tried to depict clear running water before, and my drawing became another battle.

By the time Krorn showed up on the opposite bank, playing his flute to the tune of the trickling stream, I'd erased my vacful work. Instead I'd found my embarrassing rant, and, realizing how much it brought that part of fending for myself back to life, I'd begun a short trip journal. If I never escaped the Center, I wanted some way to relive Outside.

'Oh, sorry, Taje, I'll move on—"

"No, please don't. Your music is perfect!"

Krorn's golden face lit up, and I gradually floated off into peaceful water and forest dreams.

JOURNAL ENTRY 33

The early chill of sunset woke me up. On my hike back I finally scanned Shandy, perched high in a treetop, swaying with the wind. "What are you doing up there?"

"Humans evolved from tree-climbers. I think it's still part of our genes. Come on up!"

I wanted to join Shandy, but I stopped on a branch a meter below him. I'd made the mistake of scanning the distant ground, and I suddenly discovered I couldn't climb any higher.

So now I gazed forward, at layers of forested mountains marching out to the horizon of this red-purple world. Sunset pinks and oranges flooded the vast cloudy sky, and the colors made me ache with a fierce joy.

"It's strange. I never know what I'll fear out here, and what I won't," Shandy said.

"I know what you mean." My branch creaked and swayed in the wind, and I clung more tightly to the sun-warmed, rippled bark of the trunk. Meanwhile, the wind roared like a river through the distant trees, and I longed to follow it on foot.

"Shandy, I don't want to go back to the Center! We've barely touched the surface of a tiny sector of this planet. I want to hike on and on, and explore all of it!"

"I know," Shandy said, with a longing but tired look on his quick-heal coated, sunburned face. At least the messy cream made our faces hurt less.

"But I guess we should return to camp soon." I sighed as the sky colors shifted towards various shades of red, purple, and dark blue, and Kem popped up on our wristcoms. "The sun's going down," she said. "Everyone come back to camp."

We found Hannen and Taemar sitting at a table and arguing ecological philosophies, while other classmates finished artwork by stove light. Another group had put together a foot-stomping music band, and Kijan and Aerrem sang an ad-lib song making fun of all our misadventures on Darwin.

Golden Lorratian Nikk and coppery-scaled Dainer stumbled into camp arm in arm, shoulder spines fully retracted, and translated expressions similar to Tarnek and Kem. And lastly Krorn's flute piped up as he marched in with his pants wet up to his muddy knees. Yet like me, he refused to join in with the teasing song's refrain, claiming he couldn't sing either.

We all stayed up too late, nibbling on our food, talking and laughing, singing and listening to folk songs from various homeworlds, and enjoying the smell of tree sap and loam carried by the wind, on our last starry night in Byrne Park.

JOURNAL ENTRY 34

"Well, what do you think?" Tarnek said from inside the ship's hatchway the next morning.

I'd reluctantly boarded our ship last, and I finally wrenched my eyes from the scenery to face him. "I think I learned more out there than I expected."

Tarnek laughed. But back at the stuffy old Center three days later, he nearly flunked most of us.

We'd exchanged data and recorded our reports on our quieter trip back. We all worked hard (plus I hurriedly finished my private trip journal). But, curiously, it was reports from some of our classmates who'd never lived outside of cities that received Tarnek's highest praise. We had to review those reports on our deskcoms upon our return.

For instance, unlike most of us, Krorn and Tarknes hadn't ignored the clash between guests and native life in Byrne Park, when they ran their extra thorough data integrations. And Taemar and Hannen had also questioned a ranger, who suggested they make some predictions—for instance, potential effects of improper nutrition on the 'giks and in turn on their natural forage and predators.

That seemed like cheating, but I suppose only because the rest of us hadn't thought to use "local data resources." And I thought some prior experience Outside would have helped the rest of us more.

Instead we scanned our disappointing grades, and worked extra hard at our classroom lessons, each determined to out-do ourselves next trip. Well, maybe I wasn't quite so bothered, as I wasn't trying to become a top-notch ecologist. Still it was hard to give up good grades when I'd gotten so used to them.

Our focus in labs also changed, now that we knew how a Real World could zap us. And in our little workshop we learned how to repair our gear, as we were quietly reminded that no Central Supply existed on distant outposts.

We also exercised harder than ever in gym. We divided our class into two teams, the Ectotherms and the Endotherms, for grueling games during lunch and most weekends. And we got Shandy to play on a team, arguing his need to keep up with us.

We also began a self-defense class that turned serious the very first day, as our instructor demonstrated how a weapon that could be snatched from our belts might be worse than no weapon at all.

So when Tarnek handed out our next field trip assignment at the end of our second-quarter finals, we felt ready. Everyone now understood the need for adequate sleep on the trip over, and we didn't have to be tricked into it ahead of time with sleep deprivation.

Onboard we resumed piloting sims, attended Kem's lecture on FIL paraspace S.O.S. signals and laws, practiced emergency evac torch-cutting techniques on an already trashed inner bulkhead, and took a sobering little first-aid class on wind-chill factors and hypothermia.

We cheered the student trio who managed to safely land us on a long sloping beach between the surf and cliffs, in the middle of a heavy rainstorm.

We cheered again when ship scans showed us nothing but pristine wilderness—a curving coastline that faded into the mists. We checked our raingear seals and hurtled out the hatch, to land on soft wet sand—truly Outside!

Again the odor zapped me first—this time sort of like a saltwater aquarium with both live and dead contents, spilled into a storm. Shandy and I faced an ocean for the first time in our lives. So much blue-grey water, endlessly churning towards us! No holo could do it justice.

Under my boots I felt the surf pound like the planet's heartbeat. Shandy shoved back his visored hood, and the rain-packed wind blew his pale hair from his grinning face. I smiled back at him, and then a stronger wave surged up the beach and chased us on our way.

At first we almost ran, we felt so full of ready energy, until the sand slowed us to a hard slog.

Our trip leaders urged us on. We soon learned to hike on the hard-packed wet sand closer to the surf, and to dodge the longer waves. They tossed up tantalizing bits of segmented creatures and bulbous, dying seaweed, a feast which multi-legged furry or feathered creatures abandoned, hissing and squawking, whenever we approached too closely.

Other camouflaged creatures stared at us warily from braided purple vines spilling from the slate cliffs to our right. Our trip leaders named nothing and gave us little time for wristcom recordings. Apparently we had to race the sun to our campsite.

But I was easily distracted, I tripped several times, and I must have sealed my boots too hastily. Icy feet stole my attention from the rash of colorful, rocky tide pools below our new campsite. We set up on a generous patch of sand above the high tide line, in a large cleft where the cliffs retreated and tumbled into a natural stairway to the tangled forest above.

It was a smooth site, but I couldn't waste time appreciating it. I hastily set up our flexitent under a cliff wall, while Shandy refilled our water bottles from a nearby pool below a miniature waterfall. We'd joined forces again without anyone objecting.

I ducked inside the tent. I warmed my numb feet, which tingled painfully as they returned to life, and I meticulously dried the soggy insides of my boots with our trimode stove. I almost missed a pre-dinner rappelling lesson, and I hated losing any time our very first day, but Kem's first-aid frostbite holos remained frozen in my brain.

Getting careless for one micro about staying dry was a lesson most of my classmates had to learn the hard way, sometime during this trip. We fought a nearly constant downpour as we sorted out the complicated habitats of this littoral zone. Various sub-environments overlapped along constantly changing borders, and it was difficult even comming how to divide it up.

We all felt honored that our teachers considered us ready for such a challenge, and this time we gave it our best and more. At least all but one of us did.

JOURNAL ENTRY 35

Taemar lost track of her teammate on our fourth morning. We received her frantic report, and Tarnek overrode our wristcom screens and ordered us all immediately back into camp.

"Hannen isn't answering his wristcom!" Tears streamed down Taemar's cheeks. "He must be badly injured or unconscious!"

"Or he lost or broke his wristcom," Jael said.

"That's very tough to do—"

"Enough!" Tarnek interrupted Tarknes. "What did we teach you to do in a potentially serious situation like this?"

We gulped air like glippers flopping outside our tanks.

"Come on," said Kem. "Your classmate's life may depend on your answer!"

"We need a leader, so decisions can be made quickly," Dojan finally said.

"Good!" Tarnek said. "And since I'm your legal guardian, I'm taking over right now, and I'll expect all of you to follow my orders without hesitation.

"So first of all, Kem, I want you to accompany Taemar to Hannen's last known location, and try to track him from there.

"Meanwhile, Taemar, set your wristcom on constant call. Kem can set hers on short-range scanner mode, for any human besides yourselves, and for something inorganic that Hannen wears on his belt."

That meant if their scans couldn't detect a live body, Kem and Taemar might still find Hannen.

Numb feet suddenly seemed incredibly minor. And tracking a live person here seemed rather hopeless, considering how quickly the rain beat boot prints into mush. I shivered, and silently wished them luck as Kem and Taemar took off.

"The rest of you set your wristcoms for longer-range scanning, in a semi-circle right here," Tarnek ordered. "Now!"

We knelt on the beach in an arc facing away from the ocean, and sweated over our wristcom controls.

Fine-tuning a scan is as much an art as a science, especially when speed is important, and we certainly weren't artists yet. Tarnek paced behind us, docked over our shoulders to study our holo specs, and hollered at us.

"Set for body size! Put upper and lower limits on body temperature! Nothing in flight, for the love of space, Sheejar—lock into ground-based coordinates! No human can move that fast, Kijan—filter it out! Dojan, you're scanning too far away!

"Piel, stop there! I think you have him! It's a static location southeast of here. Kijan and Dojan, climb into the forest above camp. Nikk and Dainer, sprint down the beach in opposite directions. Let's try to get at least a small amount of triangulation for some rough coordinates. Shanden—"

Shandy immediately produced a backpack loaded with first-aid gear. Tarnek nodded at him, slung on the pack, and turned to the rest of us.

"Just in case, I want two sets of stretcher-bearers to accompany me. Branem, Taje, Krorn, and Tarknes, you're Carrier Team One. Wind, Ness, Errek, and Gkorjneil, you're Team Two. Krorn and Tarknes, set your wristcoms on continuous call. Branem and Taje, set yours for short-range scanning, like Kem did."

Branem and I filtered out the group, including equipment and clothing, and Tarnek quickly checked all our call and scan settings before giving his approval.

The triangulation teams reported estimated coordinates, and Tarnek ordered them back into camp. Next he turned again to Shandy.

"Stay in camp, monitor your wristcom, and keep communications open and clear between everyone. The rest of the class will remain here and act as standby runners under Shanden Fehrokc's command.

"All right, is everyone ready? Let's go!"

Tarnek took off at a ground-eating lope, on down the beach through curtains of rain. We took off after him. Despite being in better shape this trip, we all got winded. But none of us fell behind, if only by sheer force of will and adrenaline.

We now realized, right down to our cores, that a freak accident could injure or kill any one of us Outside. My eyes welled as I exchanged worried looks with Branem, and I briefly wondered if I should rethink my hazy loner escape plans. Maybe this class was good enough.

Tarnek led us to the base of a tall grey outcropping of cliff rock. It ran right into the water, now at high tide, a nova barricade. Our teacher cursed loudly and backtracked to a point where we could climb up tumbled boulders and make our way above.

A thick stand of purple cane trees blocked our passage, and Tarnek whipped an emergency torch from his belt and wielded it like a machete, ruthlessly cutting a smoking pathway for us. "Watch yourselves!" he shouted back at us. "The ends are still hot!"

He became our hero that day. Strong and determined, he brought us rapidly through every obstacle to get back down to the beach beyond the outcropping.

He patiently backtracked us again. As we slowed to a panting walk, I didn't know what I feared more—finding a false reading—maybe a beached sea mammal—or discovering Hannen bloody and crippled, or lifeless.

The scream of our scanner alarms made us jump. A micro later we almost stepped on Hannen, lying in the sand at the foot of the cliff.

JOURNAL ENTRY 36

When I stared down at my classmate's motionless face, horror forced me to confront my normal envy. Like Hannen, most humans possess some skin pigment, along with dark glossy hair, and smooth almond eyes—unlike me, a pasty oval-eyed freak.

But now Hannen's face was nearly as pale as mine, where it wasn't smeared with blood, and his clothes were soaked and bloody beneath torn seals in his raingear.

He must have tried to free-climb the rain-slick cliff. I looked up at it in shock.

"Tajen!" Tarnek roared at me, as he ran his medkit scanner over Hannen so fast no one else could read it. I jerked back to attention. "Unstrap and unfold the stretcher from my pack. Lowwind, get out my sleeping bag and attach it to the stretcher. But my medscanner warns against setting the bag for gradual warming until he's starting to arouse.

"Hannen is alive, but I'm reading shock from exposure, blood loss, and concussion. Hypothermia has actually saved him by slowing his metabolism. He's also got some minor external wounds, and some possible hairline fractures, so the rest of you get out the wound kits and splints."

Tarnek managed to get a catheter injected into one of Hannen's shrunken veins. He attached human synthblood, shock, and brain trauma medpacks, and programmed a slow IV fluid injector, all attached to a telescoping stretcher IV pole. We stabilized Hannen's joints and bandaged him. Then we opened the sleeping bag and carefully shifted Hannen onto the stretcher and closed the bag.

Meanwhile Tarnek called Kem and Taemar back into camp, and alerted Shandy to ready more teams for transferring Hannen from our base camp to the ship. But Shandy did us one better, sending a fresh team to meet us on the beach.

Aerrem slapped me on the back when I dragged at last into camp. "Hey, cheer up. The word is Hannen's going to be okay—you found him before he got too cold to wake up!

"Kem and Tarnek led a group back to the ship to hook Hannen up to some fast-healers in the med-niche. They left orders for the rest of us to return to work."

"No," I said, still panting.

"Yep. What else can we do?"

I tried my best. I'm sure we all did. But I felt shaky and absent-minded, and a bit crowded, as we all developed a sudden interest in finishing up our tide pool work. It kept us close to camp and each other, as the rest of our stretcher-bearers straggled back into camp with increasingly reassuring reports.

We nibbled quietly at our dinner that night, and discussed ways we might avoid a similar accident in the future.

The next morning we all agreed to finish our data collections by noon, and so we could try for a replay from our first trip. Our contemplations of art and nature turned out more subdued, but the rain relented at last, and we ended up chasing each other into the surprisingly warm sea.

We bobbed and shouted among the waves, while the setting sun lit up our faces and cast orange reflections on the water. At last we ran shivering and screaming back to our tents, to towel off and dress for dinner.

Swimming had burned off some of our excess adrenaline, so we could stand to eat the more edible parts of our seafood barbecue. Some classmates buried the rest, while others made campfire music around stoves set for heat and light.

When Shandy and I crept off to bed, we fell asleep to the last notes of Krorn's flute, playing with the splashes of the waterfall, the beating of the surf and our hearts, and the cries of the night creatures.

I felt very glad to be alive, here and now. And I felt certain most of us had done more than simply pass this test.

JOURNAL ENTRY 37

All of us commed we'd scanned an island ecology, and I took it one step further.

Through careful genetic and backup gravity measurements, I proved we'd only landed on a different part of Darwin—instead of on a whole new planet, like most classmates assumed. The weather on our second trip had hidden Darwin's moon, or everyone might have guessed it right off. So I even managed to demonstrate this was Darwin and record another little trip journal. But hardly anyone seemed impressed.

"It's not as if we won't know where we're landing to do a real job!" Aerrem laughed.

"But we also had to figure out we were working on an island."

"That's different—that part was a test!"

I shook my head, but I didn't have time to argue further. Hannen refused to say what had enticed him to attempt such a dangerous climb, but luckily he healed very quickly from his injuries, because we shipped back to an intense third quarter, which introduced us to increasingly complex analytical methods.

We studied com models for everything from simple predator-prey, symbiotic, and parasitic relationships between limited numbers of species, to world population dynamics and global environmental cycles, not to mention the latest data on interplanetary invasive species research. We also spent whole labs learning very exacting chemical and physiological analyses—one fuse-up, and often many of us had to start over.

Even our exercise sessions increased again in intensity, as our gym teacher gradually turned up the gravity and ambient temperature. This helped us get ready for our end-of-third-quarter field trip, a ten-day survey on planet Pelsus, under the guidance of a native tribe of Mumdwars, which gave us plenty of social studies as part of our prep work.

Only Shandy didn't seem very excited about this trip. While I eagerly studied Mumdwar customs, he kept obsessing over micro translator settings, whenever he wasn't lost in nostalgic holos of Istrannian scenery.

"You know," I finally said, "you didn't miss that much the day you left class sick. But I can review translator exercises with you if you think that might help. And if you really want to return to Istrann so badly, why don't you try Legal Aid?"

"Legal Aid?"

I guess no one had ever bothered to mention that office to him. Come to think of it, I hadn't known about it until this year. "Uh, Tarnek talked about it, when—I was in trouble. I think the Center must have a legal office in Admin, on Level One."

"That makes sense!" Shandy quickly looked up the office and made an appointment, which earned him a lawyer. But he never said much about it after that, and I didn't have the heart to ask.

I merely commed that since FIL scientists never found any reason to suspect the Istrannian plague was natural, the few surviving natives might not want any more alien visitors.

Nor did Shandy ever ask for help with his translator. I supposed he was too used to learning ahead of the rest of us. He used his deskcom a lot to adjust his controls, even though we had extra lessons in communications.

The rest of us became very excited, getting to plan our first trip to an inhabited planet. FIL was allowing us to interact with a so-called "low-tech" society, deemed capable of withstanding our "high-tech" presence without undue influence.

The squat grey tripod Mumdwars had actually performed this FIL service for some years, and the tribe we stayed with clearly enjoyed teaching us about their desert habitat.

We all struggled with the higher gravity, which wore us out quickly each day. But once I started my UV blocker, I at least discovered I could withstand heat better than many of my classmates, and I seemed to have a knack for translator work.

Certainly none of us understood everything our hosts tried to tell us, yet I enjoyed every attempt to communicate. But I guess I don't have as much to tell about this trip, because we were all on our best behavior, and we managed to avoid any further mishaps.

The scariest part for me was piloting our ship for the landing. But our hosts had provided such a nice level, visible landing field that the ship's com hardly had to work at it, so my job was even easier. I almost immediately began another trip journal, but it wasn't as exciting, although it contained details about the Mumdwars and their environment, which helped with my part of our official report.

The hardest part was leaving our new friends, after ten intense days working together. Perhaps I really didn't want to think much more about this trip, because in the end I found it quite sad. I'd made friends, friends I'd probably never see again. Sometimes our universe really did suck.

For this third trip we also prepared our first group report. I helped with the section covering the Mumdwar's ability to fit in with and nurture their environment. Some of my classmates ignored or dismissed as "primitive fantasy" the incredible layers of myths, symbols, and customs the Mumdwars used for this purpose.

However, I argued that if this belief system worked, it did matter and should be studied, even if this wasn't the sort of science we used. Who could guess what we might learn? But I also claimed a pre-industrial society actually gave the Mumdwars an unfair advantage.

In fact, I also argued that enhanced technology is an almost irresistible trap. Who didn't want advanced shelter, food production, medical care, transportation, and entertainment, whatever the long-term environmental costs?

Whenever reasonably intelligent species stumbled upon inventions like fire, farming, and the wheel, before reaching a full understanding of their world, ecological balances might never recover. And supposedly intelligent species could be as devastating as a major meteor strike—look at what happened to Earth!

I think I made some valid points. But I guess I'm stalling, rather than launching into our fourth quarter, because I got into trouble again.

JOURNAL ENTRY 38

After we handed in our third-quarter eco-report, we threw a class party in our student lounge. Aerrem and Dojan arranged for special food and fruit drinks from Outside, and musical students brought their instruments. We even talked Tarnek and Kem into attending, and we dressed up in an exotic mixture of homeworld costumes.

Shandy actually joined in by wearing a velvet vest and pants and a silk shirt, all such a bright orange that when I looked away from him, I saw his shape in blue. They must have been old but treasured clothes from Istrann, as they were in good condition, but his elbows almost stuck out of his cuffs, and he wore orange knee socks to cover his calves. He must have outgrown his Istrannian shoes, because he simply wore orange sneakers. Shee and Crell began to snicker, but Aerrem stared them down.

Kijan and Dojan of course wore their rugged brown hunting pants and shirts, with ceremonial knives in their belts, multi-pocketed green vests, and green feathered caps.

Branem had dressed up in tan, snug, mining coveralls, designed to fit inside space suits, and which happened to show off his muscles and a crotch I worked hard not to stare at.

I had a fair distraction. Aerrem made me wear my first bra, and I was deciding it was the most vacful invention in the entire universe. The straps insisted on sliding off my narrow shoulders, and I had to keep slipping a finger under my collar to rescue myself.

I wasn't exactly comfortable in any part of the outfit Aerrem had goaded me into wearing. Too bad I'd confessed no memory of any Donshore clothing more exotic than overalls or shorts and T-shirts. I could be wearing the latter here.

Luckily one of Aerrem's silky, beautifully embroidered tunics hid my bra battle, and I discovered that the deep teal tunic actually looked smooth with my light red hair and green eyes.

The tunic also covered up a hasty patch over the tail hole in flowing purplish-blue trousers, which were in turn stuffed into knee high dark green boots I had to wear double socks to fit. I tried not to blush as I caught our teachers scanning our rather odd mix of costumes. I was glad I'd at least refused a peacock feather for my hair.

Fortunately, Aerrem had chosen party clothes with lots of embroidery and beads, and fiery colors that rippled through her tunic, pants, and boots, and therefore drew the most attention. The pet business must have paid her well.

Of course in Aerrem's mind this party was simply an elaborate ploy to seek more information about our end-of-the-year final exam, and she expected us to back her up when she cornered our two teachers on the couch.

"Tell us about our next trip," Aerrem said from the middle of the arc we formed, standing around them.

"Trip? What trip?" Tarnek lounged back and grinned. As a joke, he wore an adult-sized set of the Center's yellow gym clothes.

Shandy just stared back at him.

"Our final exam, vac-head!" Kijan said, unconsciously gripping his fake knife handle.

Where will we go?" Branem said, frustrated.

"How long will we get to do it?" I asked, while reaching under my collar again.

"So many questions!"

"You rascal!" Kem turned on Tarnek. "Quit toying with them, and give some real answers! After all, I won't be around to help anymore." She gazed down at her colorful sari and brushed away some invisible crumbs.

"You won't?" Our faces fell. "Why not?"

"Believe it or not, I'm going on break. It happens once in a very long while. Then FIL will announce my next evil mission."

We tried to laugh, and we tried to congratulate her, but we knew we'd miss her.

"Thank you." Kem nodded. "But please don't let me distract you from your questions."

"And I thought you were on my side!" Tarnek said.

"Come on, tell us about our last test!" we all shouted him down.

"Okay, okay! It'll start at the beginning of end-of-school-year break."

"We already know that!" Branem said. It was a measure of our enthusiasm that having been told this part long ago, we were actually still looking forward to sacrificing some of our vacation for a final exam. "Tell us something new!" he said, even more frustrated.

"How long will it last?" I tried again. "Will we get to use the whole school break?" It was probably too much to hope for, but I could dream, couldn't I? If I couldn't figure out how to escape the Center, I commed this was second best. Or maybe I could run off and hide right at the end of this last trip. Sure.

"Probably your whole break," Tarnek said.

"Probably?" we roared.

"Well, it could easily take longer—"

"Longer!"

"You'll have to decide for yourselves how much time you'll need. I'll give you preliminary Scout Ship reports for several representative sectors on each of four different planets.

"FIL has ordered more in-depth surveys of these worlds for potential colonization. I'll drop you into one of these sectors, and if you do a good enough job, your data will become part of the official FIL eco-report. Sound good?"

We all cheered, except for Branem, who immediately scanned the trap: "You're not going to tell us ahead of time which sector of which planet our final exam will take place on?"

"Of course not. That would ruin all the fun!"

We had to cram all quarter long, to add those dozen Scout Ship reports to all our regular homework.

However, as if in sympathy, Tarnek began to act like he was cramming too. He took over more and more of our classes, and threw information at us as if Arrainius's sun might go nova tomorrow.

But it was us who went nova, the morning he didn't show up for class at all.

JOURNAL ENTRY 39

"Quiet down! I have an announcement to make!" A Lorratian strode to the front of our classroom, fifteen minutes after class was due to start.

We had made it through about two thirds of our fourth quarter, and this was the very first morning Tarnek hadn't showed up on time or early. What had happened? Our classroom fell deathly silent.

"I suppose you're wondering why I'm here, instead of your head instructor, Turneck," the Lorratian began, as she fingered a line of disfigured gold scales on her shiny cheek.

"Space, I guess so," I muttered softly. Already I didn't like the way her shoulder spikes poked out.

"What's wrong? Did something happen to Tarnek?" Kijan perked his furry ears as he pronounced our teacher's name with exaggerated clarity for the stranger.

"It's a staffing emergency. I'm your teacher's official replacement for the rest of the school year. My name is Rognarthe."

"What sort of staffing emergency?" Taemar said.

"That, my dear, is absolutely none of your business."

Taemar looked stunned. I'm sure we all did. But Kijan refused to leave it alone. "You don't understand. As our head instructor, I'm sure Tarnek would want us to know—"

"No, you don't understand," Rognarthe said. "This Center doesn't have to explain all its actions to you. And is this how you always greet a new instructor?"

I commed we should be above tormenting any new substitute who vectored into range, but it almost seemed like this teacher was asking for it.

She scanned us all, as if expecting another challenge. When she didn't get it, she focused on Shandy, seated at his T.A. desk near the front.

"You—why aren't you with the rest of the class?"

"I'm Shanden Fehrokc, Drehx Tarnek's Teaching Assistant." He barely concealed a scowl, obviously insulted that she had to ask.

But Rognarthe gave him an incredulous look. "Well, I don't need you. Consider yourself dismissed."

"Fine." He didn't even fight it! He locked all further emotion out of his face and began to gather up his belongings.

"Wait a micro! You can't do that to him!" I stood up and shouted over my classmate's shocked comments.

"And who on Arrainius do you think you are, telling me what I can't do?" Rognarthe turned on me in a micro, and zapped me with a glare set on kill.

My jaw dropped. This had gotten fused so quickly it was beyond belief.

"I asked for your name!"

She sounded so much like Chark that I almost laughed. "Tajen," I spat out instead, as I willed my fists to unclench.

"Your full name!"

"Jesmuhr. Tajen Jesmuhr!"

"So someone has allowed a JD to stay in this program!"

My gaze dropped involuntarily to my nearly forgotten bracelet, while my face fried. I still wasn't exactly the most popular student, but now my classmates actually began to mutter.

"Well," Rognarthe said obliviously, "at least your tracer is a sign of some discipline in here. But I want it understood right now that I will not tolerate any disobedience or impertinent behavior whatsoever."

"What a hypocrite!" Aerrem hissed.

"I can arrange an ambush for her," Branem offered in a whisper.

How well could Lorratians hear? I zapped both friends with an alarmed look as I began to sit down. But maybe I'd at least drawn Rognarthe's fire away from Shandy, who now stood frozen at his desk.

"Did I tell you that you could sit down?" Rognarthe snapped at me.

The class had the decency to gasp as I stood back up, shaking with anger. "I suppose I'll have to ask you for permission every time I need to pee?" Sympathetic snickers peppered the room.

"That kind of language will land you right back in Discipline for the rest of the quarter—just try me once more!"

I was finally too stunned for any reply, and the whole class fell silent.

"That's better. You may sit down now. And you, sir, were dismissed," she immediately turned back to Shandy.

I sank into my seat, and felt ashamed of my lack of courage, while Shandy walked out in bitter silence.

Aerrem leaped up, her tail whipping so wildly she almost whacked several classmates in the face with it.

"I'm not putting up with this vac any longer! I don't care who you think you are! No one can come into our classroom and act this way—"

"Aerrem—" I tried to stop her.

"Shut up, Taje! Let her pick on a student with no record! I'm going to talk to someone with more authority over this fused mess!"

A micro later we heard her turning on all the locker room showers on her way out, and Rognarthe couldn't stop any of us from laughing. But after she shut off the water with a simple switch at her desk and regained control of the classroom, she zapped us with one final blow, in answer to Hannen's cautious inquiry.

"I still don't understand," he began.

"What's left to understand?"

"You said you'd teach us until the end of the year?"

"Yes. Isn't that perfectly clear?"

"No. Who's going to supervise our offworld final exam, during our break?"

"I'm afraid that's simply not my concern."

"But Tarnek's already arranged all our trip passes—are you going to cancel them?" Lowwind asked.

"And he's given us a huge amount of material to study for it," Nessel objected. "How will you adequately test us?"

"Look, let me lead you down the garden path, since you can't seem to find it for yourselves," Rognarthe said. "I have been hired to teach you through the end of the quarter—which means I'll direct your written and lab finals.

"Beyond that, I have no authority over what happens, nor do I care."

JOURNAL ENTRY 40

"How'd it go after I left?" Aerrem stood waiting for Branem and me by our hall lift exits after class.

"About how you'd expect," Branem said, shaking his head.

"Did she teach you anything new?"

"It was all boring review. Rognarthe has no idea how far we've gotten."

"Did you vector anywhere helpful?" I asked Aerrem.

Aerrem's tail slumped. "I tried! I made a total pest of myself until they let me talk with a real person in Admin. And he told me Rognarthe is completely qualified—she's successfully headed FIL planetary ecology edprograms several times."

"Did he at least say what happened to Tarnek?" Branem asked.

"No—he said it's completely confidential, but not to worry too much." Aerrem didn't sound comforted.

"Not to worry too much." I snorted. "Well, that's it for me!" I stopped just outside my door's range. "You were right all along, Aerrem. School's simply not worth caring about—"

"Taje, if you skip school, Rognarthe may order you locked up again!" Aerrem halted in her tracks, and Branem docked alongside her.

"I'm already locked up in here, with nowhere left to go!" At least I'd gone on three field trips. I might have to live on those memories, sadly enough. I was glad I'd recorded them.

"I'm going to call for a class meeting tomorrow night," Aerrem said. "Since it's an emergency, maybe we can track down Kem and talk her into returning. We'll start a petition—"

"Why not do it all by deskcom? Set up a class comcall."

"Taje, this is far too serious. The Center doesn't guarantee com privacy, so Branem and I will get in touch with all our classmates by com, but we need to hold this meeting in person, privately. We have access to our own classroom, which I'm not sure Rognarthe knows. Shandy also knows the com controls in there, so he can shut them down if he finds any of them on."

"Well, I sincerely wish you luck with all that." And did the Center actually have enough staff or com power to spy on all our com calls? That was one conspiracy theory I'd always choked on.

"You're not coming?" Aerrem said.

I shook my head. "I'm sorry, but this already feels too much like banging my head against another bulkhead."

Aerrem sighed, but nodded. "I understand."

Inside I found Shandy lying on his bed. Sheefharn stood on Shandy's chest so he could stroke her soft chest feathers with his long, gentle fingers.

Sheefharn turned her head and shrilly scolded me, snapping her crest at me, as if the whole rotten day was my fault. Her screeching woke up Max, who pelted off my bed while Sheefharn flapped up to the divider.

I scooped up Max. "I'm sorry, Shandy. I should have tried harder—"

"Forget it." Shandy wiped his eyes with his long thin hands. "You didn't stand a chance, and it's not even worth fighting for."

"I'll say. You didn't miss anything today."

When he said no more, I quietly slipped into my room to give him some privacy. I dropped into my seat in front of my deskcom. Max chuckled softly in my lap while I checked for new messages and answered some unexpected notes of sympathy.

Next I cleared out a neglected backlog of old junk, and confronted Tarnek's notice, with our end-of-year trip pass verifications, and his dozen planetary eco-reports.

I'd spent so much time studying those reports, and discussing and speculating over them with classmates, that I discovered I couldn't bring myself to delete them. Well, let's start with eliminating the torment of trip pass notifications—my pathetic hope for at least one last escape from the Center. No, wait!

Maybe all hope hadn't crashed and burned.

JOURNAL ENTRY 41

I did heed Aerrem's warning to the extent of testing Rognarthe. I slowly showed up for class later each day and gradually left a little earlier. Our new teacher took absolutely no further notice of me, nor did she bother to program my tracer bracelet to tell on me.

So I cut class altogether whenever I felt like it. I wasn't the only student who quickly grew tired of endless eco-concept review sessions, and I commed Rognarthe simply didn't care who attended them. The rest of our teachers had all mysteriously disappeared, many even before Tarnek had left. Maybe they knew about Rognarthe, and didn't like her any more than we did.

Meanwhile no trip pass cancellation ever appeared on my screen—another minor detail Rognarthe apparently felt no responsibility for.

So I actually had all the training, equipment, transportation, and permission I needed to depart Arrainius forever! I would have to leave as originally scheduled—the day after our written and lab finals—which didn't leave me much time to com both a remote destination and a fail-safe equipment list.

I still didn't involve any of my friends. I had to assume I risked a strong chance of getting caught and dumped back into Discipline or even rehab, and I had no desire to drag anyone I cared about in there with me. I did know I'd have to tell Shandy about my plot soon, but I put it off as long as possible.

I also realized I couldn't take my pets with me. I hadn't the heart to totally uproot them, and they would seriously complicate any attempt to escape. Unfortunately, getting into the Center is much easier than leaving.

I knew the perfect solution, but that didn't make it any easier. Apparently Rognarthe had given Shandy no alternative class schedule for the rest of the year, so he spent most of his time moping in our room. It was inconvenient but understandable.

What would happen to him next school year? Back to GIP? Or did our class give him the right to transfer to something better next year? I couldn't bring myself to ask him. For that matter, where were we all headed? Apparently no one had the courage to ask that question either.

But that was far enough in the future to ignore for now. My current plot involved waiting until Shandy had a doctor appointment to invite Cam over.

"All of them?" Cam's copper eyes glowed. "You want me to take all your pets?" Suddenly he barely kept his shoulder spines from erupting. "Why? Are you in trouble again?"

"Maybe." I bit my lip. I couldn't tell him any details without putting him in jeopardy too. "Don't ask me anything more. Do you want them?" Why couldn't I simply ask if he'd love them the way I do?

"Oh, yes!"

I guess I didn't need to ask. But I blinked back tears as I reviewed care instructions one last time, and asked one last question: "Cam, your roommate won't turn you in for keeping pets, will he?"

"No! He knows why I spent so much time here while you were gone. Sometimes he came with me to help, and he loved playing with Max."

I helped Cam smuggle all my pets and their paraphernalia over to his room, where I gave poor confused Max one last hug and kiss.

I fled to an extra loud busy dining hall for an early dinner. But the meal sat mostly untouched on my tray, except for some added salt from my tears. At last I stood up. It was time to face my roomie.

JOURNAL ENTRY 42

"What are you doing?" Shandy had followed me from his section to our divider. Now he leaned against it as he folded his arms and waited for my answer.

I had expected Shandy to ask about my missing pets. But when I collapsed into the seat at my deskcom, my face froze. I'd left my equipment list on the screen. I hastily closed it, but was I already too late? And why did it matter now?

I twisted in my chair, unable to meet Shandy's stare. "I—I have something I need to tell you," I vacfully began. Why was this so difficult?

We both waited in grim silence while I gulped empty air. Finally Shandy couldn't stand it any longer. "You don't need to tell me," he blurted out. "You're planning an escape from the Center."

I forced myself to look up at him with a question on my face. Like I hadn't given him enough clues already!

He shuddered. "Do you really think I'm that insensitive? You've only been plotting at this ever since I've known you. And now I suppose you think you have the perfect opportunity."

"Well, don't I?" I said. Why did he sound so angry?

"What about your loyalty to the class?"

"What do you mean? Taking the class ship? Who's going to miss it now? And why should I care anymore, when Rognarthe obviously doesn't? She's destroyed the only good part about living here!"

"I guess that is all you care about," Shandy muttered as he turned away.

"And what is that supposed to mean!"

He slowly faced me again. "It means," he said, "that I'm wondering—why haven't you asked any friends to join you?"

"Shandy, if you've guessed my dreams for so long, don't you understand this is what I want more than anything—to master the challenge of living on my own, on a fringe world?

"I know it sounds nova, but I'm so tired of being supervised and ordered around, through every civilized micro of my life! I'll go nova if I have to stay here any longer! And by space, I'll accept the risks, but only for myself!"

"Are you certain you understand all the risks?"

"Haven't we received perfect training for this?"

"I don't think you've really thought it through—"

"So what am I missing?" Like I hadn't commed it from every vector a hundred-plus times already! "Enlighten me!"

"Don't you think this setup is a little too convenient?" Shandy zapped back.

My jaw dropped. "You think this is a trap?"

"It could be! Perhaps it's another secret test—this time of our integrity and patience. I don't know. I'm only a fired T.A., and it was never my business to warn other students. But I did think *we* were friends."

Shandy started to turn away again, but I leaped up to grab his arm. "Okay, Shandy, what's really bothering you?" Why was he now questioning our friendship?

We matched scans for only a micro, and we both had to work at not crying.

Shandy took a deep breath, and clenched his fists as I released what must have been a painful grip on his arm.

"I've told you—" he stuttered, "—I failed with other roommates—too many—before getting you. I've never told you—how small your fight with Branem was—in comparison. I was so happy, when we got along together! Taje—why haven't you asked me whether I wanted to sneak out of here with you?"

There it was, the question that deep down, I must have expected and most dreaded. "Shandy, I'm so sorry! You're one of my best friends ever! Which is why I don't want you launching into a trap with me, if that's what it is.

"And if it isn't, I'll still have to land illegally. To get away with that, I'll have to land on a planet far too under-populated to provide you with good medical care."

"I've managed all the class field trips without any problems," Shandy said. "Why do you think I can't handle this? I even ran away on my homeworld as often as you did!"

"But that was so you could stay on Istrann!" I said.

"You were trying to stay on your homeworld too!"

"I'm old enough now to realize I no longer have a home on Donshore. But you're still fighting to return to

Istrann—isn't your lawyer working on it as we speak? And the nova security surrounding Istrann since the plague attack would make it impossible for me to smuggle you back there."

It wasn't like I hadn't thought about it! "You'll simply have to wait until the Center is willing to release you and the Istrannians are willing to let you return."

"But you can't wait?"

"I can't pass up this chance! I just can't! I'm sorry you have to wait, Shandy, I really am. I care about you—enough to know I shouldn't risk taking you with me."

"That's just it, Taje—how can you commit yourself to such dangerous isolation?"

"I won't pick a totally uninhabited planet. But I am basically a loner, and I'm aching more than anything for a Real Life, Outside! It can't be any more nova than feeling so homesick for a world inhabited by a nearly decimated race of native telepaths! Can't you understand?"

He'd be equally alone, maybe more so, all his family and friends dead and buried there, and a few living natives who could read his every thought. I could only assume that he must yearn for a wilderness he missed deeply.

But Shandy's face locked up, like back in Rognarthe's class, and he headed for the door. Deep down, then, I knew I'd said something wrong, but I foolishly didn't know what.

"Where are you going?" I asked as the door slid open for him.

He scanned me from the doorway. "To the class meeting Aerrem called. Aren't you coming?"

"Another meeting." I groaned. "This time it's about the petition failure?"

"Yes."

"Forget it. What more does Aerrem think any of us can do?"

"I don't know. She couldn't put it in her message."

I paced restlessly after he left, and at last headed for Level Three, where I checked out sweats and a pair of ice skates. I whipped around and around the small rink until I felt ready to drop. I returned to my room, deliberately shut down my com without checking messages, and curled up in bed, all alone. I already missed Max's warm little body nestling against me.

But maybe the worst part was over. Now that I was so close to my lifelong dream, why did it have to feel so fused?

JOURNAL ENTRY 43

Our door buzzed, jerking me halfway out of a disturbed sleep. I managed to squint at my deskcom time meter. Great Galaxy, this late it had to be a mistake. I turned over, and it buzzed again. Well, let Shandy get it. He was closer. It kept buzzing.

"Who is it?" I grumbled, still unable to open more than one eye. Wasn't Shandy back yet?

"It's Aerrem! Quick, it's an emergency! Open up!"

I launched out of bed, nearly dragging my covers with me. Shandy's bed looked untouched. "Open!" I hollered as I stumbled towards our door in a T-shirt and underwear, my heart banging against my ribs. The next micro I was staring into the muzzle of a stunner, in Aerrem's hands. Aimed at me.

"Wha—"

"Get dressed, Taje!" Aerrem marched inside, the hackle of her tail making it look twice as big. Branem and Dojan flanked her and trained their stunners on me too.

"What is this?" My pulse raced as I struggled to breathe on my way back into my section. What had gotten into all of them?

"No questions!" Aerrem ordered. "Just put on some pants and sandals!"

I shook so hard I had trouble dressing, which was infuriating, because I commed intimidation had to be one of Aerrem's goals. And it was working—I could barely think. I scanned my deskcom out of the corner of my eye as I pulled on my pants, and after I slipped on my sandals, I lunged for the emergency button.

I never made it. Aerrem must have scanned that move before. She shot me first.

I felt the beam hit me with a stinging zap, and suddenly all my muscles went slack. I fell against my desk, and slid sloppily to the floor, banging my chin on the way down.

"Ouch," I wanted to say, but only spilled some drool down my face. From here all I could see was that the servocleaner had missed the giant dust monsters lurking all over the green carpet under my desk for months, if not years.

"You shot her!" Dojan complained.

"Now what will we do?" Branem wailed.

"Stick to our plan!" Aerrem snapped. "Call honor guards, and report Taje for trying to start another fight. That should keep her locked up long enough—"

"But you shot her!" Dojan insisted. "You don't think we'll also get into trouble for that? This is getting too complicated—"

"All right, all right, we'll let the stun wear off first! But let's move Taje before Shandy returns. Maybe we should carry her into an empty lift—"

"Why do we have to worry about Shandy?" Branem said as he and Dojan lifted me up by my armpits.

"Save your questions for later—hurry up! I think she's coming around!"

Indeed a strange tingling spread through my limbs as they dragged me out of my room. To Aerrem's credit, she must have set her stunner very cautiously. By the time we passed through Shandy's room and reached the front door, I was able to dig in my heels and make my own threat.

"Haul me out this door, and I'll yell loudly enough to wake up the whole hall!" I croaked, uncertain I could really carry out my threat.

"Try it, and I'll shoot you again!" The fury on my dorm sib's face was almost enough to stun me again.

"What did I do?" I pleaded softly. "Please tell me what's going on!"

"Don't play innocent with me!" she zapped back. "Just tell me what turned you into such a selfish traitor!"

"Aerrem, I don't know what you're talking about!"

"The class ship, you nova thief!"

"So Shandy went to the class meeting to tell on me!"

"He did no such thing! He didn't even come to our meeting. We found him afterwards, crying in the student lounge." She paused to let that sink in and burn deeply. "He totally refused to say why—until we told him we'd voted to go ahead with our final exam eco-survey—without a teacher!"

"Ohhh." I was such a vac-head! "I never thought our class would use the ship again!"

"Right." Aerrem sneered.

"You know what a fused liar I am! Aerrem, why don't you believe me?"

"Why didn't you believe in me enough to tell me your plot? Afraid I might want to come along as badly as Shandy?"

I winced, while Branem and Dojan kept me locked in their tense grip. What could I say, besides the truth? "I didn't want to get anyone else into trouble with me—"

"Nobody can avoid trouble around you, Taje!"

I gulped, and my unchecked tears washed a little of the scorn from Aerrem's face.

"What do you want us to do with her?" Dojan asked quietly, while Aerrem stared back at me. All of us almost jumped as the door slid open for my roomie.

"Get the full story from Shandy!" I blurted out.

Aerrem groaned, and lowered her weapon. "Is this really your loner syndrome again, Taje?" she said, her tail fur still as erect as an upset Lorratian's shoulder spikes. "You truly thought we'd never consider using the ship without a teacher?"

"What's going on?" Shandy said, with alarm on his tired face.

"I wasn't trying to steal the ship from you!" I insisted. "Aerrem, what's gotten into you?" Tears continued to stream down my face, and I was still too weak to wipe them away.

"Since you didn't bother to attend any of our meetings, you don't know the class voted me leader of our expedition. So now I have to decide for everyone whether you're telling the truth."

"Honestly, I won't take the ship if the class needs it. I simply didn't com that anyone would—and I'll be glad to join the class final. But if you don't believe me, maybe you can at least trust Shandy!"

"That's true, I guess. You'd better hope I can also trust what he believes about you. Branem, Dojan, maybe you two should wait outside—"

"Are you sure?" Branem exchanged doubtful looks with Dojan.

"Keep your stunners handy and guard the door," Aerrem said. "Don't let anyone in or out until I say so!"

They reluctantly exited, after dumping me on Shandy's bed. I rubbed my tingling arms while Shandy tried to talk Aerrem into comming the truth. But she had already launched too deeply into her new role of class leader, and her anger simply morphed into raw anguish.

"I can't take any chances. Not with less than a week to go! Can't you two com my predicament? The whole class is depending on me, and I can't let my friendships bias my decision. I know how much you've wanted to escape this dump ever since you arrived, Taje. If you were willing to leave even your best friends behind, how can I trust you now?"

Shandy slumped against a wall, and I suddenly worried that maybe we'd exhausted him to the point of another collapse.

"What's the matter?" Aerrem looked as alarmed as I felt. "Maybe I should take Taje back to my room to com this out—"

Shandy shook his head, and covered his face with his long fingers.

"Shandy, what is it?"

"I can prove Taje isn't lying." But he scanned as if he was about to start crying too.

"Great! So what's the problem?"

He pushed himself away from the wall. "Aerrem, I have to talk to you—here. Alone."

"Okay." She rested her hand on his trembling shoulder for a micro, and he told the door to open so Aerrem could order Branem and Dojan to haul me away.

I was finally able to wipe my face and nod gratefully at my roomie as I was escorted out. If Shandy needed some privacy to admit to Aerrem that he'd snooped my deskcom screen, that was fine with me. Let them read all my prep in my deskcom, which I hadn't remembered to lock. I had little left to hide now.

JOURNAL ENTRY 44

Branem and Dojan marched me around the hall, only to vector into another surprise. Taemar, Hannen, Jael, and Piel all stood outside Aerrem and Branem's door, despite the late hour.

"Where's Aerrem?" they demanded.

"She's busy." Branem ignored further questions, but he let everyone in to wait for her. No one seemed particularly surprised to scan me under guard, or to find both bedrooms stuffed with noisy cages and bubbling aquariums. I guess Aerrem hadn't quite finished with the pet business.

Branem and Dojan sat down with me on Branem's bed in the front room, while everyone else took seats at the deskcom, on animal crates, or on the floor. We all sat in an awkward silence that sucked up an eon before Aerrem returned, her tail dragging with exhaustion.

"What now?" she said, and the crowd erupted. "Quiet, everyone!" she ordered almost too softly to be heard, but everybody obeyed. "Hannen, you first. What are you doing here?"

"I—uh—have a confession to make."

"You should have told me before!" Taemar turned on him. "I was so worried!"

"I told you, I couldn't!"

We all stared at Hannen. Had he given the whole scheme away already?

"Launch it now, Hannen!" Aerrem's tail quivered.

"Well, I think you'd better know—the whole class should know—I didn't get into a real accident on Darwin. Tarnek and Kem set it up as a class exercise, to give us emergency experience—"

"That whole accident scene was a sim?" Aerrem looked shocked, and then she laughed with nervous relief. "Oh, Hannen, how did you ever make it scan so real?"

"I wasn't supposed to tell—anyone. Darwin actually has satellites, so you really didn't even need your wristcom scanners to find me." Hannen held his head in his hands. "But now that Tarnek can't help us, I'm guessing he'd want everyone to know.

"We used stage make-up, medkit and med-niche practice programs, and saline injections to fake my injuries and treatment. I just don't think anyone should feel too over-confident about our emergency skills."

"I still think you should have warned me!" Taemar said. But Aerrem managed to quickly intercede. She hustled the two teammates out the door, after promising Hannen that he could make a full confession at the next class meeting.

Aerrem rubbed her eyes as she turned back to the rest of us. "Okay, Jael, what are you doing here? Are you still suffering doubts?"

"Talk some sense into him." Piel's antennae twitched. "I want to go, but not without my teammate!"

"I don't believe in peer pressure for this," Aerrem said. "It's simply a very personal decision, isn't it, Jael?"

Jael returned Aerrem's hard stare. "I won't tell on the rest of you, if that's what you're asking. Tarnek would want us to remain a team in spirit, whatever each of us decides to do.

"But no matter how good everyone thinks this scans, FIL could condemn us as runaways, and dump us all into Discipline."

"And you aren't willing to take that chance?"

"I need more time to think about it."

"Sorry, but we're almost out of time. I wish I could give you longer, Jael, but you'll have to let us know by our next meeting, so Taemar can order enough food."

"And you're really going to ask Fehrokc to join us?"

"Of course—he's our T.A.!"

"Exactly. You don't think he'll tell on us?"

Aerrem's tail thrashed despite her obvious exhaustion. "Weren't you there when Rognarthe ejected him like a piece of space junk? You have my word that we can trust Shanden Fehrokc."

Jael looked down, nodded, and left, his Telmid teammate still pleading with him. But now it was my turn for Aerrem's attention, and my pulse pounded in my throat. Had Shandy managed to convince Aerrem I was telling the truth? I nervously scanned Aerrem's frowning face as Branem and Dojan gripped their stunners more tightly.

"What did Shandy say?" Branem said at last.

"He thinks it may all be a trick." Aerrem collapsed on Branem's desk chair.

"What!" Alarmed, Dojan and Branem both stood up, stunners aimed at me, while I cringed.

"Shandy suspects another sneaky class test," Aerrem said. "He says Rognarthe possesses one obvious skill—the ability to goad us all into rash reactions."

The stunners dropped, and even Aerrem's zoo fell eerily silent.

"But," Branem finally stuttered, "but what kind of test could this be?"

"Of our patience and integrity? Who knows. Hannen's confession tonight just adds to the evidence. When has the class ever *not* been a test?"

JOURNAL ENTRY 45

"How certain is Shandy?" Dojan asked.

Aerrem shrugged. "He's not," she repeated wearily. "He wasn't told any more than the rest of us. Less, actually, since Rognarthe jettisoned him so quickly."

"So you think we should cancel?" Branem said.

"I don't know. We'll have to discuss Shandy and Hannen's warnings tomorrow night, and let the whole class decide all over again. It's too nova for me to com by myself."

"I don't care what we're risking." Dojan sniffed. "I'm sick of the Center. I'll chance it if you want to go."

"Same here!" Branem said, and I almost added my personal agreement aloud. But I still didn't know whether they'd let me join the expedition.

Aerrem gave Branem and Dojan a weary smile, but her face grew wary again when she scanned my questioning look.

"Shandy cleared you—"

"Oh, smooth—"

"But I haven't," Aerrem cut in. "Instead, I'm setting some new ground rules. Break any of them, and we'll not only leave you behind, we'll also arrange for your return to Level Two, and it won't be to Medicine. Is that clear?"

"Very." I swallowed hard.

"Okay. One, you will return to perfect attendance in class. Two, you will cause absolutely no more trouble in there, no matter how badly you're provoked. Three, you will attend all the rest of our meetings. Four, whenever not in class or at a meeting, you will stay in your room."

"Agreed!"

"I'm not finished. I'll also have Trist monitor your bracelet, to make sure you obey these terms. And lastly, tomorrow night you will stand up in front of our class and relate in excruciating detail what Discipline is like, so no one harbors any delusions about the chances we're taking."

"Okay," I squeaked, my face turning redder than my hair.

"Fine. Now everyone go to bed. I'm tired, and we still have way too much to do."

I escaped Aerrem's wrath gladly, although I had to face my roomie again, and thank him for whatever he'd done to rescue me. Luckily Shandy seemed too embarrassed to offer any details. And soon we both became too busy to care.

JOURNAL ENTRY 46

Aerrem talked again about the "nauseating trip excitement" which overcame a lot of us as we exited a translift into the Admin lobby. We were already sweating, from fused nerves, as well as packs bulging with cautiously redundant gear. One wrong question from anyone on Level One, and we'd never even make it through the security gate for the tube station lifts.

The class had voted, after much debate, to go ahead with our final exam, even if it was a trap for runaways. How bad could it scan if we planned to carry out Tarnek's original plan, including returning with a proper report?

But maybe that was all nova wishful thinking. And now suddenly another worry zapped me, and I ducked out of our line.

"Taje, where are you going?" Aerrem whipped around from where she and Branem were about to lead our class through the security gate.

"I've got to jettison to the back of the line!" I hissed. "What if Tarnek didn't clear my tracer for this trip before he left? At least the rest of you could get through the gate before I set off an alarm—"

"Forget it." Aerrem gave me her first sympathetic scan since the night she stunned me. "I was deluded when I said Trist would monitor you. She told me Tarnek must have ordered your signal killed. She hasn't been able to track you for the sheer fun of it since our first field trip."

"And no one told me?"

"Keep it down! Here we go!"

Miraculously the gate allowed us all through, and a tube lift smoothly delivered us to an underground station. We gave each other stunned looks, and deliberately took over a whole tube car, laying our packs across empty seats.

Aerrem gave us a galaxy-spanning grin from her seat. Then she scanned Shandy's face. "What's the matter, Shandy? We made it this far! Are you still worried about a trap?"

Shandy turned his face to the window, which showed nothing but a speeding grey wall. "No," he said.

"He had to ask an interplanetary vet to put Sheefharn into stasis," I explained for him. Leaving our pets behind was the hardest part for both of us, but it was worst for him.

"Sheefharn never ate very much or did very well whenever we went on field trips, and Shandy was afraid she'd die if he left her any longer," I said. Stasis gave Sheefharn much better odds, but a few animals never woke up from it.

"Oh," Aerrem said. "I'm sorry, Shandy." She quickly changed the subject. "Ready for your job, Taje?"

"Kijan's launching us, right?" I said, suddenly panicked.

"Yeah, since he helped pilot our most recent space station launch. But you get to copilot—warm-up for piloting all our landings!"

"Argh, don't remind me!" Once more, Aerrem hadn't given me a choice, so I'd had to steal study time for piloting review. I would not get nicely prepped, level landing fields this time.

Most talk died after that, between post-finals exhaustion and useless worry. But our wristcom passes got us into the busy shuttle port, onto a crowded shuttle, and into the even busier orbital station, without anyone giving us a second scan.

"Amazing," Jael gasped when Aerrem's wristcom let her open the ship's hatch. But Launch Control wasn't quite so happy with us.

"Blast!" Kijan said from the pilot seat. "Launch Control wants to know why we don't have any teachers aboard yet!"

I sat down next to him and checked my comscreen. "Kijan's right." I was already sweating again, even though my main job was to land us at our chosen destination, Planet Taron. If we ever reached Planet Taron.

"Taemar to Aerrem!" Taemar used emergency override on all our screens.

"What?" Aerrem said behind us. She and Branem had comscreens in our seatbacks. "We're rather busy right now—"

"Aerrem, we've already finished our count, and we don't have enough food!"

JOURNAL ENTRY 47

"Are you sure?" The tip of Aerrem's tail spasmed in the cramped cockpit.

"Yes, I'm sure! Of course we're double-checking, but there's not much here to count—"

"Hang on, Taemar!" Aerrem switched her com back to the insistent Launch Control call and her face to a cheery smile. "Hi, I'm Aerrem Nathegorn, a student in Drehx Tarnek's Planetary ecology Class—"

"We seem to have a problem here, Nathegorn," a brown-skinned Altruskan said on the screen. "You're already requesting timing and coordinates for launch release, but we have no record of any instructors boarding—"

"I know!" Aerrem pulled a face. "Our teachers sent us ahead and told us to get the ship ready for launch. They're on the next shuttle up, and if we fuse this, they'll lower our trip grades."

"How typical!" The Altruskan snorted. "It's a little irregular, but I'll check with my supervisor and see what I can do for you. Stand by."

"Thank you!" Aerrem quickly closed the call, while putting her hand over Branem's mouth to muffle his "I thought our licenses were good enough!"

"Space, I'm such a vac-head!" Aerrem slapped her own forehead. "Why did I say that? If they check shuttle passenger lists, they'll find out I lied!" She switched her com back to Taemar. "How much food do we have?"

"Enough for round-trip travel, plus a week or two, if we stretch it. Oh, and there's a crate full of salt I never even asked for!"

"We were supposed to have received a three-month food supply, plus round-trip! I verified your order delivery yesterday—"

"I know, I know! The station either mixed it up, or lost it. This mostly looks like our all leftovers from Pelsus—"

"Aerrem, someone else from Launch Control is on my com, with our launch release data!" Kijan's furry ears jerked upright. "Should I stall?"

"If we request a delay, we could go buy station supplies," I said. "The prices are nova, but I should have enough credit in my wristcom—"

"Launch Control will probably com us, if we take that long," Aerrem snapped. "No stalling, Kijan! It's probably a fuse-up in Launch Control, and if so, it won't last."

Kijan took the data, I double-checked it, and ten heart-pounding minutes later the orbital station released us. At our assigned time and position, we vanished into paraspace.

JOURNAL ENTRY 48

"Quiet everyone! We have a situation to discuss!" Aerrem brought our class to order in the ship's lounge. "We're on our way to Planet Taron, because we got lucky with Launch Control, and I commed we had just one chance to slip away. But we're only hauling enough food for a round-trip flight and a week or two on Taron!

"We all know that's not nearly long enough for a proper survey report. So if we really want to try to pass our final exam, we'll also have to pass a survival test.

"Therefore I'm calling for another vote. Do we continue on, or do we return right now to Arrainius? If anyone requests it, we're turning back. I don't want to drag anybody with second thoughts into a mission this hazardous."

Everyone got noisy again, and Aerrem let it go on for a while. Then she insisted that we raise our hands and take turns. "If there's debate, let's all hear it. Dojan!"

"It's not as if we haven't been taught how to forage, and we did choose a biochemically compatible world to study. I don't see any reason to give up so soon!"

"We could start rationing right now." Hannen put his arm around his forlorn teammate. "We can stretch out what we have, while we're learning."

"And we could insist on setting aside enough food for our return flight, so even if we have to quit early, we can return quite safely," Nessel said.

"Or we could re-direct to a semi-civilized planet and lose ourselves there, so no one can ship us back to the Center!" Lowwind said, and I grinned.

Gasps and bursts of laughter erupted around the cramped lounge. Obviously this was a new idea for some but not all of my classmates.

Aerrem put her hands on her hips. "Okay, who else favors setting up an isolated colony and living with each other for the rest of our lives, because that's the only way we might succeed at running away! And do any of you really think we can deviate one micro from Tarnek's plan and not get caught by FIL?"

My face burned, everyone else quickly relented, and we voted to proceed with our plan. Even Jael didn't want to give up, now that we'd gotten so close to reaching our yearlong goal. But now we had a lot more homework, reviewing a preliminary Scout Ship lifeform list for potential Taron food resources.

As I scrolled through it, Aerrem accosted me. "Are you going to keep another trip journal?"

I nearly jumped out of my seat. "How did you know about that?" I whispered.

"People talk. So are you? It could help defend us, later on."

"I don't know. And it's private! Why don't you compose a trip diary? You're the writer."

"I do fiction. And it doesn't include holos."

When I said no more, Aerrem shrugged, and moved on. She knew better than to argue with me.

I returned to our new homework. We never did get a real chance to celebrate our escape. And I found myself too wound up for easy sleep. I could hardly wait for our new adventure to start. (Of course I'd record it. How could I resist?)

"But will it be enough?" Shandy asked, during a private moment. I assumed he meant in the place of permanently running away. I wasn't sure if he was only asking me, or wondering the same for himself.

"I don't know," I said. But I was lying. I never wanted to return to Arrainius, but a memorable experience and a record of Taron would probably have to do.

out a gap in the trees to land Aerrem and Branem on the crest of the range, so they could camp in a roughly central position of command.

Then we landed Jael and Piel down the other side of the range a ways, on another rocky patch, and Dojan and Kijan near the base of the mountains. Now Shandy took the copilot seat, and we let Hannen and Taemar off in a small clearing in the lower but still woodsy region farther on, and Tarknes and orange-eyed Krorn in some rolling plains beyond that.

At last Shandy and I became our own team again. Shandy checked my comwork for our final destination, a chain of lakes the two of us wanted to investigate. The rapid flow of com data came to a halt with our ship's soft field landing, and I sat back with a sigh of relief.

Shandy rubbed his temples and frowned.

"What's the matter?"

"A small headache. I can take something for it."

"Not surprising, after all the suspense," I said.

"Scared?" Shandy said.

"A bit," I admitted as I initiated the ship's shutdown sequence. "But unlike the other teams, we can return more quickly to the ship if anything goes wrong."

"We could even use it as our main shelter."

We looked at each other. "Nahhh!"

We ran a visual scan before exiting the cockpit. This continent possessed at least one predator we didn't want to meet unprepared, although the noise of our landing had surely caused any alert animal to bolt.

"What's that?" Shandy pointed at a rapidly receding, dun-colored cloud—a whole herd of large animals, running away from our ship!

"Herts? Smooth—they're why I wanted to study this area! Come on, let's go Outside!" I launched out of my seat and we raced each other to the hatch.

But when I dropped back down to the surface of Taron, I discovered the damage I'd already done.

The metallic, salty tang of blood, on top of herbivore dung, urine, and drying grass, zapped my nostrils. I bent over the yusahmbul-sized ungulate lying dead on the ground, its chest crushed by the nearest ship strut.

Pulse galloping, I touched the smooth tan coat, avoiding the orange-red blood still rapidly pooling around the strut from exposed, mangled organs. "Great Galaxy! I didn't even think to run a bioscan during my landings!"

"Neither did I." Shandy nobly tried to take some of the blame, even though I was head pilot, and therefore ultimately responsible. "But we landed so slowly," he added, "it shouldn't have mattered—"

A scream at our backs interrupted Shandy, and we both spun around to confront the rest of my mistake—what was probably the dead hert's calf. It was nearly two-thirds the size of its recently murdered parent, but its horns were newly erupted, instead of forming complete coils like the beautiful pair on the lifeless body.

What a fused beginning! "Blast it all, I've made another orphan!" Tears streamed down my cheeks as the splay-legged calf bawled at us.

Shandy put his hand on my shoulder. "Taje, the rest of the herd escaped." He pointed out the grazed, widely trampled grass surrounding our ship. "Only one member was too ill or injured to leave. We probably just put it out of its misery."

"But why didn't the calf follow the rest of its herd?" I wailed. "Maybe it can't survive without this parent!"

"Most herd animals are altricial, remember?" Shandy adjusted his wristcom controls as he knelt for a close scan. "At birth, they almost have to hit the ground running. There's still hope—"

"Hope?" I said, staring hopelessly at the mangled corpse.

"Maybe if we load up our packs and hike out of here, the calf's herd will return for it."

"Shouldn't we move the ship first? Even the sight of it might terrify the herts—"

"And risk more noise and damage?"

"I suppose you're right." I bit my lip as I glanced again at the wreck under the strut. "It's such a fused waste!"

"No, it's not." But Shandy scanned equally upset as he stood up.

"It's edible?" I said, my mouth going dry.

"Yes. And we need her."

"But—but you're a vegetarian, and I—killed her."

Shandy flinched. "As copilot, I do share responsibility for this death. But neither of us can bring her back to life. Perhaps we should instead remember a lesson from the Mumdwars. They apologize to their prey and thank it for their lives."

I shook my head. The adult hert was dead and it would never know or care what we said. But I ran my own scan, and couldn't deny the fact that we indeed needed her.

JOURNAL ENTRY 50

So we spent our first morning on Taron salvaging and cooking up mother hert meat for our food bags and trying not to retch over it. Meanwhile, the poor calf paced nervously beyond stunner range, crying and hooting until I thought I'd go nova.

Although our stomachs craved a solid meal, we chewed and swallowed the hert meat with difficulty. After a quick water safety analysis, we rinsed off in the shallows of the large sparkling blue lake nearby, which we hastily named First Lake.

"The other side of this lake should do nicely," Shandy said, as we finally heaved on our heavy meat- and equipment-laden packs. I nodded, and we set off on an animal track winding through the greenery around the lake.

Greenery! I was shocked at how right it felt to my human eyes. Gradually I began to relax as more singer birds chimed along our passage, and golden glitterflies flitted from bloom to bloom while completely ignoring us. Iridescent diver birds and rainbow fish splashed in the lake. Lakeside nut tree saplings periodically thickened into cool, breeze-rustled woods. No wonder FIL wanted this world analyzed for possible colonization. But part of my brain suddenly hoped it wouldn't work out.

We stopped at the next sunny beach to change from hiking pants into shorts. We strapped back into our heavy packs and tromped onward.

But days here ran a bit swifter and gravity a bit higher than we were used to, so we didn't make it all the way around the lake our first day. The sun was threatening to set beyond a hazy inland mountain range by the time we dumped our packs and swiftly made a lakeside camp.

We gagged down another meat meal, to save our limited share of ship rations. The only part of dinner that kept me from feeling sorrier for myself was the look on Shandy's miserable face. Sheer determination must have kept him from throwing up.

Afterwards we propped our packs against a tree trunk within close visual range of our mesh tent door. We crawled into our bags, exhausted and counting on the inexperience of local wildlife to see us through our first night.

"We can star-gaze some other night," I said.

Shandy mumbled an incoherent reply, and we both fell soundly asleep. But after what felt like a couple hours of the calf screaming at me in my nightmares, I awoke with a start and realized the screams were for real.

JOURNAL ENTRY 51

"Wake up, Shandy!" I tugged on his arm. I was astonished at what he could sleep through. Another scream ripped the air, and my scalp tried to crawl off my head. "We're surrounded!"

"Huh? What?" Shandy wiped his eyes, and sat up and shuddered at the next searing shriek. "Dats?"

"I'd guess so." I sat up, told the tent light to turn on, and fumbled with my wristcom controls. "Scout Ship data says they're nocturnal hunters." And dats were probably the only predators on this continent large enough to make so much noise.

Shandy ran a scan on his wristcom and confirmed our suspicions. "Lovely." He peered through our tent door, and starlight glinted eerily on his pale hair.

I shivered. "I guess our hert meat attracted them." Our camping food came in scent-proof packaging, so it normally took time—and help from very foolish people—for wildlife to learn about it.

"But we cooked the meat," Shandy said. "Shouldn't it smell all wrong?"

"What do we know? Humans have the worst sense of smell in the known universe! How could we have been so vac-brained? We should have hung our food—and our packs—in a tree!"

"Well, we didn't bother. So now what?"

I reached for my utility belt, plucked my stunner from it, and released the safety. "Cover me. I'm going to retrieve our packs—"

"That's nova! You can't go out there alone—"

"There's no sense risking both of us! Who'd be left to give first aid?"

"But you'll also drag the smell right in here with us!"

"We don't have any choice. We'll have to stand guard over them or we won't have packs or any food left by morning! Tell me I'm wrong!"

Shandy shook his head, frustrated, and yanked his stunner off his belt. We both knew from class exercises that he also had better aim.

"Okay," he said. "But get completely dressed—including utility belt, coat, gloves, and boots. I'll do the same, in case I have to come out after you. That'll give us at least a little extra protection."

Blast it all, he actually agreed with my nova plan! I dressed, and we both palmed our stunners after releasing their safeties. I sealed my coat with trembling hands, and popped the door release. "Wish me luck!"

"Good luck!"

I launched myself for our packs, whipped mine open to yank out my stove, and cranked up its light mode. My stove revealed flashing golden eyes and sharp fangs of dats close to waist level, who veered away, howling at the light. I left the stove at the base of the tree and clung to my stunner while I dragged each pack into our tent.

"Get out your stove," I told Shandy as I quickly shed my extra clothes to towel off my sweat. "I don't think they like bright lights."

"Apparently not."

We set both stoves on full power for light, one on each side of the tent, and took turns standing watch while the other tried to sleep.

Eons later I witnessed the growing silence of dawn, I turned off our lights, and we both slept in. Until another orphan calf nightmare woke me up, and I heard the real one bawling outside our tent.

JOURNAL ENTRY 52

"More meat for breakfast?" I moaned. I wasn't sure my bowels could take it.

"It'll spoil soon in this warm weather if we don't eat it, and we shouldn't waste it." Shandy sat back against the tree trunk our packs had rested against last night, and shut his eyes. The bark above him was shredded, almost as high as we could reach.

I looked away, but my gaze fell next on the momentarily silent calf, lapping water from the edge of the lake. It raised its head, chin dripping, and began crying at me again. "Why on Taron did it follow us?"

"It must have smelled its mother on our clothes. And its presence may be why the dats were such a problem last night."

"In that case, how did it survive?"

"By staying close to our lights? I'm guessing we'd better do laundry before we move on." Shandy rubbed his face wearily, instead of making a painfully obvious alternative suggestion. I gratefully agreed. I didn't want another killing on my hands.

But it took us all morning to lake-wash and sun-dry our clothes and everything they'd come in contact with, including our packs. So we ended up eating a very repetitious lunch in camp, before we packed up, hefted our heavy packs onto our sore bodies, and trudged on around the lake.

Maybe today we'd leave the calf behind, for everyone's sake. Although I couldn't help wondering if dats would bring the calf down before its herd returned, and whether swiftly killing the calf and adding it to our food supply would actually be more merciful.

"I'm not scanning any new lifeforms we could name," I said hours later, while stopping briefly to apply synderm patches to threatening hotspots on my feet. Various specialists would assign the scientific names, of course. But like the Scout Ship patrol, Tarnek had told us in one of his lectures that we could give common names to any new species we scanned, and I thought we could certainly invent more exciting names here.

"The Scout report did suggest unusually low speciation." Shandy got up, stumbled over a root, and his heavy pack almost tipped him over.

"So far I've only noted two types of songbirds—or one, if there's sexual dimorphism. And I've only scanned nut trees and meadow grass—how about you?" I limped after Shandy.

"Unless there are subtle differences we haven't detected yet, I'd agree. Too bad the Scouts couldn't come up with more original names. They must have been quite tired or in an unusual hurry. I've seen berry bushes but not the berries. Have you seen any nuts?"

"I haven't looked, to tell you the truth. But low speciation would simply launch a different question, wouldn't it?" I said, embarrassed that I hadn't looked for any new foods.

"Science rarely answers why questions."

"Yeah, but it's fun trying—wow, this won't work for a campsite!"

Hidden by trees until we nearly toppled over it, the far edge of First Lake spilled over a rocky lip, and pelted down a creek bed so steep it was almost a waterfall.

Shandy peered down through the foliage. "I think I can see the second lake."

"Why don't we look for a campsite down there? It would tuck us nicely out of sight."

Climbing down was a trick, however, with our overloaded packs, which kept threatening to dump us down the fast way. Instead we had to change into pants and bushwhack rough switchbacks through the brush to safely reach the smaller, more woodsy second lake basin.

Now only breeze-ruffled leaves and water lapping at the edge of the pebbled shore of Second Lake broke the peaceful silence.

We dropped our packs on the beach against a log, and sat down on it for a micro. "This is smooth," I said. "Nice and quiet and private."

Shandy wiped sweat from his face, smearing dirt across it, and nodded.

We both knew we couldn't afford much of a rest. This time we raced the sun to make a proper camp. I set up the tent with our sleeping bags inside and a stove outside at one end of the beach, and a kitchen area with our second stove, cookware, and food at the other end.

We'd take the second stove with us to the tent after dinner.

Meanwhile, Shandy searched uphill, away from the lake and camp, for a tall tree with a narrow but strong branch for our packs. He'd stuffed a rock into a sock and tied it to one end of his rope, and I heard it crashing into the brush, accompanied by angry curses, countless times before he finally hurled it over a suitable branch.

Neither of us complained about our dull dinner, in our haste to get to bed for a solid night of sleep. And what a sorry hope that turned out to be.

JOURNAL ENTRY 53

When the screams and howls woke us up a couple hours later, at least we were better prepared. We immediately dressed in more layers, grabbed our stunners, and switched off the safeties.

Shandy covered me again, while I jumped out of our tent and turned on our nearby stove lights. (We had discussed leaving them on all night again, but they might run down before we could get them back to the ship to recharge them.) I dived back inside, as if mere tent walls could protect me.

"How many of them are there?" I asked.

Shandy checked his pre-tuned wristcom scanner. "Looks like half a dozen. But there's also something too big for a dat—"

"A bigger predator?" My heart sped up. We'd learned that the primary mission of most FIL Scout Ships was to seek valuable planets. So FIL usually only allowed Scout Ship teams enough time to decide whether a planet had resource, colony, research, or membership potential, before they had to move on. Which is why

Tarnek had emphasized that we must consider any Scout lifeform list dangerously incomplete.

"I'm not sure," Shandy said, "but fuse it all, I think this reading is the same size as the calf!"

"So how close are the dats?"

"I'm looking! Blast, I can't tell exactly how far away they are with one reading, but their direction lines up with the tree we hung our packs in."

"Well, that'll distract them from ripping through our tent walls—but can dats climb?" I suddenly wondered. I was certain they were strong enough to break our rope branch, even if they were too big and heavy to climb out on it.

Shandy switched his wristcom to report data, and we studied a Scout dat holo, but it wasn't very helpful. The lean but muscular creature looked like a short-haired, dun-colored cross between Terran canine and feline species. Bushy dark tips on upright ears and at the end of the tail added a handsome touch, despite nasty carnivore teeth.

But the holo wasn't taken close enough to scan whether the claws could scale trees. Specs simply showed that the largest adults would actually outweigh us.

"They didn't climb the tree they mauled last night," I groped for hope.

"Are you sure?" Shandy said.

"So we could lose our packs and everything in them!"

"We can't do anything more about it tonight. There are too many dats out there now to risk retrieving anything."

And soon our tent was serenaded as well. So we spent another long night of alternating guard duty with nearly futile attempts to sleep through the noise, and the bright lights glowing through our tent walls.

More than once I scanned the calf in those lights, and more than once I wanted to yell or throw rocks at it. But of course I didn't. After all, we'd camped here to try to save its life!

Shandy and I tried to sleep in after dawn at last brought us peace, but worry about the condition of our packs soon drove us out of the tent.

I kept my relief to myself when we didn't scan any young hert parts strewn about. We found the calf quietly grazing beyond stunner range of our camp. And our packs still hung from their branch, counter-balanced. It wasn't until I picked up a dead branch and used it to snag a pack down that we discovered the damage.

Something had chewed right into our packs, eaten or stolen—or dropped for the dats—most of our hert meat, and even ripped into and consumed the contents of several of our precious camping food packets.

From the size of the scats, we guessed it was some critter bigger than a 'gik but much smaller than a dat, not to mention a lot more clever. Some animal we hadn't even tried to scan so far.

Shandy's pale hands shook as he examined what was left in his food bag. He gazed back at the calf, and he had a terrible look in his brown eyes that I'd never seen before. "We haven't done it any favors."

"I know," I said quickly, before he had to say more. "We should kill it and eat it before the dats get it. But we may have to wait until the calf is back within range tonight. And I'm not sure I can take much more meat right now."

I wasn't totally stalling. My bowels felt like they'd locked up. "Let's eat what's left of this torn-up breakfast packet, and then look for something with more fiber to add to a soup today. We need to start general scans and hunt for other food sources anyway."

Shandy nodded. Neither of us talked about heading back for the protection of the ship today, although we should have. We were both too dangerously tired to even consider it.

JOURNAL ENTRY 54

I shivered as I scanned the dat skeleton.

I wasn't cold, but while exploring around this smaller lake—staying close enough so I didn't need my wristcom compass to remain oriented—I'd stumbled across the remains of a dead dat, tucked between some boulders.

Something had stripped the body down to bones and dried ligaments, and I couldn't detect any skeletal injuries. It looked like it had merely curled up and died.

Of course without any other body parts to study, I really had no idea what had happened. When I finished recording the scene with my wristcom I decided to return to camp. Shandy should have some soup ready for lunch by now.

Along the way I checked my traps, mostly set in the lake. I had commed even fish might give us a decent break from hert meat. But all my traps remained empty except one I'd placed too close to shore, drowning a whole bunch of tiny blue-green amphibians known unimaginably as "phibs" in the Scout listing.

I sighed as I hauled my dripping catch out of the water. The poor little creatures looked like they'd take more energy to prepare for cooking than they'd replace. But I'd carry them back and at least analyze them for edibility and our report, since I'd already thoughtlessly killed them all.

Camp seemed oddly quiet upon my return, except for a pot simmering on one of our stoves. In it I scanned our last shreds of meat, plus tubers and greens Shandy must have gathered from the lakeshore and surrounding woods. Next to it sat a panful of red berries.

Of course Shandy should not have left the cook pot untended, but suddenly I heard sick retching. I followed the sounds to find Shandy vomiting up-slope.

"I didn't want to contaminate our campground with any food scents." He glanced at the trap I still clutched, full of stiffening little slimy bodies. He tried to look quickly away, but he dry-heaved some more.

I hid my trap behind me, and almost vomited in sympathy with him. My pulse sped up. Why had we camped so far from the ship with its med-niche? Back at the Center, my roomie's doctors were always adjusting his meds. "Shandy, what's wrong?"

"I thought it might be the berries. I was so thrilled when I found a patch! I scanned them twice and couldn't find anything wrong. I guess I've just allowed myself to get too tired." He pulled his water bottle off his belt and rinsed his mouth out. "Can you guard our camp for a while? I've got to take a nap. I'll give you a turn later today."

"Of course!" But as soon as he disappeared into our tent, I set my wristcom controls with trembling hands and checked the berries again. Nothing. I scanned my catch of the day, and found a mild skin toxin, as well as too much rot already.

I buried the whole sorry lot uphill, before returning to the stove. I tried a sip of soup—decent—but I'd lost my appetite.

I commed we should try to hike back to the ship, as soon as possible, before Shandy got too weak. But would he make it now, carrying his pack? I wasn't even sure I could.

I so wanted to lie down and sleep! Colorful rainbow fish gently splashed in the lake and iridescent singer birds hummed lullabies in the trees while I struggled to keep alert. Time crawled, and I almost nodded off.

I jerked myself awake and got up to throw cold lake-water on my face. Was everyone having this much trouble? We had all agreed to a weekly call-in, but I was ready now!

I sat down on a beach log and put in a call to Aerrem. She looked so sleepy I guessed I'd waked her from a nap, but she didn't complain when she saw my face. "What's wrong, Taje?"

"Are dats screaming at your camp all night long?"

"Yes, they're making almost everyone nova, along with the makkon raids—"

"Makkons?"

"Named after the unfortunate Scout who managed to scan one. Makkons have six limbs, they climb trees, and they can chew through packs like the 'giks. But they're about twice as big, with noses and stomachs to match—"

"Oh yeah, I think I did study them on the way to Taron." I simply hadn't put the raw description together with their obnoxious reality.

"I doubt they can smell through our food packaging, but I think curiosity drives them to chew through everything," Aerrem said. "Everyone is struggling to hang on to the food they have, while searching for new sources—"

"Has anyone mentioned any bad food warnings?"

"Nothing except a mild skin poison in the phibs, which are too small to bother with anyway. Why?"

I told her about Shandy and the berries.

"He is probably just too tired. Send me your berry analysis. From your description, I suspect we've safely eaten the same bush berries, but we can verify it. Taron is proving a lot more challenging than anyone expected."

"Will we have to quit soon?"

"Maybe. Or you may have to pick us all up, so we can regroup and everyone can use the ship as a safer base. But Hannen and Taemar turned their flexitents into hammocks high in a tree last night, and they report the dats couldn't climb up to them.

"Out of reach of the dats, perhaps we can safely sleep with our food to protect it. Branem and I are going to try that tonight, with alternating watches, to be extra careful."

When Shandy woke up, he did seem better, and I gave him the good news about the hammock idea. I took a quick nap, and then we rigged up both our tents and finished the soup.

We weren't brave enough tonight to sleep with the remains of our food, but we strung up our food bags in an adjacent tree. We hung our packs near our hammocks, left our stoves at the base of our hammock and food trees, and set our wristcoms for a dat proximity alarm.

We took almost no time to pass out, and managed to get a few more hours of sleep before our next emergency.

JOURNAL ENTRY 55

My wristcom woke me up. "Aerrem to Taje and Shandy! Please answer right now!"

I moaned. I'd managed to sleep through the usual dat chorus so far, but I couldn't ignore this. I replied into my wristcom while I struggled to open my eyes. "What is it?"

"Branem's hurt—dat attack." Aerrem's voice sounded loud and shaky. "I've stopped the bleeding, but his wounds look nasty. I want you to fly the ship back here, so we can check him out more thoroughly with the med-niche scanner. Give the ship's com the same coordinates you used to land us here—we're camped very close—"

"Ohhh," I groaned, face burning in the dark. "Aerrem, we've camped a couple days' hike from the ship," I said. How vac-brained could we get?

"What? Why on Taron would you do that!"

"Well, you see, I accidentally killed a mother hert with our last landing, orphaning her calf and driving the rest of its herd away—"

"Never mind! How fast can you hike back to our ship, if you leave all your gear in a tree?"

"I don't know. But I'll find out!"

"Good. Call me as soon as you reach the ship. I've started Branem on treatment for shock, and so far it seems to be working."

I had to shake Shandy's hammock to wake him up and tell him the fused news.

"I'm coming with you," he said.

"Are you sure you can make it?" Without slowing me down, I wanted to say. I felt sick from lack of sleep, but his face looked downright ghastly in his tent light.

"I have to. No one should hike here alone at night."

"That leaves nobody to guard our food."

"We can carry it in our day packs."

"No, it's too dangerous! We're not in good enough shape to carry any extra weight, especially dat bait!"

It wasn't a cold night, but we wore long pants and coats, and we did carry lights, first-aid kits, and water bottles on our utility belts. Stunners in hand, we dropped to the base of our tree and cranked up both our stove lights. We hollered and hurled stones at the calf and the nearest dats to clear a path. Then we shut off the stove lights and ran.

JOURNAL ENTRY 56

I never thought we'd reach the ship in one night. But abandoning our heavy packs gave us mobility and speed, and I was amazed at how well Shandy kept up. We finished the most difficult stretch as soon as we climbed back up to First Lake, and guilt and fear became our motivators.

Every time I tripped over a rock or root, I imagined Branem's injuries and quickly picked myself up to move on.

We couldn't run the whole way, but we rested by walking, not stopping, which wasn't safe at night. And away from our food and the calf, the few dats we encountered seemed as scared of us as we were of them. Especially when we learned to join together to look like an animal too large and loud to even consider an attack.

When we became sleepy, we talked our heads off, and even became brutally honest, since no one else could hear us.

"Did you really want to become an ecologist?" Shandy asked me. "Or simply get away from Arrainius?"

"At first I only wanted to escape, and ecology seemed like a fun way to do it," I said. "Now I'm not so sure. FIL has spent a lot to teach us about a very important career, and I'd get to travel and spend time Outside." Had Tarnek infected me after all?

"But?" Shandy said.

"I can't decide. What about you?"

"If I didn't have to kill, maybe. If I could return to Istrann and use my knowledge to help there, well, of course. Otherwise this is all just a vacation from Arrainius and the Center."

"Some vacation!"

"Yeah, I know," Shandy said. "But I liked the Mumdwars."

"So did I." I sighed, missing them again.

Dawn faded the stars by the time we made it back to the ship. I'd never felt so glad to return to it before.

Shandy leaned against a strut to catch his breath and cover me with his stunner, while I climbed up and triggered the hatch release. Inside I turned around and covered his climb up.

I staggered to the pilot room while he sealed the hatch and turned on the med-niche. I dropped into my seat and asked the com to begin the warm-up sequence.

Shandy sat down in the copilot seat a few minutes later, and found me cursing. "What's wrong?"

"The ship's com keeps asking me for a lock-down release code!"

"What lock release code?"

"Exactly!" I threw off my coat to sweat openly in the ship's stuffy air. Next I used the ship's com to verify that no one in our class had heard of the code, much less knew what to do about it.

"I'm so sorry, Aerrem! I guess Tarnek and Kem always handled it, so why bother to teach us?"

"And I suppose the lock itself makes sense," Aerrem said wearily. "We wouldn't want any stranger to walk up and fly away with our ship during our field trips."

"How's Branem?" I barely had the courage to ask. Imagining the stretcher relays to haul him here was not a pretty holo.

"He's doing better. I disinfected and sealed a bunch of long cuts across his shoulder and chest, and medkit pain meds helped a lot. So unless there are unusually adaptive and resistant microbes here, he should do okay."

"An infection would be very bad luck."

"I know. He'll probably just end up with a bunch of scars he can brag about if he doesn't bother to have them mended—"

"Nice!" Branem joined Aerrem on the screen. "I'm fine, so quit worrying!" He had on a soft, loose shirt, so I couldn't see any of his wounds.

"But how did you get hurt?" Shandy asked. "Did the tent hammock idea fail?"

My heart sank. I didn't relish having the whole class camp in the ship with us, but it would have to, if no one could stay safe where they were.

Branem looked chagrined, however, and Aerrem filled us in. "It was Branem's grand idea to stun a dat from the safety of our tree, to add a meat source larger than a bird to our diet. But when Branem slipped to the ground to finish the dat off, it attacked with front claws and teeth—only the dat's back end was paralyzed."

"I must have only grazed its hindquarters with my beam," Branem said.

I gulped. "Sounds terrifying!"

"Yeah," Aerrem said, "and Branem dropped his stunner when the dat took its first swipe at him. They quickly got so tangled up I couldn't shoot from the tree—I was too afraid I'd hit Branem instead of the dat! So I had to scramble down, dodge my way in, and fire my stunner point blank. And all for a dat body so starved it looked like a skeleton."

"Are you hurt too?" Shandy asked.

"Only a few scratches—and about a decade of life scared out of me! But how are you, Shandy? Taje said you were sick earlier."

"I just needed more sleep. I'm fine."

"We'd better pass on some warnings," I said. "Especially now that we know we can't fly the med-niche to anyone."

Aerrem nodded. "And we'll need another vote."

"Another vote?"

"For when to set off the ship's paraspace S.O.S. signal. Kem warned us it can take a while to get a response, especially for a fringe world. But if the ship won't budge, that's the only way we'll ever get home!"

JOURNAL ENTRY 57

The ship's com buzzed us that afternoon in the ship's captain and pilot cabins, where Shandy and I had crashed in our teachers' bunks. We'd talked Aerrem into waiting this long before calling for the S.O.S. debate and vote, since we'd felt too exhausted to think without more sleep.

I sat up, better rested but now extremely stiff and sore as I headed for the pilot room. Shandy joined me there and we exchanged grimaces. But almost everyone else had enjoyed more rest in the trees last night. So no one felt ready to give up.

We decided to try to stick with our three-month survey plan. Afterwards, we'd meet at the ship to combine our data and decide if we felt ready to write our report and leave. We could do most of this by wrist-com, of course, but we were used to real meetings now. And although no one said it, I suspected we'd feel a strong need to for more company by then, not to mention better shelter.

As Hannen also pointed out, since Taron was remote in normspace, but not necessarily in the weird geometry of paraspace, an immediate S.O.S. response was as likely as a long delay. So why ask for rescue before we really needed it? We could vote again to quit any time, but we couldn't take it back once we asked for help. Meanwhile, we decided to save our return trip food for any emergency waiting period that might follow our S.O.S. transmission.

Everyone also promised to approach dats and any nighttime activities with a lot more caution. We did discuss a stretcher relay system for emergencies we simply hoped wouldn't happen. But somehow Taron hazards simply made us more determined than ever.

"So what's next?" I turned to Shandy after we finished the group comcall.

He shrugged. "Hunt for some food?"

My empty stomach twisted hungrily. "We could borrow a bit from ship stores, and replace it with some of our pack food."

"If we have anything left in our food bags. And I don't think we can count on that."

"You're probably right." I sighed. "I'd suggest heading back right now to rescue what we can of our packs, but I know we're still too tired. What a waste! Oh well, I suppose it's our punishment for not staying with the ship. Not that it matters so much now, but do you want to move back here?"

"No. But I think we should. It's safer."

I nodded. Sometime last night, during that fear-filled, endless run, Outside had lost a little of its romance for me. And I'd actually enjoyed sleeping on a soft bunk, surrounded by safe, quiet walls.

"Okay," I said, "this afternoon we hunt for food. But tomorrow we'd better leave at dawn to retrieve our gear. Even so, we'll probably have to spend at least one more night Outside, before we can return with whatever's left."

We vectored for the hatch, but another surprise awaited us outside the ship.

"I don't believe this!" Shandy hissed. He raised his stunner as he gave me a questioning look. As if I'd become the judge for the calf's destiny.

"Do you think maybe it imprinted on us?" I whispered, while the calf stood there, half-chewed grass hanging from its peach-colored lips. It stared right back at us—within stunner range.

"Isn't it too old for that?"

"We have no idea how quickly animals grow up on Taron." I was stalling again. Why was I stalling?

"It's trouble, Taje. And I hate to say it, but it's also protein we need very badly now. We're lucky that dats haven't already consumed it!"

I scanned my pale, thin roomie and almost relented. If only the calf didn't remind me of my favorite childhood yusahmbul mount, with those big brown eyes gazing back at me so trustingly. But wait a micro—that was my answer!

"What if the calf could serve a much more important purpose? What if I could train it for emergency transportation?"

I had forgotten to whisper this time, but the calf held its ground, as if it knew its fate hung between us. Shandy gazed back at it with misgiving.

"Is it old enough to ride? Can you train it quickly enough to make any difference? Do you even know how to train a mount?"

"I don't know," I had to say to all his questions. "I didn't train any of our yusahmbuls, but I learned a lot, to become a decent rider. I'd—sure like to try. I wouldn't want anyone to die on Taron simply because we couldn't carry them back to the ship fast enough."

Shandy turned to face me now. "And what will you do when we must leave this world, and the calf here?"

I swallowed hard. "Say goodbye. Its fate can't crash much more."

"Are you sure? I think you two could be headed for some serious suffering if you do this."

"How could I make this creature's life any worse than I already have? I'm sure."

Shandy lowered his stunner. He was a true roomie.

JOURNAL ENTRY 58

Not much was left by the time we made it back to Second Lake. As I predicted, we also had to spend an extra day there, patching and repairing our ravaged packs, so we could carry our remaining gear back.

Our lighter packs did make our return to the ship and First Lake faster, and even chew-holes in our tents didn't matter now. So we dared not complain to anyone else when we moved back into the ship.

And Ked—named after my favorite yusahmbul—did grow and learn amazingly quickly. First to trust me, next to come to my call (for berry treats), then to accept a halter for work on a lunge line and, later, ground reins.

In fact, whenever I tried to slow our training pace, Ked quickly grew bored. I found out she was female as soon as she let me handle her closely enough to get a baseline scan. I also injected her with a wildlife tracking chip, so I could locate her whenever I needed her.

And I discovered I did need Ked. I missed and craved the affection of a warm fuzzy creature, the unspoken but precious bond with a trusting animal. I stole bits of guilty time to try to capture her low-slung, tan, short-haired, muscular beauty in journal sketches.

I worried whenever she roamed free, as I had to let her do frequently, so she could learn how to fend for herself. At first near sunset I turned on landing lights to attract the calf, and next the ship's force field, so my trainee ran no risks at night.

But soon I had to strap an extra wristcom from ship stores onto a rope collar around my restless hert's neck, and let her wander as far as she wanted whenever she wanted. According to the ship's com, she never worked very hard at fully rejoining her herd, which we scanned a long way out along a stream in the grasslands. But she did head towards the fringes, probably hanging out with other misfits. That seemed to provide enough protection from rare dats so desperate they tried to attack scattered herts.

So I felt my spirits soar whenever she readily left her herd and came to my call over the wristcom. She hooted back at me as her brown-tufted tail flew behind her and her cloven hooves churned up the drying grass and dirt when she got close enough to spot. I had to wash away her sweat and dry her coat to gently work with her, and bribe her to stick around for more than a day to do more. That wasn't difficult. She seemed to enjoy my company as much as I enjoyed hers.

But work with Ked was about the only time my spirits did soar on Taron. Every sunny day came with the burden of seeking more food, which meant we often had to kill for our own survival. I was horrified by how much Shandy and I had to consume from the landscape to support ourselves, and often we didn't find enough.

Each evening at least brought the peace of knowing we couldn't do more damage that day, but that peace often came at a price. Hunger became our most constant companion. It even skewed our survey efforts, which had to focus on food sources first and ecology second.

For instance, we rarely microchipped any critter for habitat tracking, because we rarely released anything we caught. We simply had to get better at following individuals with our scans.

Our hunt for food even colored how I came to see the ecology of this continent, or at least this small slice of it: as vacful little food chains that vectored nowhere fast.

Phibs ate green bugs (an unimaginative name for local water insects), which ate their own larvae as well as water lilies (a fused name borrowed from Earth, since they weren't the same). Rainbow fish ate water lilies, green bugs, weak diver chicks, and their own young. Adult divers ate all of the above except their chicks, and were eaten by no one, but lost most of their eggs to makkons. Singers ate bush berries, grass seeds, and glitterflies, and again suffered only from makkon egg predation.

But what on Taron did dats eat? It was a persistently vexing mystery, fueled by the dangers of following them when they left their dens at night, and the skinny dats we did find by day, dead from no apparent cause, with empty stomachs whenever we got to them before—you guessed it—makkons.

The only bodies the makkons left alone were phibs, who seemed to possess no natural enemies. So how did phibs die? Naturally short life cycles? A surprisingly limited number of microbe species took over the decomposition process.

On the other hand, was there nothing else the makkons wouldn't try to eat? We learned to pick nuts, seeds, and berries before they'd quite ripened, or they'd be stripped by the next day.

Fortunately local plants generously regenerated their most edible parts quickly. But we lost all manner of baits from our traps, in some whimsical fashion we could never com, beyond obvious makkon tracks.

We had to take elaborate precautions to trap anything else—mostly rainbow fish from deep in the lake. Soon we even had to quit tying retrieval lines to our traps.

Makkons happily chewed up or carried off totally non-nutritional items like ropes, seemingly in simple revenge for not being edible. Leave anything unprotected on Taron, and chances were you wouldn't own it by the next morning, or you wouldn't want what was left.

Our poor classmates had to do nightly guard duty and devise increasingly devious food protection schemes. Eventually most resorted to heavy, closely fitted rock cairns, or awkward underwater storage.

Even sleeping with food—too dangerous in most environments—didn't work, because everyone was too tired and the makkons were too sneaky.

Makkons ran about day and night, subtle tan and brown flickers and soft rustles in the bushes. They left scats everywhere, and showed up in astonishing numbers on our scans. They also participated in a nonstop joyous orgy of litter productions, which put even queets to shame.

And they managed to remain slightly beyond accurate stunner range. It was completely fused that we couldn't catch any of them for our dinners, much less for close analysis.

Most troubling of all, how did any of Taron's sketchy ecosystems manage to work? Despite our teams' broad geographical range, we never found more than one species of tree.

Fortunately it was a bountiful nut producer. We found one species of bush—ditto for berries, not to mention edible magenta flowers. One seed grass, one "reed" plant with starchy tubers, and one water plant with edible greens and lovely sky blue, gas-filled surface flowers. ("Lilies.") That was our complete photosynthetic inventory. Now I suspected the lack of imaginative names resulted from shear Scout boredom.

We noted one type of shimmering green water bug, the "green bugs," and one shiny gold-winged insect plant pollinator, the "golden glitterflies." One species of amphibian, the poison-skinned "phibs" everyone left alone. One waterfowl "diver" bird species and one sexually dimorphic "singer" bird species, all so brilliantly feathered and noisy they should have attracted predators for themselves, not just their eggs. "Makkons," "dats," and at least one large herd of elusive "herts."

That was our entire list of multicellular wildlife, when we compared info over our coms, even before our meeting. Taron was an artist's wonderland of color, sound, and motion, if you didn't mind all the repetition.

The meeting itself loomed over Shandy and me, as we struggled to finish our survey scans and analyses, and forage for our classmates and ourselves. Since we were the only team that didn't have a long hike, we were expected to provide meals for everyone upon arrival. We didn't know how on Taron we'd manage that, and our tempers fused.

"What are you doing?" Shandy caught me raiding a trap full of stunned, pithed fish next to his stove one morning.

"Setting a new trap." I picked out a large shimmering body for bait. I mixed up a pan full of lake mud and another with greens mashed in water, and set my comscreen on mirror.

"What are you doing?" I asked him.

Shandy irritably brushed wet hair from his face, and painstakingly filleted another fish for his grill. "I'm drying fish for the meeting."

Fish leather for a week—yuck!

Shandy frowned at me. "I could use some help. And you're wasting my fish in that trap. You know makkons will raid it—"

"Exactly." I stuck a finger in one of my pans and began to paint my face.

"What are you thinking? It won't work!"

After finishing my face, I began on my arms, giving myself artistic brown and green swirls. Some color for me at last! "I'm going to hide near the trap, and when makkons come, I'm going to stun at least one of them! We haven't analyzed a single local specimen for our report!"

Shandy scanned like it was a nova waste of time, and he was probably right. But I did learn one new fact that miserably long hot day, as I doggedly followed my prey through dense scrub and overgrown streams—nothing nearly as direct as Rognarth's "garden path."

Oddly, the color of my foe kept shifting randomly between dun, rust, and sienna, in the leaf-filtered sunlight. It took me most of the day to realize makkons loved playing chase, and they took turns at it, leading their poor confused predators on a relay race to exhaustion.

JOURNAL ENTRY 59

The makkon I finally caught was dead by the time I picked it up to carry it back to camp. Yet I felt no sense of victory, relief, or revenge. I couldn't help admiring the furry brown makkon's delicate, pointed face, with large golden eyes.

I studied its pair of intricate, hairless hands, each possessing three pairs of opposable digits. Four more limbs ended in sharply clawed, six-toed feet. No wonder makkons could get into everything!

I scanned its heart one more time. Nothing.

I wasn't surprised, but I brushed a rush of tears from my crusted face. I'd resorted at last to such a powerful, broad, long-range beam that I'd drained my weapon to stun the makkon, along with any other creature hiding in the same clump of distant bushes.

Not only was this a terrible waste of power I could only justify with my ready access to recharge facilities aboard the ship, but any other random victims would be wide open to excruciating carnivore attack. I'd simply wanted an end to the hunt, and my only hope was that every critter in those bushes had died instantly from heart failure.

Well, at least now I didn't have to make the nova choice between tag-and-release and eating my catch. I hiked back to our kitchen area of camp, carefully recorded a complete anatomical scan during dissection, then butchered the makkon for our dinner.

"You did it," Shandy said quietly. I nodded wordlessly, and somehow he knew not to ask how.

Instead he worked on another batch of fish, while I gathered some greens, grains, and tubers for a makkon stew. I set my stove on simmer next to Shandy's grill, so I could walk down the dusty beach. I shed my boots, and waded into First Lake.

With my back to Shandy I cried into the lake while I scrubbed away dried mud, sweat, and green stains. I was so sick of murdering everything I was supposed to be studying. I now hated ecology, and planned to transfer out as soon as I could escape this tortuous test. What I'd do next was anybody's guess, but almost anything had to be better than this.

Of course, I knew I wasn't being fair, because ecologists normally brought their own food supplies, and I found the intricacies of how life fit together like an interlocking puzzle fascinating. If I stuck with it, I'd also get to travel to all sorts of worlds, if we didn't land in too much trouble for pulling this stunt. I was just sick of this particular puzzle.

Taron wasted a subtle orange sunset on me as I choked on my sobs, and I'm amazed I heard anything. A rumbling sound like distant thunder silenced the squeaking phibs, the last bird calls, and the evening insect hum. But I scanned no storm clouds.

I whirled around and splashed to shore, grabbed my boots, and joined Shandy at the ship. We climbed the rungs to the roof. There we could safely watch while Ked's massive herd gradually returned to First Lake, off to the right side from our camp. I spotted Ked among them, and while I loved seeing her so close, I worried about whether I'd have to explain her at the meeting.

We watched the magnificently sleek, curly-horned beasts move back in with the self-assurance of overwhelming power. But, sadly enough, our little stunners contained more power. So the hert herd's presence now solved most of our food problems, even though Shandy's last batch of fish and my makkon stew burned up on our untended stoves.

JOURNAL ENTRY 60

Only when I scanned my classmates arriving for our meeting did I wonder how much Taron had changed me.

Our closest neighbors, Tarknes and Krorn, hiked in nearly a week early to help Shandy and me prepare. They looked thinner but stronger, and wiser but tired. Once they caught up on their sleep in the ship, and on their protein intake with hert meat, they helped us build a log-bench circle and a latrine.

They also foraged ruthlessly to add to our berry and nut stocks, and helped us with another hert hunt the day before the big meeting. Even with their help, we had to butcher in the field. We used two stretchers to carry the remains back to camp.

Branem and Aerrem arrived so early on the official day that they had to buzz our cabin doors to wake us up. I tottered to my open door.

"Open," Shandy slowly muttered as he sat up on his bunk and rubbed his eyes.

"Space," I yawned, "what did you two do—camp just beyond sight last night, so you could be the first here?"

"Bad night," Branem muttered.

"My, my, what a life of luxury!" Aerrem put her hands on her hips. "Ever try to find a decent tree in the middle of a huge prairie? Get up and give us a turn in those beds right now!"

They dumped their packs in our cabins and dropped into bed as quickly as we could jettison. They were filthy from their travels, but we didn't have the heart to demand they wash up first. And they fell asleep before we could bring them breakfast. We tiptoed out through the stripped cabin where Tarknes and Krorn slept, and made our way to the log circle outside.

Jael and Piel hiked in next, surprisingly enough, considering Jael wore a first-aid injector on his good arm and his other arm in a sling made from a shirt. Tiny Piel carried most of their gear in his towering pack.

Tarknes and Krorn must have heard our exclamations, because they came tumbling out of the ship.

"A nova dat pack zapped us, in the middle of the day!" Jael grimaced. "We had entered the foothills, this side of the coastal mountains."

"Are you hurt too?" Krorn asked Piel, as we helped remove their packs and passed them up into the ship.

Piel poked self-consciously at a small dent in one of his antennae. "Nothing that won't grow out, but my stunner is nearly drained. Let's get Jael into the med-niche. My medkit scanner says his arm is broken, but we're not sure how bad it is."

"You have a fractured radius," I read from the med-niche scanner while Krorn ran a sterile line from the niche to Jael's injector, and Tarknes removed Jael's field bandage.

The smell of sour human blood hit the air, and suddenly I wasn't the only person looking pale.

"Breathe!" I reminded everybody, since everyone else seemed frozen. "The scanner reports minimal fracture displacement, and that the nearly parallel ulnar bone will help brace it, so the bone should heal fine with routine wound care, a splint, and a fast healer."

"Are you sure that's all? I don't have the nova luck of some alien Taron infection, do I?" Jael lay down on the bunk while Krorn and Tarknes followed med-niche instructions for local anesthesia and wound flushing. Piel dragged the nearest chair to the bunk and I boosted him up into it.

I shook my head. "The medcom says you have a mild infection, but only from your own skin bacteria. And the medcom says you're metabolizing your pain meds too quickly. The niche is giving you better meds for both now."

"Ah, good." Jael closed his eyes, and Piel bent over to give him an excellent imitation of a human kiss. The rest of us quickly left to give them some privacy.

"Space, I hope that was the worst injury we'll see," Krorn said as we rejoined Shandy, who had remained on guard duty over our breakfasts at our log circle outside.

"We'd get a comcall if anyone was in worse trouble." Tarknes put a hand on Krorn's shoulder.

Unless both members of a team got zapped too badly. But I didn't say it aloud. And Hannen and Taemar marched into camp next, as if to cheer us up with their muscular, glowing good health.

Hannen had shot up in height, and had obviously outgrown his boots, for he was hiking in handmade sandals—blister-free. Taemar looked short now in comparison, but she had grown as tall as I had, and the front of her shirt had filled out a lot more than mine. The teammates stashed their packs in the ship and then volunteered for lunch-making duties.

Nessel and Lowwind arrived next. Lowwind didn't have any obvious injuries, but a fresh scar slashed across Nessel's face, denting her upper lip and scanning like it had barely missed one of her eyes.

"What happened?" Krorn asked.

"Dat attack—what else?" Lowwind snapped. "She stayed out too late one evening, and after the attack she insisted on treating her own wound—"

"It's nothing that can't be fixed once we go home." Nessel let her dark overgrown hair slide over half her face. "It's no big nova deal—"

"Not unless you consider the fact that by putting yourself at risk, you endangered both of us—"

"My medkit scanner said I was okay!"

They kept arguing as they vectored for the ship to stow their packs, and Krorn slammed his lunch down to go after them. "They'll wake up everyone!"

The rest of us rolled our eyes.

"It sounds like one team is ready for divorce," Taemar said, and she and Hannen exchanged such sappy looks that the rest of us groaned.

Suddenly a couple of low voices chanted from nearby berry bushes: "Taemar and Hannen, sitting on a log, K-I-S-S-I-N-G! First comes *love,* then comes—"

"Who's that!" Taemar jumped up, and our two Tliesjians giggled as they popped out of the cluster of bushes.

Jaws dropped. Kijan and Dojan had leaves tangled in their overgrown, curly brown hair, and they wore nothing synthetic except their wristcoms, their stunners, and the frames of their packs.

They'd cobbled together everything else we could see—their shorts, vests, moccasins, and pack compartments—out of patchwork leather and fur. They also possessed impressively carved bows and reed quivers full of bone-tipped arrows strapped on their packs. Dat teeth and colorful feathers decorated their necklaces and armbands.

"Carnivores," Lowwind muttered as she and Nessel rejoined our circle.

Kijan curled his lip. "Hey, omnivores, you'd be dead meat right now if we'd been hunting you!"

"What happened to all your stuff?" Taemar retorted.

"What do you mean?" Dojan snuffled, trying to sound hurt. "It requires talent to hand-make clothes—do you have any idea how many makkons it takes to sew together one fused vest?"

"One does holo quite a debacle." Nessel grinned, and most of us couldn't help snickering as Kijan and Dojan shook their heads.

"We don't have to listen to this," Kijan said as they turned to the ship.

"What happened?" Krorn asked on his way down from the hatch, and we all laughed again as the Tliesjians shook their heads and scrambled up inside.

"Well, I think they look cute!" Tarknes said, and secretly I agreed.

"I wonder if they have any underwear left?" Taemar said, triggering another round of laughter.

Next we had to explain our amusement to Errek, Gkorjneil, Nikk, and Dainer, who'd found each other on their way in, and arrived in decent condition—at least, no more skinny, sore, tired, or patched up than the rest of us.

Errek had a big ugly scab on one knee. Gkorjneil's horns had grown and one was chipped. And both Nikk and Dainer were missing a few scales, but that was about it.

Dainer's copper scales had taken on a suspiciously golden hue, but that was no surprise, as Lorratian bodies often changed sex arbitrarily at puberty. However, I wondered how Dainer—or any Lorratian, for that matter—felt about switching sexes. Maybe it felt perfectly natural, but it wasn't my place to ask. I also wondered if the two Lorratians would remain a couple, especially if gold-scaled Nikk stayed female?

JOURNAL ENTRY 61

Then Aerrem, obviously upset, exited the ship.

I set my pan down, classmates stood up abruptly, and this time nearly everyone asked, "What happened?"

Aerrem's frown turned into a yawn, and she sagged down beside me. "Sorry! I didn't mean to alarm anyone. I'm only annoyed—everyone else worked so hard to arrive on time today, while Crell and Shee wandered a bit off course."

Well, not my favorite classmates anyway.

"Compasses not working?" Taemar asked dryly.

Aerrem shrugged. "Their wristcoms worked well enough to call me. They claimed they'd gotten distracted, and forgot to check their compass readings often enough. They agreed we could start our meeting without them. They should arrive in time for data exchange. So the next question is, do the rest of us feel ready to start now?"

I don't know that any of us felt ready, but we were all eager to talk in person, after months of isolation. I got up and started serving hert steaks.

Aerrem stared at her pan, pleasure warring with distress on her face. "The herts came back? Why didn't you tell us!"

"We wanted to surprise you."

She had to work at cutting off a tiny bite to try. "It's tough."

"It's dangerous to hunt prime members of the herd," I said. "We have to kill stragglers." I exchanged smiles with Aerrem. We both understood this tactic had as much to do with mercy as safety.

Branem exited the ship and yanked a shirt on, over multiple long pink scars slashing across dark new chest hairs on his milky brown chest. Piel and Jael slowly followed, and Branem and Jael traded stares. Jael now wore a brace on one arm and a new drug injector on the other, and another round of explanations ensued.

"Are you sure you're ready to do this?" Aerrem asked Jael, who began to eat eagerly.

"I feel a lot better now. And if we're deciding on whether to go home, I must be included in the vote!"

"I don't know that we'll decide that this afternoon," Aerrem said. "I commed we'd talk about our preliminary findings and theories today. Tomorrow we can start on actual data exchanges, and that will help us see where we stand."

So we started talking, with Aerrem insisting we raise hands and take turns. Nikk immediately brought up the lack of diversity. She was already familiar with all our food sources except herts, and like me she could quickly list every plant and animal in this sector. And that seemed especially odd, considering the many environments Nikk and Dainer had hiked through to get here.

"I'd hate to scan other Taron land masses," I added. The low number of wildlife species had disappointed me here. "This continent possesses the longest Scout Ship lifeform list, which isn't saying much. Until we began exploring, I had assumed Taron Scouts were unusually rushed."

"I'd understand Taron better if it didn't have any flowering plants," Branem said, "and if phibs were the highest lifeform here. But why aren't more species radiating into and adapting to open niches at this evolutionary level?"

"You're right," Piel said. "Whole environmental niches remain unfilled. For example, the niche of intelligence—"

"Space, that's still considered at least partly a matter of chance—" Dojan said.

"Yes, but has anyone identified any parasites here?" Piel insisted, and suddenly we fell silent with embarrassment.

No one had. It was indeed a totally empty niche. "Except for the makkons!" Gkorjneil smiled his big-toothed grin, and everyone laughed.

"But Piel's right," Kijan said. "And the birds here can show off as many colors as they want, because they have no predators—"

"Except the makkons!" we all chimed in.

"Obviously the dats should stand at the top of the food chain." Dojan snorted. "But look at them—what do they manage to eat? We haven't found much beyond undigested grass in their bowels."

"I think the makkons run them to death on wicked relay races," I said.

"Dats aren't fit to survive," Kijan said.

"Maybe," I said, staring at his dat tooth necklace and remembering the sad skeletal remains at Second Lake.

"This sector is all out of balance!" Nessel said. "I think the makkons in our area are about to reach a crisis level, they're so resourceful and their reproductive rate is so out of control!"

"We've scanned streams choked with starving rainbow fish," Dainer said, as she served herself a voracious second helping of lunch. "Don't the fish have any predators besides the waterfowl I've seen diving in your lake?"

"We've got masses of gold "glitterflies" getting into everything," Krorn added. "I've even found a few in dats' stomachs."

"I may have swallowed some," Tarknes said grimly.

"So," Aerrem said as she set her emptied pan aside, "we've detected minimal diversity despite some advanced evolution, and lots of imbalances—we can all come up with data to support that. Okay, so the real question becomes, what's the underlying cause? And could it endanger a FIL colony here? Theories, anyone?"

"A catastrophic environmental event could explain all of this," Errek said. "Major volcanic activity, a serious meteor strike, a big ice age, an intelligent species gone nova—any of these bottlenecks could indiscriminately wipe out many species, leading to further food-chain disasters."

"We're not geology or archaeology students." Branem moaned. "We can't prove any of that!"

"That doesn't mean none of it is true," Gkorjneil defended his partner.

"The preliminary report doesn't back any of it," I had to say. "Initial scans found few active or dormant volcanoes, no huge impact craters, no above-average glacial evidence or activity, and no traces of a past civilization."

"But that's all it is—a preliminary report," Wind said. "And the explanation could be even simpler, like a geologically recent temperature change causing an increase in wildfires—"

"Have you found any evidence for that?" Kijan retorted. "Charcoal, perhaps, or singed tree trunks?"

Wind shook her head. "If it happened, it was too long ago for us to scan the evidence. But again, that doesn't rule it out—"

"If it happened that long ago, why aren't we seeing better adaptation to it?" Dojan insisted.

"Something odd happened quite a while ago," Taemar said. "Something quite toxic, I suspect. There are still traces of it everywhere, if you look carefully enough."

"Toxins?" Jael exclaimed, equally taken aback as the rest of us. "Everywhere? Why didn't you tell us about this sooner?"

JOURNAL ENTRY 62

Taemar couldn't defend herself until Aerrem broke up the clamor by banging her fork against her empty pan. "Quiet everyone! Let's hear what Taemar has to say."

Taemar stared back at us, dumbfounded. "Didn't you all carry out basic water, soil, and atmospheric analyses on arrival?"

"We acquired a desperate little side-project called survival," Jael retorted. "The prelim said Taron was compatible for our species, so we focused on edible life-forms, and made sure our water bottles could filter out local microbes—"

"I ran quick scans our first day," I admitted, without confessing that I'd done it more to briefly escape the carnage of our first kill, and to make sure we could safely wash the blood from our hands in the lake, than as a scientific baseline. "Anything that seemed a little off was too minimal for us to worry about—"

"Exactly." Taemar nodded. "We found a whole array of odd chemicals in the soil, water, and air—"

"Oh, that's all!" Lowwind snapped, and she had a point. After all, we were entirely dependent on Taron's soil, water, and air!

"It's all merely tiny traces at this point," Taemar said. "Nothing sufficient to harm any lifeforms here now, especially short-term visitors like us. But didn't any of you get curious about them? No?

"Well, I did, and it wasn't easy to research, but I've concluded that they are remnants of both organic and inorganic poisons."

"How does that fit in with the rest of our findings?" Piel asked.

"We're not sure," Hannen said. "But it doesn't take intelligent life to make toxins. Perhaps in the past a kind of biological warfare occurred, maybe between competing plant species. And maybe it escalated until one or more species were too successful, wiping out their own biotic environments."

"With inorganic toxins?" Kijan said.

"Living tissues can concentrate them," Taemar argued.

"Long-lasting poisons would build up the worst in the higher trophic levels," I slowly reasoned it out. Eaters of eaters and so on would get more and more intoxicated. It was an interesting idea.

"Right," Hannen said. "That would explain the shortage of animals at the top of the food chain here. And it might also explain why the dats don't appear very skillful. Perhaps the biggest measure of success on Taron is a prime filter organ, rather than top hunting skills—"

"This all sounds terribly weak," Kijan objected. "Whatever happened, I suspect that theory is too far in the past to explain what we're seeing now—"

"We're not claiming our theory is any better than anyone else's," Taemar said. "It may be, however, that as freshmen ecology students, we lack sufficient training to uncover the real answers on Taron—"

"So you're ready to give up?" Kijan flattened his furry ears.

"Why shouldn't we?" Jael countered. "We did manage to collect three months of data, despite totally fused conditions—"

"I knew it!" Lowwind said. "You never really wanted to vector here in the first place—"

"We can also clarify the problems," Dojan began a heroic argument, "so FIL scientists know what to look for—"

"And I think you two just don't like seeing that a carnivorous lifestyle isn't very successful here," Nessel confronted Kijan and Dojan. "How many poor makkon bodies did it take to make up for all the clothes you lost?"

That did it. Dojan and Kijan stood up, pulled wooden stoppers out of leather flasks, and squirted the contents at Nessel and Lowwind. Both girls promptly snatched up their water bottles and retaliated. Crossfire splashed other classmates, and the water fight quickly escalated.

Jael and Piel escaped into the ship, and Shandy muttered something about guarding camp. But the rest of us ended up in the lake shallows. We divided naturally into our gym teams and flung water at each other.

That's how Crell and Sheejar, breathless and open-mouthed, found us.

"Stash your packs in the ship, get down here, and help us out!" Kijan, leader of the out-numbered and beleaguered Ectotherms, shouted at them.

"It's a great way to cool off and clean up!" Aerrem, leader of the Endotherms, added cheerfully.

Sooner or later we all got doused or drenched. Late afternoon most of us dribbled back to the ship to dry off and change, leaving flirts like Hannen and Taemar to finish up. We cooked a quiet dinner and went to bed at sunset.

My classmates were worn out from their travels, and I was tired from more social interaction in one day than I'd had for months. But I argued eco-theories all night long in my sleep—with a dat and a makkon. They seemed to think all our ideas were nova, and I wasn't sure I cared.

JOURNAL ENTRY 63

Aerrem and Branem kicked everyone out of bed at dawn, and organized ruthless assembly lines for our meals, so we could spend every possible micro of our second day sharing and correlating hard data. But it didn't lead to any immediate answers or surprises.

At the end of the day, Taemar and Hannen took dinner up into the ship for Piel and Jael, who had quit early for a nap. I heard they demanded our results as soon as they awakened. Meanwhile, I was scanning numbers in my soup.

Then musical classmates broke out their instruments to play foot-stomping music, within the ship's lights and force field.

When the dancing began, I stepped back to a ship strut and quickly scuffed some large bones and horns into the shadows under the ship. That's when Jael reappeared, Piel carefully helping him down out of the ship, so the two guys could join in with a slow dance of their own. Jael rested his splinted arm on Piel's low but strong shoulder. They swayed together as they gradually moved away from the ship. My heart warmed to see how close they'd become.

"My oh my, an interspecies love affair—don't they realize their pheromones will clash?" Kijan quoted our most infamous sex-ed teacher, as he clapped to the music.

"Ah, get over it," Jael said, his eyes closed and a look of bliss on his face. "Piel saved my life."

Kijan also got a well-deserved glare from Aerrem, who was dancing with Branem. "Okay, okay," Kijan said, "you know I was kidding!" He grabbed up a pair of sticks and a hollow piece of log, so he could join the enthusiastic band with his improvised drum.

I leaned against the ship strut, tapped my foot to the rhythm of the music, and soon began to plot how I might duck into the ship without Aerrem noticing. Company was good, but I'd experienced more than enough already today—

"Taje!"

"What?" I jerked to attention.

"You've got to dance with Krorn!" Nikk said, arm in arm with Dainer. Both Lorratians were still breathing hard from their most recent dance together, a sweetly enduring pair despite Dainer's sex change. "Tarknes has abandoned Krorn!" Nikk insisted.

Sure enough, Tarknes and Dojan were dancing furiously together. I seemed to remember them also lingering in the lake, along with Hannen and Taemar. When had this started? For some reason, I'd assumed that as a team, Tarknes and Krorn had also become a couple, but of course that was a silly presumption. Was that what other classmates assumed about Shandy and me? My face turned red.

I scanned Krorn leaning against another strut farther from the action. He'd left his flute tucked into his belt, and he never sang. Maybe this wasn't his kind of music, and maybe it wasn't even his kind of dancing—

Nikk persisted. "Come on, Taje, Krorn looks so lonely, and you're not dancing with anyone—"

"I'll go get him!" Dainer offered, and Nikk joined her.

Krorn and I both tried to plead Total Dancing Ignorance, but no one would listen, and we were harassed into a tentative dance together.

I wondered about Krorn's fiery orange eyes, but didn't have the courage to ask. He stared at my weird green eyes, and was kind enough not to say anything about them.

So we continued dancing through more than one piece, my pale fingers in his golden hands. And when we had to stop at the end we thanked each other, and it felt like more than politeness.

Gravity released me and I floated up into the ship, where I found Shandy already bedded down in his sleeping bag. We'd let classmates take turns in the real beds. "Have a good time?" he mumbled.

"It was all right." So why did I suddenly feel guilty? I quickly got ready for my own sleeping bag. I did need some rest. Tomorrow we planned to split up after breakfast to mull over our data, and meet at lunch to try to pull it all together. I wished I could forget it all instead, and ride away on Ked.

But when I managed to fall asleep, I dreamt again about annoying eco-computations. And the numbers kept slipping through my fingers, to escape into a dark crack which twisted down into the strange heart of Taron.

JOURNAL ENTRY 64

"None of this data looks new," I complained as Shandy and I finished our calculations late the next morning. "What do you think the problem is here?" Couldn't we solve this, or pretend to, and so we might relax as long as possible?

So far Shandy had remained curiously quiet during our big meeting. I knew he enjoyed socializing even less than me, but surely he was smart enough to com some ideas of his own.

Shandy glanced up at me and blinked with surprise. "I think it's a value judgment, to say something is wrong with Taron. And I have no idea why, but whatever is happening, I feel certain we haven't come close to the real answer."

I stared back at him while an odd shiver crawled up my spine, and I lost all courage to question him further.

That afternoon our second log-circle meeting dragged out for eons, and resolved nothing. We simply rehashed all our questions and wild theories until we drove each other nova again.

At last Aerrem banged her pan with her spoon to bring us to order. "Okay, so we either call a halt, and write up what we have while we wait for an S.O.S. response. Or we go back out there, maybe cover some new territory, and try again."

"I think we'll only add to the pile of unanswered questions," Lowwind said. "I'm tired of feeling dirty and sleeping in trees. Let's go home."

Jael looked surprised, but he nodded. "What more can we hope for?"

"The dats may make life impossible for any colony," Piel agreed. "So this could all be academic—"

"You don't think anyone in FIL can outsmart dats?" Kijan looked shocked. "They're the most vac-headed predators I've ever scanned—"

"And more scanning is going to change that?" Wind said.

"I think we'll need at least several more months of scans and analyses to put this together." Taemar folded her sun-browned arms. "We haven't even begun any genetic analyses to confirm our presumptive species classifications—"

"Several more months!" Jael's hands became fists, and he grimaced. "We never agreed to stay here that long—"

"No, but we agreed to vote on it if we made it this far," Aerrem said. "Are you objecting because you're worried about your broken arm?"

"The med-niche said it would heal okay."

"That's not good enough. I want an honest answer. I think if anyone has a medical concern, they should say so, and request a priority S.O.S. signal right now."

Silence fell around our circle. I caught Aerrem glancing at Shandy, and he shook his head.

"Jael?" Aerrem asked Piel's teammate one more time.

"I think we should vote," he said quietly.

I think most of us were actually more afraid of returning to the Center and facing up to what we'd done than we were of putting in more time here—in the hope, no matter how micro, that we'd return with results so brilliant FIL would welcome us back.

So the majority of us voted to stay. And then Ked stepped into the middle of our circle.

JOURNAL ENTRY 65

I had hoped this simply wouldn't happen. I knew Ked's herd was within walking distance, but our early hunt made life safe from my classmates so far. At least if she didn't try to come to me, and I certainly didn't call her. I'd also hoped the presence of so many people would temporarily scare her off. I'd rather not have to explain her, unless she was needed for an emergency.

But Ked's curiosity had won out. She sniffed and snorted as she stepped daintily into the middle of our meeting. Alarmed and excited classmates stood up and swiftly drew their stunners.

"No!" I roared as I leaped up. I threw my arms around my hert's velvety, muscular neck. Ked moaned sorrowfully, mistaking my exclamation for a scolding.

"It's okay, Ked." I forced my voice to soften. "It's okay." I scratched the itchy bases of her growing horns, and she leaned into my hands and grunted with pleasure.

"Oh, Taje, what have you done?" Aerrem groaned. "Is this that so-called calf you were babbling about—"

"She grew fast," I said, while Ked pretended to nibble at my hair with her big rubbery lips. "Lots of species grow and reproduce quickly here."

"I've even measured tree growth in the short time we've lived here," Taemar agreed. "But you certainly know this flouts every commonsense rule against wildlife handling and interference—"

"She's not just a tamed pet!" I interrupted Taemar's lecture and my classmates' growing uproar. "She's our ambulance!"

Silence. "You can *ride* her?" Branem asked, with quiet wonder.

"I'm close."

"How close?" Aerrem put her hands on her hips.

I backed Ked out of the circle, slid my hands along her shoulders, and slowly levered myself onto her low-slung, tan-furred back. "This close," I whispered. "Easy Ked, easy now. Whoa."

But I didn't have her bridle or even her halter on her, and she did not stand still. I felt her big sigh between my legs as she peered around, and winked a large brown eye at me.

Then she took off, snorting at birds we flushed squawking from the bushes, and hooting with pleasure as she ran into the grasslands this side of First Lake.

"Are you okay, Taje?" Aerrem's voice came over my wristcom. Ked galloped figure eights while I clung desperately with my knees, and at last she headed back.

"I'm okay," I said, barely hanging on with sweaty hands to a tuft of fur at the base of Ked's neck. "But maybe—you'd better—watch out!"

We broke up the meeting as everyone scrambled from our path. Ked hurtled straight into the lake, whirled around, and dumped me off her slippery rear with a huge splash as she lunged back up the bank.

My face fried as I waded to shore and my patiently waiting mount. No one else could stop laughing.

JOURNAL ENTRY 66

Aerrem shook her dark fluff of hair against the orange and blue sunset. "Don't you ever run out of luck, Taje?"

"Of course. That was my unintended first ride on Ked," I admitted in the privacy of our circle of four, sprawled on the roof of the ship.

"That was ridiculously obvious!" Branem chuckled.

"But it won everyone over," Aerrem said. "You couldn't have planned it any better."

"Not all my actions work out that well," I insisted glumly, and Shandy nodded sympathetically.

Our class meeting had not ended immediately. Even our most eager teams found excuses to linger—exchanging haircuts, cooking or drying hert meat stocks, and coordinating new campsites. Meanwhile, Aerrem had to promise the most reluctant teams that we'd reassess our situation with a group comcall in one month.

But now only our two teams remained, and this was our last night together, on top of the ship, so we could safely enjoy the growing starlight.

"I guess you have suffered your share of bad luck," Aerrem admitted.

"Like fighting with your dorm sib's new roommate, or your nova plan to steal the class ship?" Branem chuckled at me.

"Sure," I said, too eagerly.

"There's more? Aerrem, what's she hiding?"

"It's not my business to tell." Aerrem actually held to Center custom—barely. "Only Taje can answer that question."

"Aerrem—"

"Taje!" Branem interrupted me. "What do you still have left to tell?"

"Not much," I said. "I just don't like talking about my past."

"I'll tell you how I ended up at the Center, if you tell me your story."

How did Branem guess it was that part that most embarrassed me? Maybe it was sheer fused luck on his part, or maybe Aerrem had told him a micro more than she should have. Perhaps I'd better tell him in my own words, before she finished the job in her own evil style.

So I told my story in the growing darkness, which made it a little easier. How I'd grown up on Donshore, a remote fringe world, on my mother's homestead. And how she didn't return from the field one day and didn't answer any of my comcalls. I was about eight or nine—old enough to keep an eye on our solar and wind-powered farm, but not old enough to understand my loss.

"But I knew I wanted to stay on our farm, with my animals."

"So how did you get caught?"

I frowned at Branem's quick assumption, but he was right. "I got tired of keeping up with my com lessons and tests to stay out of trouble with Central Ed. So I sent them a tube tank full of our premium riddleberry jam, with highly unlikely hopes for the outcome."

That earned some laughter from Branem and even Aerrem, although she'd heard it before.

"Yeah, very funny," I said. "Until they traced the shipment back to me and asked a local family to foster me while they searched for my mother. That's when I started running away.

"I thought I'd managed our automated farm quite fine, and I was anxious to return to my animals. I was shocked to find them all gone—shuttled to other farms for proper care in my absence, of course. It was never the same after that, but I kept trying to go home anyway—even when I was shipped across the continent."

"Stubborn Taje!" Aerrem said, half scolding, and half proud. "All those poor well-meaning foster parents—didn't your conscience zap you at all?"

"I guess not. Not then. But I couldn't look any of them in the eye now."

"Guilt—a lovely gift from our dorps," Aerrem said.

"Well, I suppose dorm parents have to serve some purpose." I sighed. "So what's your story, Branem?"

"Have you finished yours?" He chuckled. "I still haven't even heard whether you're a PD or a CO!"

"Oh," I said, cringing in the creeping gloom. I never enjoyed this joke, because I was a CO, and because it was all in such poor taste.

"I'm classified as a Case Overload. But that simply means Donshore authorities finally gave up on both my mother and me. They sold our homestead and made me watch the credit transfer to a FIL account in my name. Next they shipped me to the Center on Arrainius, where no one can run away without seriously criminal connections."

"Or a very vac-headed teacher!" Branem chuckled. "But seriously criminal connections didn't keep me out of the Center."

"What!" both Aerrem and I yelped. Startled, I scanned Aerrem's silhouette. She was Branem's roommate and teammate! Was she losing her touch?

JOURNAL ENTRY 67

"My dad," Branem broke into our shocked silence, "was not only my clone-father, but also a space pirate. So when FIL caught him, I had no friendly neighborhood relatives to take me in."

Aerrem and I gulped. Great Galaxy, good reasons truly existed for not prying into Center residents' pasts! But suddenly Shandy spoke up, for the first time that night.

"All right, Branem, tell the rest of it—"

"Oh, I'm not finished," insincere innocence now took over Branem's voice. "When I landed at the Center, Admin immediately declared me a Planetary Disaster!"

Aerrem and I couldn't help laughing, even though this was a very tired Center joke, and we'd been had. But we tickled Branem into submission.

"Fair's fair!" Aerrem said. "You made an agreement—now you have to tell your true story!"

"Okay, okay—just stop it—long enough—for me to talk! I really am—a clone—of Branem Fordem the First!"

"Right—"

"Let Branem tell his story, Aerrem," I said. "Maybe he actually is a clone—"

"One of over fifty," Branem insisted. "Completely human, not that it matters."

"What?" Aerrem's tail banged against the hull. "Wasn't your father ostracized by his fellow citizens for such greedy reproduction?"

"I said he was a pirate—of sorts. He lived in his own space mansion, where he ran his asteroid mining business. He was so rich and isolated he could do whatever he wanted.

"But he wasn't all that old when he died, for reasons no one tried very hard to investigate. And he didn't leave behind enough family to adopt us all. Not to mention hardly anyone wanted us—"

"Well, that's not too hard to believe—" I teased, but immediately felt mean. Clones who revealed themselves tended to run into almost as much harassment as transgenics. No wonder Branem had needed a very unbiased roommate like Aerrem.

"If you don't believe me," Branem said, "look up the other Branem Fordem II on Level Five, if you ever get the chance. Every Center that'll even look at a human has taken some of us."

"Your father didn't even give you different names?" Aerrem asked, outraged.

"No."

"I'm very sorry, Branem." Now I really regretted my sarcasm. "That's totally fused! How can you stand being the clone of such a nova person?"

"I know even clones aren't exact replicas. I will never be my father!"

An awkward silence took over as we listened to the warm wind hissing across vast fields of dry grass. Finally Branem made another effort to cheer us all up. "Hey, no wonder we get along together so well. We're all CO's!"

"Shandy's a PD," I blurted out, making my face heat up. "I'm sorry, Shandy. That wasn't my business to tell."

"Why don't you tell us about it yourself?" Branem asked my roomie.

"That wasn't part of any promise here—"

"I'll tell my story next," Aerrem interrupted Shandy's surprisingly contrite answer. "Though there's not much to say, and you know most of it already. My parents left on a vacation years ago, but their spaceflight fused, and the cruise ship disappeared into paraspace limbo."

"That's vacful luck," Branem said. "But what I haven't commed is why your parents had no family to take in Trist and you." Then Branem swatted his forehead audibly in the darkness. "Oh, sorry, Aerrem, is it because both of you are transgenic and nobody wanted you?"

JOURNAL ENTRY 68

"Oh, yeah, we're an 'irresponsible, unnatural experiment,'" Aerrem quoted our worst Center sex-ed teacher. He'd showed us grotesque holos of transgenic kids too crippled by incompatible genetic inserts to ever leave a hospital. Apparently he'd considered the prevention of interspecies romance a vital part of his Center mission.

But I'd had to comfort my dorm sib afterwards while she puked in the nearest bathroom. Aerrem will have to perform the same "experiment" if she ever wants kids of her own.

"Trist and I have suffered some prejudice," Aerrem dryly admitted. "But I can't say we ever face anything like what espers have to put up with. And Trist and I even have families on three different planets willing to take us in.

"But that's actually part of the problem. They're all still fighting over us. Meanwhile, FIL can't even decide whether to declare our parents officially dead. So Trist and I landed in zero-land at the Center on ugly Arrainius, where no one wants to pay for an expensive trip just to visit us."

"Still, it must be nice, having that many people fighting over you," I said, ever jealous.

"I guess it's a backhanded compliment. Now, isn't it time for bed? Branem and I have a hard hike tomorrow."

I didn't want the night to end, if only because I'd miss my friends when they left in the morning. But it was Branem who made the night last a little longer.

"Come on, Shandy, tell us your story first. Can't you enter into the spirit of the game? We won't bite you."

An awful pause ensued, while I cringed in the darkness. Why would Shandy ever want to relive the slaughter of a worldwide plague? But Branem didn't know that, and it wasn't my business to tell him.

"I'm sorry, Branem," Shandy answered at last. "I lost my spirit for this game long ago. I'm tired, and I'm going to bed now."

Aerrem turned on Branem the moment we all heard the hatch thud shut. "You should know better than to press anyone for information like that!"

"Okay, I'm sorry! I'll apologize to him in the morning, before we leave. But can I ask you one last question, Taje?"

"What?" I said warily, although Branem never sounded more sincere.

"Well, I was wondering—you never mentioned a father. Are you a human clone too? Or a transgenic, which made your skin so pale?

"A clone of my mother? Or even a mostly human transgenic? I suppose it's possible," I said. "I don't remember a partner for my mom, or any story about me, but that doesn't prove anything. I've considered the possibility, but I never had my DNA checked, and I'm guessing you can com why." Who in the universe wants to feel like somebody else's copy, or near-copy with a few extra oddball genes?

"Yeah, I do understand. So have you told all your secrets tonight?"

"No! Why?"

Branem snickered. "Well, at least you've always been honest with me! So I'll tell you one last secret, if you promise not to tell anyone else besides Shandy."

"Sure!" Aerrem and I chorused. A guy offering gossip—who could resist?

"Okay," Branem said. "Drehx Tarnek is a clone!"

JOURNAL ENTRY 69

"What a fused idea!" Aerrem said. "Where did you hear such vac? That's deep ID stuff. Even Trist couldn't ferret out data like that—"

"Tarnek told me."

"What!"

"He told me," Branem insisted, all lightness vanishing from his voice. "He made a big point of it when he talked to me, after the fight. I thought Taje should know. Tarnek was trying to become buddies with me, and I think that's why he crashed you so hard, Taje. I was just a nova teacher's pet—"

"Branem, it wasn't your fault!" I had to remind him.

"Someone must have hurt Tarnek very badly, for him to want to tell you that," Aerrem added.

"It's still no excuse for what Tarnek did to Taje—"

"But I did treat you badly, Branem—"

"But not because I'm a clone. And he even called you a 'pale vac-head.'"

I cringed. That stung. I was used to name-calling from other kids, but not a teacher.

Aerrem hissed. "So he's a bigot too. But isn't this all an ancient holo? Forget about Tarnek. Scan all those brilliant stars up there."

Indeed only the desert night sky of Pelsus could match this intense display. Darwin had too many trees and clouds, and Arrainius too many city lights. As I gazed up in awe, I couldn't help wondering how many people on other worlds were scanning Taron's sun tonight.

Branem yawned. "We should leave early, while it's still cool. I'm going to bed."

"I'll join you in a bit," Aerrem said, and as soon as the hatch sealed shut again, she asked me how Shandy was doing.

"Okay, I guess. That day he got sick at Second Lake was scary, but he's seemed fine since."

"He's using meds from the ship? His prescriptions must have run out by now. Is he sleeping okay?"

"What do you mean?"

Aerrem moaned, for once acting like she knew she'd said too much. "You didn't know? He needs meds just to get decent sleep."

"I didn't know. But if he's using the med-niche, I haven't scanned it." That's why Aerrem made me pilot, I now vac-headedly realized—so Shandy could stay near the med-niche. "Now tell me why you didn't know Branem's story before tonight?" I asked, to cover up my own embarrassment.

"Oh, I'm not losing my touch," Aerrem warned me. "Everyone knows the Center allows boy-girl roommates only for special cases—a fact you might com a little harder for yourself, dear dorm sister. I was told Branem was moved in with me for his sake, and I was strongly urged to respect his privacy."

"Right. You only spied on his deskcom homework to find out about the ecology program."

"Now that was hard to miss, and it kept me somewhat updated. And we don't talk about it, for obvious reasons. But I didn't cheat on the test, in case you wondered."

I hadn't. "How is it?" I asked instead.

"How's what?"

"Living with Branem?"

"Ah. He's a clumsy guy. It's hard work, keeping him and his shaky ego out of trouble! But it's worth it—he's a very strong and honorable fellow. So how's life with Shandy these days?

"Fine." So why was my mouth turning dry?

"And what secrets are you still keeping, from your dorm sister no less? Have you two finally done it?"

"Aerrem! Of course not! It's not like that between us."

"Taje, aren't you tortured by any hormones yet?"

"Yes, of course, but—"

"And riding a hert takes care of it?"

"Aerrem!"

"Unbelievable—all this privacy out here, and you don't take the slightest advantage of it—"

"What about you and Branem?"

"What do you think?"

We ended up in a big tickle-wrestle, like we did as kids in our dorm, until we rolled near one end of the ship and heard a dat snarl from much too close below. Ked had already returned to the edge of her herd, so the force field was off to conserve power. We turned on our belt lights and released our stunner safeties so we could cover each other as we climbed down to the hatch.

JOURNAL ENTRY 70

I felt surprisingly sad when I scanned small forgotten belongings and classmates' boot prints over the next several days. Was I less of a loner than I'd assumed? Maybe I was lucky I hadn't ended up on my own. But having to return soon to the crowds and confinement of the Center was now a far more scary thought.

I'm sure that threat haunted all of us, as we struggled to find some new or enlightening data over the next grueling month. Many teams chose to investigate new areas, but no new discoveries zapped anyone, and when Aerrem set up the one-month group call, even Taemar and Hannen felt ready to quit.

Fortunately I'd gotten my riding skills sorted out with Ked, and we could help. I rode Ked all the way to the coast—enduring one awful afternoon in a foothill canyon. Ked took the lead, running full blast, while I used my stunner to fend off unusually alert dats—perhaps the same pack that had attacked Jael and Piel in broad daylight.

Errek and Gkorjneil had taken a turn at coastal analysis, certain they'd learn more than Sheejar and

Crell. But the region was surprisingly barren. And Ked and I arrived too late for us to all head back the same day. So Ked and I rewarded ourselves with a gallop along the beach at sunset.

I never felt freer, with the strong muscles of a loyal animal surging under me, the sea wind and spray in my face, and Ked's hooves churning in the wet sand. We whooped and bellowed for sheer raw joy. And we made Errek and Gkorjneil happy the next morning, by carrying some of their heaviest and bulkiest gear.

By the middle of the trip back, we made a whole pack train. Ked got totally spoiled with handouts and attention, but she earned it. She ended up so loaded with everyone's junk that I had to walk and carry extra stuff too. I also insisted on complete rest for Ked whenever we stopped to camp—no rides.

Truthfully, I was a jealous rider. Soon after we returned to the ship, we triggered our S.O.S. signal. Legally we couldn't set the urgency level very high. But our upcoming departure suddenly felt a lot more real, and I dreaded parting with my hert.

So whenever I could escape work on our report—which was depressing enough with lots of data but no final conclusions—I rode away from camp, and tried to pretend I had run away, with Ked as my only companion.

Some of my classmates quietly asked if they could also try riding her, and a few, like Branem and Sheejar, weren't so quiet. But I always had an excuse ready. For instance, "It's too hot today," "She seems a bit lame," or "I've already ridden her far enough this morning." It was selfish, but I couldn't help it. She was mine, and I wanted her for myself our last days together.

But with our final doom nearly upon us, and no one used to living in large groups anymore, tempers flared easily. And classmates like Aerrem and Taemar, who worked hardest to keep our camp organized and functioning, often ended up doing the dirtiest work.

And so came the day on Taron that I rue the most. Krorn had volunteered to catch fish that day, and before I could escape, Aerrem volunteered me to join him. That meant we started out with lots of swimming and diving, to set our traps beyond reach of the greedy makkons.

I had to admit it was better than doing dishes or digging a latrine, during one of Taron's typically long hot summer days. Today's cooks had begged us for a break from hert steaks, hert stews, hert roasts, hert shish kabobs, broiled hert, barbecued hert, baked hert, and stir-fried hert.

After setting our traps, Krorn and I sat on a grassy tree-shaded bank well away from camp and more work. We chewed on hert jerky, ate berries, and watched Taron's two moons set while we waited for our traps to fill.

Krorn also played his flute while I worked on my journal. My record of our trip might help prove our diligence, if I had to let any authorities review it. I hoped not. It was full of holes, but I'd still have to carefully censor it, and leave some real blunders to prove the honesty of the rest.

At last I wrapped up my stylus in my screen and stuffed them into a cargo pocket. Krorn uprooted some hollow reeds, showed me how to carve a crude flute, and tried to teach me how to make music. That creatively wasted the rest of our day, and we ended up rolling with helpless laughter over my musical incompetence.

Lastly we dove for our fish-stuffed traps. We gutted our catch and left the entrails in some bushes for the makkons. We washed our knives in the lake, closed and slipped them into our pockets, and hauled our dinner contribution back to camp.

"Did you hear?" Tarknes asked as she turned on a stove. "We received an S.O.S. signal reply today. I tried to call you—"

"We were swimming and diving," Krorn reminded her as my heart lurched. "So when will they pick us up?"

"We don't know. The signal acknowledgement only said they'd relay our message to FIL authorities. They had a strange accent, and we suspect that's all they could say in UC."

"So we might still have a long wait," I said hopefully. Everyone nodded but no one smiled.

Krorn stayed to help the cooks, but I felt sweaty and fishy and suddenly very unhappy. I walked down the sadly trampled beach for a sunset bath.

On my way I shed my boots and belt with my water bottle and medkit, and dropped my wristcom into a boot. I found myself blinking back tears, so I rushed down to the lakeshore, comming I'd undress as I waded in. That's when I heard galloping.

I spun around as Branem and Sheejar yanked Ked to a halt. They had four adult dat bodies between them on poor Ked's long back. I stared at them in disbelief. I thought Branem at least had better sense than this.

"We tried to call you." Branem grinned proudly. "A dat pack just attacked at the edge of the hert herd, and lost the fight. Of course herts are herbivores, but we commed the makkons would clean up if we didn't act fast."

"You tried to call me?" I said, appalled. Didn't he know I was on the fishing team?

"Yeah—but you didn't answer. So Shee and I decided to try using Ked—"

"You should never use Ked like this!" I stomped over to her foaming flank and tugged at improperly tied knots. "Get off of her right now!"

Sheejar slid off Ked's rear and stood vac-headedly open-mouthed right behind Ked's powerful rear legs, before slinking away. I pulled out and opened my pocketknife to hack off the ropes.

Branem remained stubbornly astride Ked. "I thought we were finally friends. But I guess you still think you're better than everyone else! Why won't you let anyone else try Ked? We didn't do so badly!"

"Ked is still very young!" One by one, I yanked the limp dat bodies off her steaming back and dumped them into a bloody heap on the ground. There was hardly enough meat on their broken bones to feed a makkon, much less a person.

"Have you ever seen me ride Ked at a fast gallop with this kind of load?" I said. "The dat smell coming from her back probably also scared her into running too hard. How dare you endanger her like this, so close to when we'll have to leave her!" I was almost in tears. "Now get off!" I gave Branem a nova shove, knocking him into the dust on the other side of my trembling hert.

Branem rolled and jumped back to his feet, as our self-defense instructor had taught us. His voice roared with rage, but I ignored his words as I leaped onto Ked's back and grabbed her reins. I cursed at Branem, swung Ked around, trotted her on the beaten path around the lake, and checked her gait for any lameness.

At last I sighed with relief, gave Ked her head, and she

surged into a lope, scattering indignant members from the edge of her herd. They brayed at her and Ked hooted back—laughing at them, I swear it! Then Ked veered away from the lake and snorted happily as she bounded over the tall dry grass.

I'd allowed Ked plenty of opportunities to fully rejoin her herd, but she hadn't. I'd worried that my scent on her coat might lead to her rejection, but she never even tried to return farther than the edge.

Now I wondered why I hadn't abandoned my herd, to live on my own. Ked never acted lonely or sad—why should I feel any differently?

Together we bellowed at the sunset as it faded into stars, and together we became the freest and most vac-brained creatures on Planet Taron.

JOURNAL ENTRY 71

We got lost at nightfall. On Taron.

Ked gradually slowed to a walk, and I realized we ought to head back. I circled Ked around, and discovered we'd run too far, and it was now too dark to spot First Lake or our ship.

Unlike some people, I don't possess a built-in sense of direction. I knew I should at least vector back towards the coastal mountains, but now I couldn't tell if I was scanning their fading silhouette or the inland mountain range. I'd never really bothered to study Taron terrain or star formations after sunset. It wasn't very safe, or on any test—until now.

I absentmindedly lifted my wrist, ready to humbly call for directions. I tugged at my dead tracer bracelet instead.

Smooth. I was stranded with no wristcom or utility belt—which also meant no light, no medkit, no water bottle, and no stunner. I patted my shorts pockets, to check what I already knew—my entire equipment list now consisted of my pocketknife, comscreen, and stylus. I wasn't even wearing my boots. Brilliant. Aerrem would kill me, if the dats didn't clobber me first.

I slid off Ked and slowly led her back along her trail through trampled grass, until the light grew too dim and howls echoed in the distance. Ked abruptly halted, her tufted ears twitching. I got back on her, and decided to pick the direction away from the howls. Ked agreed.

Maybe we'd intercept a tree. I could spend the night in it, and freed of my weight, Ked stood a better chance too.

The growls grew closer as I trotted Ked up a series of hills, in desperate search of any useful view in the growing starlight. From a hilltop I at last scanned a curiously sunken valley, deep and dark, below. I hoped for woods, with lots of trees.

Ked's chest heaved hotly under my legs as she began the descent, the steepest so far. I loosened her reins, grabbed the tuft of hair on her withers straight-armed, and leaned back, trying not to slide forward painfully onto her shoulders, while she stepped and slipped downhill.

A scream split the night and Ked almost fell to her knees at the bottom of the slope. She stumbled and scrambled, while dat eyes flashed starlight at us, and Ked lunged forward.

A jagged branch scraped my arm. Now we galloped through dense woods, gnarled old trees threatening to block our escape from a whole pack of hunger-maddened dats. Why did I think this was a good idea?

I let Ked take complete control. I couldn't see or react fast enough, much less leap like an acrobat into a tree from Ked's bouncing back. Even worse, a small dark ravine appeared on our left, another barricade against escape.

I could hear a stream rushing at the bottom of it and curving ahead of us. I snatched out my pocketknife so quickly I almost dropped it.

I clenched my shaking hand as I sliced off Ked's rope bridle. She'd never make the jump over the ravine with me onboard, and I didn't want her reins tangling her escape. If we split up, maybe we both stood a better chance.

I closed and stashed my knife back in my pocket after tossing Ked's bridle into darkness. The little ravine loomed ahead. As soon as I felt Ked's muscles begin to bunch, I jettisoned over her side.

I tried to roll into my fall, but the bank crumbled under my hip. I sledded down to the shallow stream at the bottom, and the back of my head banged against a rock.

Darkness flew overhead and dirt clods fell on my face. Ked skidded for a micro on the opposite bank. Then her powerful hind legs caught some purchase on the collapsing ledge, and she surged out of view.

The howling pack pelted down into the ravine, splashed across the stream, and flowed up after her. I lay there, stunned, while one dat actually stepped on my hand in its mindless hurry to keep up.

Dat cries peaked and gradually faded into the gentle wind, sifting through tree leaves overhead. I slowly rolled over and got up on my hands and knees, trembling hard. My back felt bruised and soaked, and rocks bit at my knees and palms. I held my breath as I gently traced a bloody swelling in the middle of my wet hair on the back of my head. Next I crawled and clawed my way back up the dirt embankment. If only I could reach a tree now—

Golden dat eyes glinted in starlight as they jerked around to stare at me from less than two meters away. I nearly pissed in my shorts as I let go and fell back to the stream bank below. Ked hadn't led all the dats away.

Now I ran alongside the stream, mud sucking and rocks jabbing at my bare feet, while adrenaline shot through my circulation like a fiery anatomy lesson.

This must be the end. I gasped for hot air, bloodied my feet on sticks and stones, and my vision grew blurry.

Well, I'd enjoyed a good if rather short life, filled with friendship, and I discovered I didn't care I was still a virgin. At least now I'd never have to return to the Center. I ran faster than I'd ever thought possible, but the pack stragglers panted and roared at my heels.

The ravine walls dropped to the level of the stream and we all spilled out, yelling at the top of our lungs as we hurtled into the woods. Branches raked my face and almost tore off my shirt. A moment later teeth sank into my left arm, I screamed, and together we fell through the ground into darkness.

JOURNAL ENTRY 72

That's what it felt like, anyway. Night and fallen branches had camouflaged a hole in the ground. Twigs cracked under my feet, and I fell into a crevasse with my attacker.

We slammed into a stone-hard ledge with a yelp and a grunt. The dat let go of my arm as it disappeared over the edge, freeing me too late for a controlled fall.

I landed on my right knee with a sickening crunch and skinned my palms. More sticks, rocks, and dirt pelted me, as I heard the rest of the dats circling the hole three or four meters above. They pawed and whined at the edges.

I had to work too hard at catching my breath to curse them. Instead I slid the tips of my fingers along the smooth borders of my rocky perch. I discovered enough room to lie down and ease my swelling knee, aching arm, and bleeding hands.

Until sunrise I dared not move, nor escape into sleep, for fear of falling farther. At least I had no wrist-com time meter, to count all the excruciating minutes and hours of the longest night in my life. Instead I endured endless throbbing pain, and wasted too much moisture on tears.

Dawn caught me dangerously dozing. I jerked awake, and as sunlight slowly seeped in, I realized I'd jettisoned from an exploding ship into space vac.

I wasn't lying on a ledge over a deeper pit, but rather on a caved-in slab on the floor of a long narrow cavern. A matching door-sized hole yawned in the center of the ceiling above me. And the stone walls were too smooth, steep, tall, and far from the hole for me to even think about climbing out.

Tree leaves fluttered in the sky above the hole, now abandoned by any creature. I shivered in the strange silence. Where was the dat that had fallen with me?

I glanced over my shoulder, and tumbled backwards, falling the short distance from the stone slab onto the cave floor. I cried out with the shock of landing on my injured knee. But the dat didn't move from where it lay, crumpled between the slab and the opposite cave wall. I finally realized my foe wasn't even breathing.

I carefully crawled back onto the slab and reached out to touch smooth tan fur. Rust-colored dried blood mottled the bruised muzzle and bitten tongue, and the dat's head felt too loose when I pushed on it. Our fall had broken its neck. The eyes stared dully at nothing, accusing me of another mindless Taron death.

But maybe this dat had found the easy way out. I collapsed on the coffin-sized, branch-strewn stone that had fallen sometime in the past from the roof of the cave, creating this trap. Could wristcom scanners penetrate down here? We'd located Hannen beyond an ocean cliff wall on Darwin, so I clung to hope.

I decided to stay put, in sight of the hole all day, as a missing person should. Meanwhile, I missed everything, especially my water bottle, wristcom, medkit, and friends. Pain pulsed all the way into my hip and my foot, until I found it difficult to remember which joint I'd smashed. It was so bad I barely noticed the bite on my arm, but of course it still hurt and oozed blood, along with my palms.

As often as I could, I pushed all my pain into loud yells for help. Next I waited in suspense for some answer, any answer from a classmate.

Midday I had to scoot over to the wall opposite the dat to escape the hot sunlight, now beaming directly down on the slab. On its way, the light had gradually revealed broken skeletons littering the grey floor. More dats, and makkons, all slaughtered by the same trap. I tried to distract myself by working on my journal, but now it contained too many regrets.

How could I have done this, to Ked, myself, and my classmates? I could only hope Ked had escaped the dat pack and found her way back to camp. But that meant my friends would face another terrible mystery upon her return.

Tarnek should have kept me locked up! I didn't know how to act like a proper friend or teammate. Now I might die for it, my last words a shamefully angry curse at Branem.

That afternoon I returned to the slab and awaited any replies to my hoarse shouts for help. How far from camp had I landed? Tomorrow I'd have to start searching for water, if no one found me. Tomorrow. But first I faced another long night of dark pain and fear.

Our self-defense teacher had taught us the rule of threes for humans. Humans can't last three seconds without hope. Three minutes without air. Three hours without shelter from challenging weather. Three days without water. Three weeks without food. And three months without companionship.

My priority was obvious. My source was not.

JOURNAL ENTRY 73

Second day. I woke up with a throat so dry it hurt to swallow. Now I'd have to explore the cave for water or a way out, or I wouldn't last long enough for rescue, not in this heat.

I recorded a brief summary of my plan on my screen, and wondered whether I should delete any part of my trip journals to protect the privacy of others.

But I couldn't back it up or remember how many bits I should quickly erase, and I was wasting time. So I forced myself to leave my screen unlocked and uncensored, on the slab.

I picked out the longest, sturdiest fallen branch, stripped it down to a crude crutch with my pocketknife, and used it to stand up. But as soon as I put my full weight on it, the rotten stick shattered, and I crashed to the ground and howled.

Minutes later, I got over it. I reminded myself how frightened my friends must be, and how much worse they'd feel if they found me dead down here.

I crawled over to the wall, away from the dat, and used it to brace myself. I slowly stood back up and slid my right hand along the wall as I hopped on my left leg. There was something to be said for being in shape!

Soon I left all light behind and had to place blind trust in the cave wall as my guide. I'm still not sure when I realized I'd learned to expect regular, vertical cracks in it. But I discovered I was even counting them to measure my progress.

As I slid to the floor for a rest, I traced the nearest crack down and across the floor. It ran in a straight, smooth line, as even and perpendicular as the floor and the wall—this was no cave!

This was constructed—from synthetic slabs, similar to the defective one that had fallen from the ceiling and led to my capture. I couldn't believe how long I'd taken to com I'd fallen into an underground building! Even after living for months in a wilderness, I still took floors, walls, and ceilings for granted!

So a civilization had lived on Taron—perhaps that explained all the anomalies! Intelligent life could wreak so much havoc, including self-destruction. I'd come up with answers even FIL hadn't found—

Yeah. Right. If powerful Scout Ship scanners hadn't detected this structure, what made me think my classmates' wristcoms could penetrate it to locate me? This explained why they hadn't found me. Until now, I'd simply assumed they hadn't tracked Ked and me far enough to get within scanning range.

I needed to stand up and keep moving. No matter how bad I felt.

JOURNAL ENTRY 74

I hit the wall at the end of my second "day." Literally.

I smashed into it nose first. I tasted blood as I collapsed in another spasm of pain at the base of this new barrier. I hadn't found any right side exits on the way, and now I avoided wasting more water on crying. Instead I concentrated on tilting and pinching my swelling nose to get it to stop bleeding. My curses echoed back through the hallway.

I got up and groped the end of the tunnel, and even jumped as high as I could on my good leg. But I felt no gaps, and no breezes either. I'd crashed into a dead end. How appropriately symbolic. I sank back to the floor and decided it was time for sleep. It was certainly dark enough.

When I tired of waking from sore body parts trying unsuccessfully to make some peace with the hard floor, I slowly stood up and felt my way to the opposite wall, so I could lean against it and hop my way back. Third day, and probably my last.

Maybe I'd find a doorway or exit along this wall, but I was quickly losing hope, while dizziness and weakness slowed my pace.

I could still hope Ked had managed to survive. I also wished I'd worked harder on my friendship with Branem. Maybe my classmates would at least find my body, so they wouldn't have to wonder forever what happened, like Aerrem and Trist wondered about their parents. And I missed my roomie. Suddenly I crashed again.

I'd tripped on the sunken edge of a flawed floor slab along this wall, and it dumped me right into a puddle of ground water. I was so astonished I forgot to curse at the hurt it caused me. Instead I carefully rearranged my battered body so I could suck the puddle dry.

Luckily I couldn't see it, because it tasted muddy and slimy, and it might be packed with leached toxins and lethal microbes. I couldn't afford to care. I had to have it. I was so dehydrated I couldn't remember when I'd last peed.

I didn't get up again until I licked every last drop up. My heart quit pounding, and I actually made a little grudging, hot urine along my way. My stomach cramped a couple times, but I didn't know if it was because the water was bad, or if it was simply due to my abrupt intake. I worked hard to avoid puking, and sweated instead.

Back at the fallen slab and its silent guardians, heaps of bones and teeth glowed in the orange light of sunset. I retrieved my untouched screen and shouted up at the hole. Still no answer.

The stink of dry rot crept past the clots in my nostrils, and I gazed at the desiccating dat. I'd known not to try to eat it without a source of water, but too late I realized perhaps I should have drunk its blood or at least the fluid in its eyes. Yuck. Oh well.

I sank down against the opposite wall, and every empty-eyed makkon and dat skull stared back at me. This is what happens when you fall down here, they seemed to say. And you deserve it.

"Stop it!" I shouted senselessly, while their broken bones beckoned like puzzle pieces. I gently poked my purple, swollen knee. It remained dented, and broken bones inside ground painfully whenever I shifted.

The evening light also revealed pus oozing from the bruised punctures in my left arm, and I realized that not all of the bad smell came from my dead attacker.

I didn't sleep very well that night either.

The next morning only tree branches waved at me from above. Again I left my plan on my screen, and set off to explore the other end of this accidental hell.

JOURNAL ENTRY 75

The wall soon curved gently but relentlessly to the right, and the cruel floor sloped downward, in a slow and seemingly endless spiral. Round and round she goes, and no one knows where she'll end up!

I dragged myself ever deeper into dark despair, sadly hoping to stumble into another pool, because surely I'd never find a route back to the surface this way.

Why didn't the stream in the ravine end in a waterfall down here? Visions of puddles, ponds, lakes, and rivers filled my head. I yearned for water bottles and water fountains, fogs, clouds, and rain, while again all chances of sweat, spit, piss, and tears ended. How far could I afford to explore before I'd have to return or give up? And weren't they the same thing?

I took frequent breaks, but no position felt restful now, and I had no measure of time before sleep finally took me by surprise. And I couldn't say how long I slept. I scrambled amongst snagging tree branches with a hungry dat pack at my heels, before a loud howl echoed through the dream and I shuddered awake.

What was I doing down here in the dark? Why had I assumed no dat could survive the same fall I had? Did a real shriek wake me up? Dats could easily possess better senses than humans—so I was a blind crippled target down here!

I fingered my pocketknife, a feeble weapon against so many sharp teeth and claws. I had to get back. Back to the light. Maybe I could use my knife blade there to focus sunlight on tinder and build a signal fire below the hole. And I might get more water from the seep hole at the other end. Why hadn't I thought of all this sooner?

Hopping uphill, however, was harder. Much harder. I probably took almost two days to return to the fallen slab. I had to stop and rest too many times, until pain drove me on, and nearly out of my mind. So it's hard to say exactly how much time I lost. But when I reached the fallen slab, the sun was too low to try to start a fire, and I doubted I'd ever make it back to the seep for more water.

I collapsed on the fallen slab. My lips felt cracked and crusted, and my parched tongue filled my mouth.I tried to say hello to my dead companions, but my mouth and throat were too dry. So I used my stylus to record a short, shaky, vac-brained apology, and tucked my screen and stylus into one of my shorts pockets.

As the walls faded into darkness, the skeletons got up and danced a furious ring around me, while their nails and teeth clacked. They herded me backwards, until I tripped and fell into a clattering pile of hert bones.

It's not all my fault, I tried to claim. But you still made the wrong choices, they chanted. I found Ked's chip in the pile and knew they were right.

I'm so sorry, I said, but won't anyone help me now? Shandy, where are you? I need you! Shandy!

I yelled and yelled for my roomie, until a light raked my face. I opened my eyes, clawed at the beam, and squinted up at its source.

Shandy peered over the edge of the hole. "I'm here, Taje, I'm here!"

What a cruel dream, I thought, when I tried to answer, and discovered I still had no voice.

JOURNAL ENTRY 76

After that I remember a series of largely miserable moments. Rappelling classmates, a screeching med-scanner, someone propping me up for slow sips of water that mostly ran down my face, while an IV injector took forever to find a vein in me. Someone else sluiced me with cool water, which was smooth.

But I knew if the injector couldn't find an uncollapsed vein, I was done. Well, I'd lived a good life full of friends and animals. I hadn't gone back to the Center, and friends surrounded me now.

As I decided I was satisfied with my life, the injector found a vein it could slip an IV catheter into, and I heard cheers.

A few classmates with strong stomachs did quick wound care while others applied a hasty leg splint. Still others attached fluid and med lines to my IV. Then a bunch carefully moved me onto a stretcher and strapped me in. They tied ropes to the stretcher to both steady me from below and haul me up into the woods.

But they set my stretcher down next to the hole, and we didn't leave right away. They adjusted my fluids, and I imagined some curiosity over where they'd found me, but instead I think I overheard someone crying down below.

At last I endured an interminable, nauseating ride by stretcher relays, through night and day, back to the ship.

The first time I asked to stop along the way to pee led to mortifying excitement among my caretakers. Apparently it meant my kidneys were still working. Everyone felt relieved when we finally reached the med-niche, and classmates could hook me up to it and let it take over all the decisions.

Voices woke me up sometime later in the ship.

"What are you doing here?" I heard Taemar demanding. "Taje is stable, but you look terrible! You were supposed to rest in camp at the first rendezvous—"

"I have to talk to her!"

"We've flushed Taje's wounds again, bathed her, re-splinted her knee, and the med-niche is running her fluids and meds." I guess that as a member of the smartest team in the class, Taemar was now my unofficial doctor. "There's nothing more you can do right now. She's asleep, which is what you should also consider—"

"No, I'm not!" I gasped out in a raw voice. "Let Aerrem in! I want to see her!"

My dorm sib barged into the ship's lounge, sunbrowned Taemar hot on her tail. "Okay, but only for a micro," Taemar had to relent. She had tied back her lengthening dark brown hair into a pony tail to keep most of it out of her face.

Both classmates had brown almond eyes filled with concern. Aerrem pulled up a chair, and Taemar frowned at it. Aerrem looked filthy, and I scanned dried tear tracks in the dirt on her cheeks.

I winced. "I'm so sorry, Aerrem!" I managed to whisper.

Aerrem shook her head, her wild, tangled hair appearing more nova than ever, and her ginger-colored skin looking more the color of Taron dirt. "Taje, you already apologized to us, repeatedly—don't you remember?"

"No."

"Good. Your pain meds worked. Taemar, could you please give us that micro, alone?"

"Five minutes. That's it. Then both of you must rest!"

Aerrem put her chin in her hand and her elbow in her lap and shut her eyes until we heard the door slide shut behind Taemar.

"How much do you remember?" Aerrem asked at last, a wary look sneaking out from under her weary brow.

I could feel my heart thumping in my chest. "I remember—I remember Shandy finding me," I said hoarsely. "But I thought it was a wishful dream, because I'd called for him, yet I had no voice. Was I hallucinating? Or could I still talk when you found me?"

Aerrem shook her head as she bent down to loosen her filthy boot seals with a groan. "Fuse it all. You were so dehydrated you were almost dead! How did you survive six hot days down there, without water? Or did you fall in later?"

"No. I found and drank one puddle in the hallway. How come you didn't find me sooner? Is the hallway scan-proof?"

Aerrem nodded grimly.

"Then how on Taron did you ever find me?" I had to ask. "Were there tracks? Did the dats and I make enough prints to find the hole?"

"Almost. Branem found your footprints by the stream at sunset, the second time we searched near the ravine. He'd taken our water bottles downstream, to avoid trampling Ked's tracks at the crossing. He came back so hysterical I thought at first he'd found your body—please don't say it again, Taje. You've already apologized. It's my turn. I'm sorry. We totally fused it the first time, when we backtracked Ked to the ravine."

"I didn't leave footprints where I split up from Ked," I realized. "I slid down into the ravine. It's not your fault."

"We didn't even think to scan for a tracking chip in Ked the first night," Aerrem said. "Next we had to catch up with her on foot and follow her tracks backward to find you. You can thank Kijan's hunting ability for most of that.

"But we thought at first you'd jumped the ravine on her. And it was easier for us to cross upstream, on some fallen tree trunks—"

I bit my chapped lip. "How is Ked?"

"Someone told me she made it back here." Aerrem yawned. "I hate to say it, but Taemar's right. We should probably get some rest now."

"So Branem found me?" I quickly asked, before Aerrem could jettison. It wasn't what I remembered, but that didn't mean anything. By the end I couldn't separate nightmares from the truth.

"No." Aerrem slumped back in her seat.

My heart sank as I stared at her and waited. Aerrem talks. Why wasn't she talking?

Aerrem coughed dryly and plucked her water bottle from her belt. She took several swigs, saw the longing on my face, and handed it over to me. I didn't need it now, but I still wanted it.

"We lost your tracks in the woods at nightfall," she admitted while I gulped. "They were six days old, and our search team was exhausted and nova with worry. We ended up running around in the dark like vac-heads—"

I handed back her empty water bottle. "Aerrem, if you won't let me apologize anymore, you shouldn't either—"

"All I'm saying is I'm not sure what happened—"

"So did you switch our S.O.S. signal to top priority?"

Aerrem's cheeks flushed as she shook her head. "We thought we had the skills to find you. But we should have listened more to Hannen's warning. By the time we realized we were in over our heads, we also knew it was too late to call for more help. FIL couldn't arrive in time—"

"Well, that's a relief!" I hated seeing Aerrem's shame, and even with a broken knee, I still wasn't eager for FIL rescue. "But—how did you know it was so urgent?"

"Krorn found your gear on the beach the first morning. Which confirmed Branem's suspicion that you'd taken almost no survival gear—"

"So why didn't you give up, when you couldn't scan my life signs? Why keep hunting so frantically for a dead body?"

"I'd already given up on my parents—I couldn't give up on you too!" Aerrem shook her tail as she stood up. "I had to know what happened!"

She had an answer ready for every question—in fact, too many answers—but the door slid open again.

"Time's up!" Taemar said. "Rest now, and then talk all you want."

Aerrem sped out, avoiding the suspicious look on my face. Taemar misread it and asked if I needed more pain meds to sleep. I said yes, and a micro later I put off thinking about how they'd really found me.

JOURNAL ENTRY 77

The next time I woke up I felt ravenous, and Branem brought my meal. "You're back already, too?" I asked, surprised. "Weren't you on my search and rescue team?"

"Of course." He pulled a tray from the wall, and set down a spoon and a bowl of soup for me. Meanwhile he tried to smile.

"I was on the team that found you. We were vacfully tired by the hand-off, but you know how Aerrem gets. She couldn't rest until she scanned you here, safe and sound. And I couldn't let her return alone—it's too dangerous—which is why I owe you another apology—"

"No you don't." I sighed, mortified once again. "Please don't, Branem. I can't bear it! It was my vacful decision to get lost. Just tell me, how did your team find me?"

"I discovered your footprints along the stream, the second time we tried to track you." He sounded proud, as well he should be. "But we lost your tracks again in the dark, in the woods. So we split up and spread out, and Aerrem and Shandy stumbled across the hole.

"I guess Aerrem almost fell into it too. They called the rest of us from there." Branem looked surprised. "You really don't remember much, do you? That's why I wanted to say again how sorry I am—"

"But it's me that should apologize—"

"You already did, so I guess that makes us even now."

"Fair enough—let's call it done," I quickly agreed. "Is Shandy back?"

"No, the rest of the team stayed at the rendezvous, to rest, wait for help with their packs, and direct an exploration team back to the hole. Great Galaxy, Taje, what a find!"

"And how is Ked?"

"She made it back here. Space, didn't anyone tell you that?"

"That's all anyone tells me!"

But Branem glanced at his wristcom and shook his head. "Sorry. I have to get back to our stoves. See you later."

JOURNAL ENTRY 78

"When are you going to tell her?" I heard Taemar whispering urgently, several days later. Sometimes I learned more by pretending sleep. "Look at these readouts. She's certainly well enough to make some decisions, and we shouldn't wait any longer—"

"Tell me now," I suggested as I opened my eyes. Aerrem handed over a platter of food, and my stomach growled. "What's going on?"

Taemar sighed and actually fled, while Aerrem sat down heavily in my visitor's chair. She put her head in her hands and my appetite suddenly vanished. "What?" I repeated.

"It's your knee," Aerrem said.

"Oh, good! I thought maybe Ked—"

"It's not good," Aerrem said as the end of her tail twitched tensely. "The med-niche scanner says we can't fix your knee joint."

"What do you mean? My wounds are healing—"

"It's not like Jael's simple break. You need expert surgery—and the longer we wait, the more likely you'll require full limb rejuvenation. So the class asked me to offer you a higher priority S.O.S. signal—"

"But what about the underground hallway?"

"What about it?"

"What's at the bottom of the spiral? It might answer a lot of our questions! Don't you want to explore it first?"

"One of our teams already did—"

"And you weren't going to tell me?"

"The spiral dead-ends, at what looks like—but may not be—a sealed door. There's not much to tell—"

"Except maybe some very smooth findings, if we can cut through that door. And I want to be there if we try—"

"Are you nova?" Aerrem suddenly stood up, ripped the niche screen from the wall, and shoved my knee scan at me. "The class will vote on it, but we're worried that torching our way through the 'door' may cause more harm than good.

"Meanwhile, look at this scan! Do you really want to risk making this worse?"

I stared at the screen. How odd to think those were my bones, not looking much different from the broken piles in the underground hallway. My knee wasn't cracked—it was shattered. I couldn't even count all the pieces. But I wasn't dying from it.

"How could I make this any worse?" I argued as I slapped the screen back on the wall. "I'll keep my knee splinted, and you can haul me back there by stretcher." I shuddered. "I suffered a lot for this find, Aerrem! I want to be there, and I won't okay a more urgent S.O.S. until we do it—"

"You'd blackmail us into this?" Aerrem's brown eyes bugged, and her tail smashed the air.

"No," I pressed scabbed hands against my eyes, blocking a sudden rush of stinging tears. "No, I didn't mean that! All I ask—is that you think of me—when you decide. Please! And meanwhile tell me how Shandy actually found me—"

"I'm not really sure—"

"And that's not the whole truth, is it?" I said, though it was one step closer. What a gullible vac-head I'd been! "He's an esper, isn't he?" I finally blurted it out. "He's got some Istrannian genes—that's why he's so pale and so homesick—"

Aerrem shook her head. "That's not for me to say."

"Okay, so update me on Ked!"

"I told you, she made it back—"

"That's what everyone keeps saying. Now tell me the rest! You can't imagine how horrible it is, leaving the rest to my imagination!"

"I'm sorry, Taje." Aerrem's tail slumped. "A whole pack of dats must have zapped her. Now she's so scared she won't let any of us close enough to treat her wounds, and they're really fused."

Aerrem's eyes overflowed with tears, and mine launched. I sat up and sobbed at the med-niche to clamp me off. It dispensed an arm injector, which I strapped on and hooked up to my IV cath. I found a powered knee brace in a cabinet under my bunk.

Aerrem clutched the edges of her chair and wiped her eyes with the end of her tail. "What are you doing?"

JOURNAL ENTRY 79

"I'll go nova if I have to spend another micro on this bunk!" I put the brace on my knee, adjusted its controls, and scooted to the edge of my bed. "Ked needs me! Please find my medkit!"

"Taje, don't do this!"

"How much longer can Ked afford to wait? And how are you going to stop me?"

Aerrem leaped to her feet as I struggled to stand. It hurt, even with pain meds from my injector. But I didn't care anymore, and instead of blocking me, which might have taken one or two fingers, Aerrem tracked down my medkit.

"At least let me monitor you!" Aerrem pulled a bioscanner out of her own medkit on her belt.

"Fine. Just don't scare off Ked, or call Shandy—I don't think he could handle this."

Aerrem didn't try to deny it—another clue—and they all added up to the same answer. She let me lean on her, and guided me to my hert friend, not far along the edge of First Lake.

Ked tossed her head half-heartedly and snorted, then scented me and stood still, her limbs trembling with fatigue. The terrible stench of her rotting wounds assaulted my nose as I limped close enough to touch her.

Ked's fur was crusted with dried blood and pus. Deep, festering gashes ran down her back and sides. I shuddered as I imagined the battle scene: dats outnumbering Ked, and her too exhausted to defend herself.

I braced myself to take her chin on my shoulder and wept as she rested the weight of her heavy head on me. I stroked her face and held her head up to kiss her cold, pale lips.

Ked moaned softly as she shut her eyes, and propped her head back on my shoulder. How could I fix this? I didn't even bother with my medkit scanner. Aerrem quietly approached, and Ked no longer cared. Aerrem put her hand on my other shoulder.

"Aerrem," I said, "I need help. From someone stronger than us."

Aerrem nodded sorrowfully, and talked to Dojan and Kijan on her wristcom. They arrived soon afterwards with their wristcoms on scan, and stunners and knives on their leather belts.

"We—have to put Ked down," I finally admitted. "I can't let her suffer like this any longer."

Dojan and Kijan spoke off to one side, too softly for me to hear. But I saw them release the safeties on their stunners.

"We'll set these very lightly at first," Dojan said. "Only enough to encourage her to lie down. Next we'll give a heart-stopping dose. And then we think you'd better leave."

I nodded wordlessly, and I held onto Ked as they fired. She sank slowly to her knees, and then to her side. I cradled her head. Her large brown trusting eyes gazed gratefully right back at me, and she let her last breath escape with a huge foul-smelling sigh.

I sprawled in the hot dust and stiff dry grass, with my dear friend's limp head filling my lap. I bawled as I stroked her soft short coat. Aerrem joined me.

"She must have just been waiting for you. To say goodbye," Aerrem sobbed as she hugged me.

"It's not fair. Shandy was right. I never should have done this to her!"

JOURNAL ENTRY 80

Later Kijan reported a scan showed Ked's wounded chest was full of infection. "You made the right decision," he and Dojan came to the med-niche to tell me. "She was drowning inside."

I turned my face to the bulkhead, and I asked them to remove my untouched dinner.

Dojan's ears fell back as he picked up my tray. "Shandy wants to see you."

"Taje?" he asked again, when I didn't answer.

I swallowed back more tears. "Tell Shandy thanks for finding me. But this isn't a good time for a visit."

A micro later Aerrem turned up to lecture me.

"But I don't understand why Shandy never told me!" I slammed my hand down and flinched when it bled again. I felt so stupid. Ignorant me—I had figured Shandy would simply grow into his hands and feet. I also thought he had brown eyes and eyebrows because he was like most humans, despite his pallor. So I never guessed he simply wasn't completely human. And, worse, I felt betrayed—by a roommate who never told me he could read my mind any time he wanted.

"And I don't com how you can ignore your teammate." Aerrem whipped the hot air with her tail. "It's not fair!"

"Life's not fair." Smooth—now I sounded like a dorp!

"But people can try!" Aerrem zapped my answer right back at me, since I was too fused to see it coming. "So if you won't talk to him about what happened, are you at least going to fill in the rest of your journal?"

"What do you mean?" How much had she already sneaked a look at?

"I'm guessing you probably started some sort of rant back when Tarnek had you locked up. You had nothing to draw! And I've seen you record our trips. Why not fill in the holes? Like how the whole story started? It might help you understand what happened."

"I already know what happened. And what are you suggesting? That I start with Donshore, Arrainius, or merely the whole class?" Even the idea of the latter exhausted me.

So I was stalling, because what I had left to record about the class was mostly what I didn't want to relive. "Besides, long stories are your specialty, Aerrem. I can't do anything like that."

"And when will you admit again what a fused liar you are?" Aerrem didn't wait for my answer. Instead she burrowed into my pack. "Exactly what else are you doing right now?"

She wrinkled her nose as she plucked my filthy hiking shorts from my pack and tugged my crumpled screen from one of the pockets.

My face flushed as I realized she knew exactly where to look. Female classmates had undressed, washed, and dressed me in clean clothes as soon as I could tolerate it. Who had found my journal and told her?

Dirt spilled out as she unrolled the screen from my stylus. She wiped them both off and put them into my scabbed hands.

"Just remember how it feels to be left out of all the stories," she said. "And promise me you'll make it complete, honest, and fair."

Now she sounded like one of our dorm parents. Or—even worse—a teacher. "If I do it," I retorted. I needed homework right now like another smashed bone—

"Promise!"

"Promise I'll get on the new tunnel team!" I said.

Aerrem shook her head and stomped out. I tried to escape into sleep but my busy brain refused to shut down. How would I tell my vacful story now? And how might I have avoided any of it?

Well, I could go back and blame fused tests for everything. What if I'd passed Naemar's blasted science exam the first time I'd taken it? I certainly wouldn't be here now. Where was that theoretically barely possible time machine when I needed it?

The next morning Shandy didn't ask, he sneaked in, and flinched at the sight of me.

"You shouldn't be here," I said, not sure whom I was trying to protect.

He held my hand briefly with his long pale, alien fingers. "It doesn't help to stay away. I'm sorry, Taje, I'm so sorry—"

"I'm really tired of apologies," I said, while the medniche revealed my pounding pulse. We both glanced at the monitor and then squeezed our eyes shut. When I opened mine, Shandy was gone.

JOURNAL ENTRY 81

Aerrem snatched my screen and studied it beyond my reach.

"Aerrem! That's my private journal!"

"It was my idea to complete it." Her tail swished as she totally ignored me.

"That's not fair! If I don't get to scan any of your stories—"

"Hush!" No one is supposed to know about Aerrem's fiction, at least not until she manages to publish. And then how she expects to be ready for an audience—"Great Universe," she said, "why are you filling in everything the class did?"

She'd caught me adding more to the day we'd first gotten our wristcoms. I was putting off the details of my latest adventure on Taron. The wristcom lesson and aftermath was another awful day I didn't want to relive. Yet it kept bothering me, and I kept picking at it, like an itchy scab, as I slowly uncovered the ugly wound underneath.

"Well," Aerrem said, "I suppose you can at least claim you're telling a more complete story—"

"I thought that was the whole point." I grabbed my screen back before she could see more.

Aerrem stood up and scanned my vitals. I had no privacy anymore. "You should be taking more pain meds," she abruptly changed the subject.

"Why? They make me too sleepy to think."

"Like the journal, I'm not suggesting it only for your sake."

I turned my back on her. Moments later I heard her walk out. But I couldn't record anything more that day. And I did take more pain meds.

"Taje, wake up! Special delivery!"

Annoyed, I left the escape of deep sleep that evening, and opened my eyes. Branem stood over me, with what looked like a tan furry rag dangling from his milk-chocolate hand. I quickly banished a frown from my face. Branem already felt bad enough.

"What is it?" I tried to sound interested.

He set it down on my shirt, exposing the paler skin of his palm. The creature was barely alive. Smaller than a makkon, it was little more than a bundle of small bones in a shorthaired dun sack. It scanned me with beady dark eyes, and perked dark tufted ears—

"Branem—"

"Wait a micro—" No doubt expecting an outburst, he jettisoned, but returned promptly, with a pan of watery stew he set on my bunk.

"Branem, this is a dat pup!"

"I know—I know!"

The pup slid over to the pan, sank its muzzle into its contents, and vacuumed them up.

"It must have belonged to one of the dats the herts killed! I found the rest of its litter dead—starved to death. I know I should have finished it off, but I'm so sick of killing everything in sight. And I couldn't believe this pup had survived this long for no good reason!"

The pup's belly was now so full it had trouble climbing onto my chest. I found myself helping it, with horrified fascination. Its ears perked at me again. It burped, slid from a sitting position to lie on its chest, and looked at me with hope in its little brown eyes. The same hope I now saw in Branem's brown eyes.

"I thought—he might cheer you up a bit," Branem said cautiously. "I know I can't replace Ked."

The pup put its chin down between its paws, closed its eyes, and fell asleep on me. Once more a trusting animal claimed my heart, and there was absolutely nothing I could do about it.

Of course later I heard rumors of a terrible fight between Aerrem and Branem. The dat pup was a totally fused and impractical making-up gift. But no one dared object to the pup in my presence, even when he began teething and chewing up everything in sight.

I was soon forced out of my bunk more and more often to maintain discipline. And when others began calling my pup "Disaster," for lack of a better name, I shortened it to "Dizzy."

Meanwhile restless tempers won the vote to attempt to cut through the deep end of the underground hall, and because I had discovered it at some personal cost, I was included on the team. Aerrem accepted my continued work on my journal for my part of the bargain.

But Shandy was also included. I suppose with his special skills his selection made a lot more sense than mine did, but I still didn't know how to face him.

Shandy had saved my life, but he'd hidden the truth about himself from the first day I'd met him. Betrayal, mourning, and fear overwhelmed any eagerness I'd had for the expedition, and Aerrem's insistence that I keep my promise to return the same way I'd left—by stretcher—finished it off.

Although we took shortcuts, I still endured a long slow slog by my carriers back to the hole—a trip I'd rather forget. At last we slid downhill, and old gnarled trees surrounded us. Our class had implanted a location chip in the tree closest to the hole, so we found it without difficulty. And without having to go near the ravine. Upon arrival I gazed downward. I felt nauseated and filled with dread.

JOURNAL ENTRY 82

"This is taking eons!" Branem changed his tired grip on the torch aimed at the light grey wall blocking the deep end of the tunnel. "I've barely put a dent in it!" he added.

Taemar paused on one foot, in the middle of a hop-scotch game, lit up by a stove light and our belt lights. I was refereeing between her and Aerrem, using a silly childhood game to fight boredom and nerves, a nasty combination.

"Have you set the torch on full power?" Taemar asked. Her boot had landed very close to a line in the floor, but she remained steady.

"Not at first," Branem said, "but I have now!"

Dizzy pounced on Taemar's foot. I couldn't talk anyone into pet sitting, on top of the thankless jobs of guarding the hole or waiting for a pickup signal back at the ship.

Taemar tottered. "Hey, unfair interference!"

"I'll take a turn at the torch now if you want." Aerrem said.

"Nah," Branem said. "I'm all right. Finish your game. But we may end up needing a recharge back at the ship to get through."

Great Galaxy, I hoped not. It was a long haul down here, and my classmates were amazed at how far my footprints had made it in the dust on the floor. But those prints brought back vivid memories, whether totally real or not, which made me sick.

"Anyone for a game of hangman?" Hannen offered his screen to Shandy, who shook his head. I glanced at the screen and probably turned equally green.

Shandy was huddled against a far wall. I wondered if he felt as miserable as I did. I shuddered, and forced my concentration to return to our ridiculous game. It had been so long since any of us had played hopscotch that I had to make up rules as we went along.

Hours later Aerrem halted in the middle of her second turn at the torch.

"You actually get through?" Branem jumped up.

"No, but feel it! The wall's shaking!"

It also emitted a low hum, and we all got up to feel the vibration in it. I scanned the stunned look on Shandy's face, and Aerrem noticed it too. "What is it, Shandy?" she asked.

I shivered, but he grew angry. "How should I know? We're in way over our heads!"

Dizzy slipped around me, snuffled at a crack below the middle section, and whined.

"It's opening!" I yelped.

I had about a micro to suddenly remember all the hazardous possibilities we should have worried about more—like a crash shelter with a toxic atmosphere, a tomb with an automatic defense system, or a booby-trapped military depot. A loud alarm suddenly ripped at our eardrums.

A large section of the wall shot up into the ceiling, and a dozen bipeds in rust-colored atmosphere suits stood facing us. Their three pairs of opposable digits gripped tarnished instruments, which they pointed directly at us.

We understood their meaning all too clearly.

Aerrem dropped our torch to the ground with a loud clatter. We all slowly raised our empty hands, and hoped our message was equally clear.

JOURNAL ENTRY 83

"Oh, what have I done!" Aerrem moaned into her hands.

"It's not your fault!" Taemar said. "We all voted on it, and none of us imagined anyone living down here!"

We sat in a small grey room, off the hall, not far beyond the barrier we'd tried to torch open.

Our captors had swiftly taken everything from us—our packs, our utility belts, even our wristcoms and my med injector—before we could attempt any further communication. Then they'd herded us in here and locked the door.

I would have laughed if I hadn't felt so awful. Our class had sent its leaders, its smartest team, and a team with an esper, and this was the best we could do?

I scanned the ceiling fixtures. At least they included a light. I tried to remember to breathe. How could I have already forgotten pain this terrible?

Branem joined my gaze upwards. "Looks like a sensor array up there. Are they spying on us?"

Taemar caught me wincing. "Are you okay?"

"At least they didn't take my brace." I gritted my teeth as I tightened the joint supporting my knee. Dizzy lay mournfully beside me, unusually subdued.

"Why did they take your meds?" Hannen asked.

"Why did they take our wristcoms?" Branem said. "Now we can't even talk to them!"

"Hannen's question is important," Taemar said. "If they took Taje's injector to torture her, that implies some fused purpose—"

"Maybe they're mining without a permit," Aerrem said, "using this old tunnel as a hidden base—"

"Maybe it's a military base," Branem said, "for some group that wants the benefits of FIL, but won't stop fighting so they can join legally."

The Federation of Intelligent Life doesn't allow members who fight wars. Intelligent life doesn't solve differences through violence. I trembled, and Shandy, once again sitting stiffly by himself against another wall, looked as pale as a Taron moon.

I wondered what Shandy could tell us, if only he'd admit aloud what he was and what he could do. Then I wondered if he could read that thought, and I shuddered. So did he.

"Or maybe they simply took anything that looked remotely threatening," Taemar said. "Perhaps they're just as afraid of us as we are of them."

"Why—were they—wearing—atmosphere suits?" I tried to join in, to distract myself from my throbbing knee and my silent roommate.

"Non-native lifeforms, with different atmospheric requirements?" Hannen suggested.

"No!" Shandy shut his eyes and rubbed his temples.

"Xenophobes?" Branem guessed.

Shandy shook his head, his eyes still shut.

As everyone else gave Shandy concerned scans, I looked away. I remembered our captor's gloved hands, gripping their weapons so tightly. "Did anyone—get a good look at their faces?"

"Not human, Kralvin, Altruskan, Lorratian, Telmid, or Mumdwar," Taemar said thoughtfully. "They had slightly muzzled faces, but they're too tall for Tliesjians. Dark hair, and golden to brown faces—that's all I scanned."

"That's all!" Branem said. "I was so scared, I couldn't even count their fingers!"

"Three pairs on each hand," I said, catching everyone's wondering looks now. "Like makkons! Shandy's right," I had to admit, "most likely they are natives."

JOURNAL ENTRY 84

"Why would natives hide underground in atmosphere suits?" Hannen replied with relentless logic.

"But Taje has a point," Taemar said. "Three pairs of opposable digits is a tremendous coincidence—"

"And we lived underground, back at the Center," Branem added, chuckling.

"In atmosphere suits?" Hannen snapped.

"Maybe they're afraid of xenogerms," I said.

"This whole senseless argument is fusing my brain!" Aerrem got up to pace, her tail lashing dangerously in the small room. "We need more information!"

"We'll get it when they decide to talk," Taemar said.

"If they decide to talk," Branem had to add.

"If they don't let us go within a week, our next team will try to rescue us," Taemar reminded him.

"Somehow that's not very reassuring," Branem said, and I had to agree. We'd foolishly allowed ourselves a whole week to explore. Now it simply felt like a delayed trap for anyone who came down here looking for us.

Hours later our captors woke us from a dull-witted, frightened sleep. Still in atmosphere suits, they dumped six empty bright red-orange atmosphere suits on the floor in front of us, and motioned us to put them on.

Aerrem had to stuff her tail down one leg. I had to hold Dizzy against my chest, leaving one sleeve empty, and we endured a tricky struggle when he slipped down towards my splint and began to howl.

The suits were too tall for all us, especially Shandy. Aerrem supported him, while Taemar let me hang onto her arm with my free hand. We stumbled out of the room, down a short hall, and under a heavy shower. I suspected it was for decontamination.

We passed through two sets of doors—an air-lock?—into an immense, artificially lit cavern with an amazing city, oddly vacant.

Our careful footsteps echoed on the cobblestone roadway, which skirted a market and arched doorways to what looked like apartments. Plants, some familiar Taron species, many not, flourished in pots and planters everywhere. Colorful mosaics decorated the walls.

I craned my neck, wanting to study all of it, tripped in my suit, and almost fell to the floor. Dizzy whined fearfully, but Taemar caught me, and stayed by my side. All too soon the tour ended. We passed through another door, which locked us into an anteroom. There our guards removed their suits and motioned us to do likewise.

We exchanged shocked looks while we climbed out of our suits, and traded stares with our guards.

Under their suits they wore rust-colored tunics and trousers, with black sashes and sandals. Their weapons were tucked into their sashes. The shortest among them stood a head taller than Hannen, our tallest teammate. Their short curly brown hair continued from their heads down the backs of their necks, and appeared again on the backs of their wrists, hands, and ankles.

Someone wearing a grey-green tunic and trousers entered from the next room and spoke to us in a language none of us knew.

Aerrem glanced quickly at Shandy, and he frowned and shook his head. Aerrem turned back to the speaker. "We mean you no harm. What do you want?"

The aliens stared at her and then muttered among themselves. Then the speaker slowly withdrew one of our wristcoms from a black sash, and held it out to Aerrem. The guards also raised their weapons and aimed them at her.

Sweat beaded on Aerrem's forehead as she struggled with translator settings. Hannen and Shandy quickly helped her.

"Will this device translate for us?" the person in grey-green finally asked.

"Yes," Aerrem said. "It should translate most of our words. Can you understand me now?"

"Quite clearly." The voice translated as male, with all emotion held in check. "This is also a calling device?"

"Yes, but—"

"We doubt it will work here. But you must not try to make any calls with it, or we will take it from you and lock you back up."

"We will not make any calls," Aerrem promised in a shaky voice.

"Good. We are ready now for the Council meeting."

JOURNAL ENTRY 85

They led us into the next room and we gulped as my teammates sat as instructed on pillow-seats at the near end of a huge, oval, polished stone table. Taemar helped me down to the floor, and I used my pillow to prop up my knee. Meanwhile four people in midnight blue with silver sashes, and seven more in grey-green, stood around the quartz-flecked shiny black table.

The rust-colored guards spread out around the room, while the person who'd returned Aerrem's wrist-com headed around the table to speak with the people dressed in dark blue.

"Looks like a report to higher-ups," Taemar said, and Aerrem quickly shut off her translator.

"Let's hope they're willing to listen to our story," Aerrem whispered. "Maybe it'll even be something they want to hear."

"Great Universe, please tell me this isn't a First Contact!" Branem scanned the room. "We're not trained for this—"

"Hush." Aerrem elbowed him. "We don't have any choice!"

Dizzy dropped into my lap, and I clutched him so tightly I almost made him squeal. Meanwhile, the nearest guard stared at Aerrem's quivering tail with what looked suspiciously like horrified fascination.

"At least we can assume this probably isn't a recent colony or a group of transients," Hannen said.

"I can't believe natives or an established colony would stay cooped up down here!" Taemar retorted.

"They are natives," Shandy said—guessing, or did he know for certain?

We all hushed up as the person in grey-green returned the rest of our wristcoms to us. We set their translators, Hannen and Shandy double-checked them, and we passed them out around the table.

The guards squatted around the room, and the rest of the council members sat down on the colorful, intricately stitched pillows placed around the table. I wished for a spare, but at least I had a rug to sit on.

"I am Elder Councilwoman Aviellian," a person in midnight blue and silver announced. "This is Elder Councilman Sturvnen, Younger Councilman Thorkiel, and Younger Councilwoman Jenghas," she named the rest wearing midnight blue. "The other people between us are our assistants."

"My name is Aerrem," our leader tried to speak equally boldly, and kept it simple by announcing first names only. "Hannen, Taemar, and Taje are seated on my left, and Branem and Shandy are on my right."

"Welcome to our Council—"

"Objection!" Sturvnen interrupted Aviellian. "I give no welcome to these dangerous intruders!"

"Councilman Sturvnen," Aviellian said in a patient tone, "is under the odd impression that you must be the mutated offspring of ancient soldiers."

"And Aviellian has deluded herself into believing you are harmless little aliens from outer space!"

JOURNAL ENTRY 86

Branem and I exchanged scans, and suddenly had to work at not laughing hysterically, while Aerrem blasted us with a scowl set on stun.

"I fail to see why you refuse to consider my theory," Aviellian said to Sturvnen.

"Why would aliens bother to travel here?" Sturvnen snapped. "Our solar system possesses no other living planets, and this one is broken. And to get here from another system, these insane people would have had to find a way to break the speed of light, hibernate many hundreds of years, or endure a generation ship—"

"Actually, we sort of bypassed the speed of light," Aerrem began—

"Only to land on this forsaken world, and threaten our entire population! No, more likely they're the product of some hideous military technology—"

"And how would they have survived and reproduced all these years?" Aviellian interrupted Sturvnen.

"Perhaps this isn't the first time they've broken into our refuge—"

"So why didn't we all die long ago?"

"Or perhaps they're mutants on timed release, from some military cryogenic unit—"

"Our science still isn't capable of that! Look at them, Sturvnen! How can you doubt they're our first alien visitors? Must I command you to review the scans? Their genetic material, their cellular structures, even the microbes carried by their bodies bear no resemblance to any of our recorded species, past or present!"

Now our faces reddened, as we remembered how grubby we'd gotten here. And Sturvnen's face was also turning the red-orange color of Taron blood.

"Something bad happened here, a long time ago?" Taemar carefully ventured.

"Something bad!" Sturvnen sputtered.

"It ended that way," Aviellian said, "but it started with sheer hubris—"

"You will not speak of this with Outsiders!"

"According to your theory, they belong here—"

"Let us at least hear their story first," Thorkiel quietly suggested.

"But if they don't know our history, they should be told!" Aviellian said.

"Let them earn it," Jenghas said.

"Yes," Sturvnen said. "Let these invaders earn it."

Aerrem's tail, thumping the floor, had begun to show her irritation. "We're not invaders, and we're not afraid of your questions."

I could tell she was working at keeping her voice calm, and I suppose her claims were a good if dangerous bluff. I stared at her and tried not to look surprised, in case the natives had already begun to learn our facial expressions.

"So why were you trying to torch your way into sector twenty-nine?" Jenghas said.

"We thought this was the remains of an ancient civilization," Hannen said.

"We're not all that smart," Branem had to add.

"Where did your pup come from?" Aviellian suddenly gestured at Dizzy. "We thought we had all our companion animals on record, but he has no ID."

Companion animals? I gulped. What if they wanted Dizzy back? "Branem found him—on the surface of your world—orphaned." Like the rest of us. Should I say that too? I began to open my mouth, but I looked over at Shandy first. He frowned and shook his head.

"Impossible!" Sturvnen said. "On the surface? These are dangerous liars indeed!"

"We're not liars!" Shandy finally grew angry enough to speak up.

"So what are you trying to do—poison all of us? And how did you survive Outside? Do you possess some sort of personal body-shield generators we haven't detected, or did you cache protective suits somewhere?"

"We didn't need suits or shields on the surface, or to enter through a flaw in the ceiling of one of your access tunnels," Shandy snapped. "How long have you buried yourselves down here?"

Sturvnen looked aghast as Aviellian spoke up softly. "Nearly seven dozens of dozens of years. Perhaps long enough for more than one break to occur in the concealed entrances our ancestors sealed off so long ago!"

"Maybe long enough for some species to escape your refuge and re-seed the surface!" Taemar said.

"That's it!" I said. "That explains so much!"

"But none of our alarms ever went off," Sturvnen said.

"Perhaps our world is no longer toxic enough to trigger our alarms," Aviellian said.

"Or these people tricked our scanners, so they could rob or kill us!"

"This was no trick," I said as I struggled to stand up. Taemar helped me, and I pointed to my splinted, bruised, and swollen knee. "I broke my leg, falling through a hole in the ceiling of your sector twenty-nine access tunnel. That's how we really discovered you." Maybe guilt would help our cause.

"And we're not thieves or murderers!" Aerrem said. "We're members of the Federation of Intelligent Life, a peaceful, cooperative, galactic organization. We've lived for months on the surface of your world, studying your ecosystems—trying to understand them—for a report."

Good. I doubted the natives were ready to hear about FIL colonization aspirations, which were moot now, if only we were allowed to report back.

"Ecosystems?" Sturvnen roared. "We have no ecosystems Outside!"

"You do now," Branem said. "Granted, they're rather weak, and the dats seem especially lost without your company. But if you let us finish our report and turn it in, FIL would probably be quite willing to help you more fully restore the environments Outside."

In the stunned silence that followed, Aerrem exchanged glances with Shandy again, he nodded, and she revealed one of our last secrets.

"You should also know," she said, "before you judge us, that we are merely young planetary ecology students, on an unauthorized final exam field trip. So if *you* don't get us into trouble, FIL will probably do it for you upon our return home.

"We're all orphans too, so we have no parents to ask for our return," Branem said, a grin spreading across his face even though he must have seen the looks on our faces. I could tell Aerrem wanted to clobber him. I wanted to at least drag him out of the room. We could have let them worry we had families waiting for us. I glanced at Shandy, but I couldn't tell how he felt.

"Now it's your turn," Branem said. "We told our story. Tell us yours."

JOURNAL ENTRY 87

Aviellian and Sturvnen exchanged looks I couldn't interpret. Then Aviellian began, speaking so quietly that we held our breaths to listen.

"Our people became very successful when we evolved intelligence," she said. "But we weren't smart enough to figure out that we would never run out of resources. And for a long time we got away with that attitude.

"But we also allowed our population to soar out of control. Then we wondered why we ended up living in squalor, choking on our own wastes, dying of world-wide plagues and pollution-induced mega-storms, and using the excuse of ridiculous cultural differences to murder for squandered resources."

"Gee, doesn't that sound familiar?" Branem whispered.

"Hush!" Aerrem hissed, poking him below the table. He barely squelched an "Ouch!"

"At last the Ultimate War Over Everything began. And the most ironic part is that our ancestors—the few who chose to retreat peacefully down here with whatever species they could save—were considered crazy. But no one else survived when all our worst weapons were unleashed, and the surface of Shielvelle became too toxic for any life.

"Maybe we *were* crazy. We almost died down here, several times, learning some very hard lessons about closed environments. And our ancestors most feared that we'd forget our own history. But we haven't forgotten. We will never forget. We survived down here only because we had learned we couldn't afford overpopulation, pollution, violence, or ignorance—the latter least of all."

"Shielvelle—is that your name for your world?" Hannen asked quietly.

"Yes," Aviellian said. "It also means home. A home we had to forsake a long time ago."

A respectful silence ensued, until Sturvnen snapped all twelve of his fingers, and the guards stood up.

JOURNAL ENTRY 88

I guess we'd gotten through to them, although I'm not sure how. The Shielvellens had so many old traumas to overcome, to believe our story. Maybe our last-minute confessions helped.

I was afraid they'd take us back to our cell. Instead they moved us to adjoining, more comfortable quarters, for an ongoing quarantine the Shielvellen Council also imposed on themselves, during their ensuing debate and continuing analysis of our equipment and detritus. They even gave my meds back. And their curiosity overcame their caution before our next team came looking for us, and they asked us to lead them Outside.

How can I possibly describe such a momentous occasion? I will never forget the wonder in the Shielvellens' brown eyes as they clambered up our rope ladder to the surface and scanned their world for the first time in their lives. Or their surprise, when they scanned more of us camped near the hole. We had to rush to explain.

Finally some of the Shielvellens worked up the courage to remove their suit helmets, and after a few hesitant sniffs, they took deep breaths of fresh air. But it wasn't a perfect introduction—a few, like Aviellian, took one glimpse and rushed back below.

Even more used to walls than we were, some natives were terrified agoraphobics. Most were not—we actually had to teach fear of wild dats on later tours. But it saddened me that our best defender could not bring herself to walk freely on the surface of her world.

In fact, the whole experience was so fantastic that Kijan didn't even believe our story when we made our first class comcall. He was utterly convinced that Aerrem was trying to pull off a huge joke.

Sturvnen had to get on the line and give Kijan a stern lecture about the historic importance of this moment. How would it look if future students had to study such a facetious reaction? Only then did I realize that Sturvnen—like Aviellian—served a special role.

Both also became my friends. I didn't know why, but it fell on Aviellian's shoulders to personally apologize for the neglected maintenance that led to my fall. Classmates passed the word that she wanted to talk to me about it in her apartment one evening. Needless to say, the thought of it made me so nervous I could barely keep from trembling.

"It was an accident." I sat back on my pillow seat in a sunken area around the artificial fire in her apartment. I tried to look relaxed, although I could feel my heart beating in my throat.

"And besides, the hole saved me from a wild krel pack." FIL could no longer claim the right to name anything on this world. In bits of spare time, between tours above and below ground, we worked like nova to revise our report, including all species names.

"Did Shandy also fall?" she asked.

"No. Why?"

"I thought I saw him limping—but I know so little about all of you. Never mind. I should really ask if you have also accepted that Ked's death was an accident?"

I gazed with watering eyes into the amazingly realistic fire, as I avoided Aviellian's sorrowful face. "No," I said. "I still have to take some responsibility for that."

"Then please understand why we must also apologize to you."

Aviellian placed a tiny cube in a console, and some soft, soothing music played. And even though she couldn't step Outside, she asked me the minutest details about all the scenery and flora and fauna, and she kept me up half the night talking.

Sturvnen was the one, however, who totally scared me by sternly ordering me into his office. There he handed me a paper I couldn't read.

"What is it?" Was this a citation of some sort? Was I in trouble, once again? What did I do?

"It's semi-forged ownership papers for your krel pup. We don't possess normal papers for him, of course, so we claimed he came out of one of my brother's litters. They're about the same age, so he added your pup in for you. None of us wanted to live with Dizzy's howling, if you had to leave him behind!"

Sturvnen sat back in his office chair and chirped, the Shielvellen version of laughter.

With shaking hands I took the fancy document covered with alien words and flourishes, and I had to work at not crying. "Thanks—thank you! But how did you know I needed this?"

Sturvnen wouldn't say who told him. We spent the day telling stories about our lives in and on his world. At last he picked up another certificate, equally elaborate, and gave it to me.

"What's this?" By now my voice was hoarse.

"Official proof of ownership transfer to you, of a new young sann ready for a rider-bond, if you wish. I know we can't replace Ked, but I heard you certainly proved yourself worthy on the mounts we provided for Outside tours."

I couldn't believe their ancestors had actually driven sanns down here when they fled, but that's why there were now escaped herds of them back on the surface. The Shielvellens were serious about their animal bonds, plus they obtained milk and environmentally friendly transportation and fertilizer for their trouble. Krels were pets, but they also helped with herding.

It turned out that nearly every species the Shielvellens saved served multiple purposes, and even microbes were considered precious. We toured hospital facilities that treated microscopic life as well as plants, animals, and people. Energy, food, and atmospheric production plants also appeared inextricably intertwined. It was mind-boggling. I commed FIL professionals would learn as much as they taught here.

I'd also learned makkons were one exception to the utility rule, at least originally. "You want to know about trelks?" Nlien, Thorkiel's daughter, chirped on the hospital tour. "You must be the animal lover!"

I nodded, face reddening, and then remembered to say "Yes" aloud for my wristcom translator. I never ran out of questions about their animals, so much so that many of my other questions remained unanswered.

"Trelks were pests," Nlien said, "invasive species, not even originally from this continent—"

"So neither were you—I mean, your ancestors."

She looked surprised. "Good guess. Yes, our species radiated out from the same continent. We hate to admit it, but we believe we evolved from the same distant ancestor, and we turned into pretty awful pests ourselves."

"Some day we'll tell you what a mess we made, after radiating out from Africa."

She chirped again. "I guess we'll learn a lot from each other. The trelks also snuck into our refuge—maybe smuggled in as pets. Some people do admire them. But trelks got into our food stores early on and almost killed off our whole colony! Now we use their cells for medical research, since they are distant ancestors."

"You didn't kill them off?" Crell asked.

Nlien gave her what I now knew was a disgusted look. "Of course not. We need all the diversity we can get. Come. See what our artists care about."

She took us to their art museum, filled mostly with sculptures and portraits—of natives and animals, including trelks.

"Well, what did you expect in an underground hole?" Sheejar whispered to Crell, and I hoped none of our hosts heard that. I loved the museum, and had to be dragged away for dinner.

Best of all, Sturvnen lined me up with domestic animal specialists, so I could learn everything possible about krel and sann husbandry and medical care before I left. After all, FIL might never allow me to return. The amount of information was daunting, however, even when I called a halt to the sann data.

It wasn't soon enough to avoid learning I'd ridden Ked too young, before her joints were fully developed. But I didn't turn down a new mount out of guilt over that. I simply couldn't justify taking another animal away from its natural environment, even if I knew for sure that I could provide adequate nutrition and housing. Dizzy was already a heavy responsibility.

When our pickup signal finally came through, many of my classmates generously dived in to help me finish transcribing all the information I needed. We had to cram right through our last night on Shielvelle, after our farewell dinner with our new friends.

JOURNAL ENTRY 89

By mutual consent, the Shielvellens remained within their scan-protected refuge during our pickup. We wanted to be the first to explain the whole situation to the proper authorities, and the Shielvellens wanted us—not our rescuers—to get full credit for discovering them.

"It might help mitigate your misdeeds," Aviellian said.

"We do so hope you won't get into too much trouble," Sturvnen added.

The Shielvellens had provided us with a huge bath and clean new clothes (probably so they could tolerate our presence). But now the clothing lay hidden deep in our packs. Our class stood on a fairly level field, not far from our stubbornly immobile ship and First Lake. The blue lake sparkled heartbreakingly in the end-of-summer sunlight, and the smell of warm dirt, sann manure, and dried grass filled our nostrils one last time.

At last a warm wind ruffled our hair as a very official-looking white FIL shuttle landed before us, and the sann herd fled once more.

"Think we'll ever see them again?" Branem nodded his head in the direction of the Shielvellen refuge.

"Depends," Jael said, shaking his head.

"Well, I hope so," I said, gazing into Dizzy's soulful eyes.

"How many of you are there?" the shuttle pilot now asked over our wristcoms. Anticipating fatalities, or more than one pickup location?

"Nineteen," Aerrem lied as she glanced at Dizzy. She put a hand over her wristcom. "Go last, and have your documentation ready," she whispered to me. I fished out my ownership paper, and Aerrem and Branem hauled my pack up to the shuttle, and helped load some other packs.

I was so nervous I kept my eyes on my leashed krel, until I could enter the shuttle last. I was relieved to have an excuse not to pair up with my teammate.

Yet boarding was rather anticlimactic. We found ourselves in a combined bunkroom and small lounge, sealed off from the rest of the ship. No one said a word about Dizzy.

Terse instructions came over a wallscreen. We were told to strap our packs in the luggage racks for launch and to prepare for a paraspace transition as soon as we left orbit, for a weeklong trip.

"To where?" Kijan demanded, but the comscreen had already gone dead. So we didn't even get a farewell view of Shielvelle.

Over the next week some classmates played morose tunes on their instruments, some grimly debated our fate, and some played endless comgames, between lethargic meals and long sleep periods. I worked hard to finish my journal under Aerrem's stern scrutiny, and to make Dizzy behave in a closed environment.

I had just gotten my krel into a successful crouch over the most flexible interplanetary toilet I'd ever seen, when someone banged on the bathroom door.

"Can't it wait?"

"No!" Aerrem insisted, so I let her in. I turned back to my krel. "Good boy, Dizzy, good boy! You're doing it!"

Aerrem stood there, arms folded, until the stinky deed was done. She refused to let Dizzy jump on her afterwards—soon he'd grow too big to make that safe. But she saved her glare for me. "How long are you going to let this go on?"

"What?" My stomach dropped into vac.

"Have you considered how a broken team is going to scan, when we try to convince FIL we were simply attempting to do our very best to carry out our final exam?"

How it looked? Is that what our class leader really cared about? I wasn't surprised that Aerrem was harassing me again about Shandy, but for this? "What about Wind and Ness?"

"They've made up, at least enough to finish the exam together. What have you done? Have you finished a fair and honest story?"

"You haven't checked it out yourself?" I snapped back.

"No. I'm your friend, remember?" Aerrem's tail smacked into the bathroom wall. "But you haven't answered my question." She noticed, fuse it all.

"Well, not quite," I said. "I felt so much pain that it's hard to relive it all—" including the guilt—

"Taje, we all felt terrible!"

But you're not asking everyone to describe it, I wanted to say. For some reason I didn't. Maybe because I couldn't ever remember winning an argument with Aerrem.

"Well, you have time now," Aerrem said, "and while Shandy's napping, here's a morsel you can add to it. I shouldn't be the one to tell you this, but if Shandy won't defend himself, I will! Shandy can't read your mind—"

"But if he's a human clone of his father, with some transplanted Istrannian genes—" as he must be, to look so human, but read minds like the giant pale Istrannian spiders—

"Not even full Istrannians can read thoughts! They're empaths. Do you understand the difference any better than most FIL members?"

"So he can read my private emotions?" That didn't seem much better.

"No, it's more like he can hear them, but can't plug his ears. For some reason Shandy's added genes didn't include workable native controls, and he wasn't allowed to stay on Istrann long enough to learn control. So he experiences everyone's true feelings around him, whether he wants to or not. Haven't you wondered why he gets so sick all the time?"

"I assumed it was plague damage," I said.

"That's what his doctors want to believe. But how would you feel, not being able to block all the emotions trapped in the Center? And until Shandy started keeping his ability a secret, he faced more prejudice than you or I or Branem will ever experience—"

"And he told you all of this?" I thought I was his roomie!

"Only when he had no choice—to prove how he knew you wouldn't steal the class ship. He didn't want us to leave you behind! And he was actually terrified that he'd ended his friendship with me by telling me about himself. Fused guy."

I gulped. I didn't want to cry in front of Aerrem, so I kept my mouth shut.

"Then he found you just in time to save your life!"

"But—but why didn't he find me faster?"

"I told you, he didn't know how to control his ability. Meanwhile, you didn't have to scan how much he suffered with you! Haven't you even noticed his limp?

"Each of us tried to get Shandy to turn back at some point, he looked so terrible, but I don't think the other members of the search and rescue team tried too hard, because they understood we were looking for his teammate, and possibly his lover.

"He refused all pain meds, I suppose because he was afraid they'd cloud his mind. So I put a splint on his leg, which only helped a little. Beyond that there was nothing I could do about it."

"Pain isn't an emotion," I whispered. "How did he detect that?"

"Actually, it is. I looked it up. And, I might add, especially if it's all wrapped up in guilt." Aerrem continued to glare at me. "Shandy also kept chugging water, which never satisfied his terrible thirst. But that's also how he knew you were still alive, he knew you were in trouble, and he wouldn't let us quit.

"And when your suffering became too much for him—when he was ready to collapse and maybe even die with you—I had to get mean and push him to keep going. I think he went a bit nova, but that's when he ran off and found you. I don't know how. And he kept me from falling in with you. Doesn't any of that count for anything?"

It counted for so much I felt overwhelmed with guilt. But why was it all my fault? Roomies are supposed to talk to each other. I hadn't held anything back from Shandy. Why hadn't he talked to me? Was he that afraid of losing my friendship? I felt a pain growing so terrible that I didn't know what to say. Unfortunately, Aerrem took it the wrong way.

"Well, maybe Shandy *shouldn't* trust you!" And with that final blast, Aerrem left me alone for the rest of the trip.

JOURNAL ENTRY 90

Faces turned pale as the shuttle finally docked. Dojan and Kijan looked the most embarrassed, in their patchwork clothes, although I thought they should feel proud.

"I'll bet this is an Arrainius orbital station," Piel said, his antennae shivering uncontrollably.

"With FIL police on the other side of our docking hatch," Jael muttered.

But it was several FIL personnel in blue ship uniforms who quietly greeted us on the other side and led us, once more gaping and nearly tripping over our own boots, through a vast shuttle and probe hangar to a large translift. I had to keep a firm grip on curious Dizzy's rope leash.

"Where are we?" Taemar bravely asked in the lift.

"Aboard FIL SEAR Ship *Onnarius*. We're taking you to quarters reserved for you on Level Five."

"Ah, we're moving up in life!" Branem joked, but no one laughed. Amazingly, we were assigned tiny individual cabins with doors lining one corridor of Level Five. The doorcoms displayed our names, so they obviously knew who we were. Our guides told us to wait in our rooms for further instructions, after a crew-member recorded who needed medical appointments. So the horrid suspense dragged on.

Dojan and Kijan dumped my pack inside my door, and then I was left alone with Dizzy. I dropped down on my bunk, loosened my brace, and turned up my pain meds, while my pup flopped down beside me.

So where would this adventure end? Back at the Center? In a cell? Fine. But this time I decided I would not let anyone make me feel guilty about what I'd done, no matter what Center or FIL authorities believed or where they stuck me.

They could lock me up and delete the door release code. I'd not only made significant contributions to a real ecology report; I'd also helped return the surface of a living world to its people!

I should feel proud, thrilled, and excited. I even had partners in crime to share the blame and help defend me this time, in a battle that was truly worth fighting. That is, if Aerrem didn't convince the whole class to turn against me again, because of my failed team.

But I knew something more had gone wrong, beyond my friendship with Shandy. I still didn't feel like a real ecologist. In fact, I felt like a fake.

I could say I'd learned about the full importance of ecology. When underground tour guides—mostly sons and daughters of Council members—had asked me about the surface of their world, I'd merely urged them to explore it for themselves as soon as possible.

They'd never heard the wind pouring through grass and trees. They'd never seen sunlight glittering on a lake, and they'd never smelled fields of dry grass or ocean breakers on wet sand. They'd never even seen real stars at night, and they'd certainly never thundered down a beach or across a meadow on the willing back of one of their own sanns. And when they did make it Outside, they scanned all the miracles, while I commed all the problems and hard work ahead of them.

Obviously, all of that mattered to me. But did I want to join in that hard work? Not if the wild krels had to be eliminated. I should hate them for what they'd done to Ked, but it was natural, even desperate behavior. Especially after adopting Dizzy, extermination wasn't a solution I wanted to contemplate.

Clearly, I cared too much about individual animals, and someday that would zap me, if I kept on this vector. But what could I do instead, if I was ever given my freedom?

Well, I certainly never wanted to feel as helpless as I had with Ked—that memory festered inside me. If only I'd known sooner about the hospital buried under our boots!

And then the answer for my future seemed obvious.

I tightened my brace again, gave Dizzy a fond pat on his head, and got up to sit at my room's little deskcom.

JOURNAL ENTRY 91

After an hour of research I returned to my bunk, devastated. I'd discovered that everything I'd done mattered. Everything!

I cried. I needed friends to talk to, and I had no one. Dizzy tried to comfort me, licking up my tears with his peach-colored tongue, but it wasn't enough.

I fished in my pack, and pulled out my journal, which was close to finished. I reviewed all the good parts, where friends had helped me. Every time I'd tried to launch alone, I realized, my plans had backfired—those were the parts I didn't want to relive.

Along the way I discovered Aerrem was right. Shandy had made plenty of mistakes a real mind reader would have avoided. If I hadn't learned his secret, I'd still believe he simply possessed a powerful intuition, and was an amazingly sensitive friend.

I remembered Shandy's tender bond with Sheefharn—an Istrannian bird that may have been in tune with his moods—and I sniffled. Shandy had to risk leaving her behind in stasis to come with us to

Shielvelle, and he'd done it even though he suspected a trap.

So who didn't have secrets they didn't want to reveal? Was I really so different? What would I have done in Shandy's place, after failing with a series of roommates, and receiving one last chance—with a roomie who craved privacy most of all?

And then he'd had to risk his secret with Aerrem, to save my reputation—and then with me, to save my life. Great Universe, I owed him an apology, and more—words of gratitude and sympathy. I had to talk with him in person—was I allowed to leave my room? I'd been told to wait here. What did that really mean?

What did it matter? Dizzy didn't like being left behind, but no one scanned my struggle to get my door to close without catching his muzzle in it. The corridor was empty. I limped from door to door until I found Shandy's. I opened my mouth to announce myself.

But I thought about all the awful, mean emotions I'd spewed at him and suddenly lost all my courage. What must he think of me now? How could I possibly apologize for what I'd done—for what I'd felt?

My face burned and I fled back to my room, while I wondered if he could feel this too. I uselessly hoped not.

My deskcom interrupted my Guilt Party with a critical message regarding a medical appointment, and very soon I had another challenging decision to make.

JOURNAL ENTRY 92

A crewmember buzzed my door early the next morning. "Please come with me."

"What for?"

"It's time for your interview. Bring your pet too."

I'm not a morning person, and I was glad I hadn't eaten breakfast. After a long debate with myself, I had dressed in clean new Shielvellen clothes, forsaking my lake-washed, stained and torn camping clothes. It was time for the truth, and thank the Universe my wait was over, after a long restless night filled with ominous dreams.

I was led along the corridor, where we bumped into Sheejar and Crell, returning to their rooms. Crell wiped a tear from her eye and Shee gave me an angry look. "They're sending us back to the Center. We're not good enough for them. Don't expect any mercy."

I nearly puked as we headed on around a corner to a small office. It felt like another trap. I took a deep breath as the door slid open for me. I stepped inside and confronted Drehx Tarnek.

I crash-landed into the one expensive vari-seat parked in front of his desk. I felt the seat adjust to me, while Dizzy jumped up into my lap and settled in. I let him get away with it, although he barely fit now.

My stomach churned, and I swallowed with difficulty. We really must be in deep trouble, for FIL to go to the trouble to arrange this meeting, wherever we were now in FIL space!

"Welcome back, Taje." Tarnek held out his hand.

"What?"

"Welcome back from your final exam." He was actually smiling! I felt a great weight launch from my shoulders. Nevertheless, my jaw hung vac-headedly open as I shook hands with him. "So it was a real test?"

"How does your leg feel?"

"Like—it was very real."

"I'm sorry it went that far. Your class took S.O.S. restrictions much too seriously—we'll have to work on avoiding that problem in the future. But I am extremely proud that every one of you had the courage to go, despite all the challenges we launched at you."

"What happens if a student decides it's not right to leave?" I thought about Jael, and how close he'd come to staying behind out of good conscience.

"Such students tend to make very good eco-lawyers and administrators—"

"So you have this all commed out for everyone?" I suddenly felt like a pawn, in a game I didn't even want to play anymore.

"Tell me, Taje, what would you have done with all your training, if we hadn't offered you an official version of running away?"

I fell silent.

"I think we have you figured out, quite well. We simply gave you a chance to prove yourselves, while more safely satisfying a dangerous impulse which seems to plague our most intelligent and independent Center students."

Did he actually think he could win me over with flattery? "It wasn't safe. I almost died."

"I know—I know. I've already spoken with some of your classmates, and started reading your class report—which, by the way, is the longest and most stunning report in the history of our program. I also heard you recorded a journal. May we see it? It might help us improve this program—"

"No. I'm sorry," I said as I saw a hint of disappointment flash across his face.

"So who did you write it for?" he asked, now looking suspicious. But I also had no intention of releasing it to the Center com system anymore. It contained too many secrets I had no business or desire to tell anyone.

"I wrote it for myself," I said now, quite honestly. And it had taught me what I needed to know. "You'll simply have to ask us your questions."

I couldn't possibly edit down my journal to a safe version quickly enough for his eyes at this point, so I asked my own question. "Why did you make this test more risky than it had to be?"

"You mean the limited food, and the ship locking down?"

"Yeah, and the long wait for pickup."

"We did want you to face some realistic consequences for your actions. The food shortage was also a test of your skills. What if you get left on a planet for an eco-survey, and your pickup doesn't manage to return on time?"

"And what if it's a biochemically incompatible world?" I said.

"You'd still have to forage, and feed what you found into a food synthesizer. You still have more to learn.

"If you did go ahead with your final, and found food foraging too difficult, you still had the option of sending an urgent S.O.S. So no one would have starved. As for the ship lock-down, we didn't want anyone deciding to leave the planet for a solo mission."

My face heated up while he continued. "The long pickup was simply so I could be here for you. But we also have satellite monitors for rapid S.O.S. signal relays, and FIL teams studying other Taron sectors who could respond quickly. Why didn't your class request urgent help, a lot sooner?"

I shrugged. "You didn't tell us about any of that. We thought we were all alone." And when had anyone at the Center ever taught us that asking for help was useful? We'd learned instead to rely on each other.

"I remember how grueling and scary my final was." Tarnek shook his head. "But I didn't have to face a broken leg and dehydration in a scan-protected tunnel, or a First Contact with potentially hostile natives!

"Your stubbornness gets you into more trouble, Taje, but it also sees you through it!"

I couldn't help smiling a bit now, but I didn't let him distract me from the most important question. "So will FIL help the Shielvellens?"

"Of course. And no doubt they'll help us too."

"You didn't know about them before this?" As soon as that question launched from my mouth, I knew it was nova.

"No. We'd scanned ruins—and deliberately gave you a supposedly empty sector to make your exam more challenging. But it turns out the joke was on us, for never detecting the survivors. Too bad, though—it was such a great test planet!"

"Our first report didn't even consider the possibility that we had observed recovering environments, instead of failing ones," I had to admit. "We found the right answer by accident—my accident."

"You've only had one year of training. Actually the only serious error your class made was to try to torch your way through a door, without any idea of what existed on the other side.

"You risked damaging or destroying antiquities, your own injury or deaths, or even interspecies violence. Nevertheless, that action will probably earn you FIL medals, for recruiting valuable new FIL members."

"So most of us passed?"

"Well, that's actually what I'm here to decide—"

"How many of us have you talked to already?"

"A few. You probably crossed paths with Sheejar and Crell, I'm sorry to say. But I've also spoken with your class T.A., and your class leader—I think Aerrem was an outstanding choice, by the way—"

I could tell he was trying to distract me. "Did our T.A. pass?" I asked point-blank.

"I think the real question we're supposed to answer here is whether you passed."

JOURNAL ENTRY 93

My face fried as I gazed down at Dizzy, and tickled the dark tufts of hair growing from the tips of his ears. He twitched them, but remained asleep. He'd spent a rough but loyal night on my bunk while I'd tossed and turned.

"I thought I was going to have to flunk you," Tarnek shook his head again, "when I first heard about your feral pet. But it's one thing to attempt to tame a wild creature. It's quite another to accept a domesticated animal as a gift of gratitude from the natives."

Someone had obviously lied for me, and for Branem. "I actually made pets of two Shielvellen species, before I knew either was originally domesticated," I confessed, also lying for Branem, although the truth might slip out from someone.

"The other one was my sann. I orphaned her when I landed the ship too close to her herd. I rode her too early, and later I rode her too hard, so she couldn't fight off a pack of wild krels. She died on Shielvelle, and it was my fault."

Tarnek scanned confused. He frowned as he leaned back in his seat. "Do I have this right? Are you actually arguing that I should flunk you?"

I blinked, and suddenly fought back tears. "You should, but I'm telling you all this so you'll understand why I need good grades—actually, top grades—and totally smooth recommendations. Or I'll never be able to make up for what I did to Ked." I couldn't even look Tarnek in the eyes anymore.

"What on *Onnarius* are you talking about?"

"I'm not a planetary ecologist, and I never will be! I need to go to interplanetary veterinary school."

"Oh, that's all!"

I thought he was being sarcastic, but when I wiped my eyes, I caught a rueful smile on his tired face.

"You realize any interplanetary medical program will make what you've just survived seem like a vacation?" he said.

"So you're not mad at me?"

"Why should I be? You might remember our very first day of class, when I made a serious promise. If our program doesn't prove right for you, you can always request a transfer. And I still stand by that. It's your life—"

"But I'd be going over to the Other Side!"

"What in this galaxy are you babbling about now?"

"I'd be learning how to help the unfit to survive!"

"Oh!" Tarnek laughed. "Survival of the fittest is a law of nature, not of people. And try becoming a veterinarian without caring about environments! Animals need healthy ecosystems as much as we do. You'll never unlearn the lessons you've struggled so hard to master over the last year, and that's good enough for me."

"So, uh, you don't have to flunk me?"

"For learning something vitally important about yourself, and acknowledging what you did, instead of going along with a perfect cover-up? You've managed a lot of growing up, Taje. I don't flunk students for that."

"Then—you'll help me?"

"I can definitely help you get into a prevet program. The rest is up to you. It's highly competitive—you'll still have to prove yourself to others—but you're stubborn and smart enough to stand a chance. Do you want to enter the onboard program, or return to Arrainius for this?"

"Where will my classmates go?"

"Those who pass and want to continue their ecology training will do so aboard *Onnarius*—"

"I want to stay here with my friends. There are vets onboard?"

"Oh yes. This ship circulates far from the center of FIL, and meanwhile has to act as a decent home for hundreds of personnel. For many people, that means keeping healthy pets. There are also interplanetary data exchanges, and even planetary house calls in some cases—but you'll see. Meanwhile, have you decided what you're going to do about your knee?"

"The doctor is pushing for rejuve, but says we could try surgery with some implants first. I'll probably choose the latter. Re-growing my leg from scratch doesn't appeal very much to me." And would take too long. I'd already spent a whole year on the wrong career.

"Very well. We'll fill out an *Onnarius* prevet program application before you go to surgery, so you'll be ready for transfer after physical rehab." Tarnek stood up, signaling he was done. But I wasn't finished.

JOURNAL ENTRY 94

I stayed docked in my seat. "Did Aerrem also pass?" I tried an easier question first.

"You know that's private information," he said, but he couldn't help smiling. "You'll have to ask her that yourself."

"Well, how about Shandy?" I plunged on. "He was my teammate on Shielvelle, so if I passed, I can assume he did too, right?"

"Shanden Fehrokc's case is complex, and our first interview was very preliminary—"

My stomach churned again, but I discovered I wasn't surprised. "What's so complicated about it? Shandy decided to go on the final, he contributed as much data as anyone else, plus he saved my life, and he helped with a very touchy First Contact!"

"Okay, Taje, I shouldn't ask you this. But we're a long way from Center privacy rules, and I think you have a right to know. Has Shanden ever told you he's a telepath—"

"No—"

"I suspected as much. He's kept his abilities a secret from fellow Center residents for a long time now. But we were warned, and we could never tell when he was cheating—"

"You didn't let me finish," I said. "I know he's an empath, not a telepath, and now I'm wondering if you understand the difference any better than I did! Empaths can't read thoughts, and he never cheated on anything!"

Tarnek looked taken aback, and he sunk back down in his seat. He shook his head. "It doesn't matter. Fehrokc also runs serious health risks, any time he lacks immediate access to civilized health care—"

"And shouldn't that be his decision, his risk to take?" And how much of his so-called illness was simply a very human reaction to foul emotions like this? Funny how much better he usually seemed, away from crowded civilizations!

"His class participation on Taron was also apparently substandard," Tarnek insisted. "And Fehrokc admitted that in the end, his team failed—"

"You mean our team! It takes two to crash a team! Two! And what do you call being T.A. for the whole class—isn't that considered rather generous participation?"

"Taje, I realize you've endured a tremendous amount of stress, and I'm willing to make some allowances. But I think we should end this conversation right now—"

"But why did you ever let Shandy into the class, if you really suspected he was cheating?" I demanded. Dizzy woke up now, and his ears stood erect. He didn't have to read my mind to know how upset I was!

"Were you afraid if you didn't let Shandy in, he'd expose all your secrets?" I said. "And then did you try to make it as miserable as possible for him, isolating him as our T.A., to drive him back out?

"You even told everyone in the class that he's from Istrann, during our translator lesson—doesn't that break Center privacy rules? Great Galaxy!" I swore as a guilty look zapped across Tarnek's face. Now I understood. He'd said "Unless your brain works very differently from the rest of us, a translator won't broadcast your private thoughts."

I glared at Tarnek. "Did you set up that surprise translator lesson to try to catch Shandy off-guard and unprepared, so you could force him to reveal himself to everyone? And when that failed, maybe you still hoped we'd at least leave him behind for the final—"

"It's really none of your concern, Tajen, but Fehrokc has always struggled with social isolation issues—"

"What a surprise!" I sneered, thinking about my own actions as much as Tarnek's. But as our teacher, Tarnek was supposed to set a better example! Now I had to wonder if being even more pale than me had also counted against Shandy.

"What will you do," I said, "when real, fully qualified telepaths apply for your program? Block their entrance, so you'll never have to worry about cheating? Instead of realizing they might actually contribute important skills, like locating a lost teammate, or helping with a difficult First Contact?"

"We don't know," Tarnek admitted. "This is not a simple subject, Tajen, and Fehrokc was the first such challenging case we'd ever had to deal with. We haven't got a policy fully worked out for it yet—"

"A policy? Is that what you call this bigotry? Well, if you're going to flunk Shandy, you'd better flunk me too—and throw me back into a cell—for failing to support my teammate!"

JOURNAL ENTRY 95

Tarnek stood up again, shaking with rage. I stood up too, accidentally dumping my pup on the floor. Dizzy gave me a shocked look, turned his head, and growled at my teacher.

"You realize, if I flunk you, you'll never get into any veterinary school!" Tarnek glared at me.

I was surprised to see I'd grown taller than him. When had that happened? But I'd fused it now, calling Tarnek a bigot—a terrible FIL insult. Well, this was the sort of prejudice Shandy had likely faced ever since he was shipped off Istrann. No wonder he wanted to go back!

Maybe if we both flunked out, we could at least return to living together in the Center. After all, whom did I call for, when I was dying? Oh, Shandy, I wish I had you back at my side! Where will you end up, if no one cares about you? And why did I throw your friendship into vac?

"Are you really willing to sacrifice your whole education—" Tarnek began to warn me.

"For an empath who was willing to quit the class for me?" I said. "You don't know what you're jettisoning—"

"For the last time, Jesmuhr, I am asking you to leave this office right now, before we both regret the consequences!"

That's when the door slid open. For a micro I thought Tarnek had triggered it, in a totally unsubtle hint. But he looked annoyed when he scanned it, and I turned around. Shandy, Aerrem, and Branem stood in the doorway.

"What are you doing to my teammate?" Shandy stepped forward, pale, shaking, and tearful. "You can do whatever you want with me, but none of it was her fault—"

"Shandy warned us that you were in trouble again and needed our help." Aerrem faced me with raised eyebrows.

"It's not me! Tarnek wants to flunk Shandy, and I told him if he did that, he'd have to flunk me too!"

"You'll have to flunk me also." Aerrem faced our teacher.

"And me!" Branem folded his arms.

"And at least half the class, once I tell them about this," Aerrem said in her deadliest tone ever, her tail bristling.

Shandy stared in shock at all of us, which broke my heart. He turned to Tarnek. "No, don't listen to them—this is all my fault!" he said, zapping me to the core.

"Don't be ridiculous!" Aerrem roared at Shandy.

"You asked for our help," Branem said. "It doesn't matter whose fault it is, or why you need us. We've learned to stand together, or we won't stand at all!"

Now Tarnek stared at us. "I'm not going to flunk half of this class. You're already famous! Your report exceeded all expectations, and you've recruited excellent new FIL members!"

"Okay, we'll drop out." Aerrem folded her arms along with Branem, I joined them, and we all firmly nodded our heads.

"We were your first teaching assignment," Aerrem angrily reminded Tarnek. "I bet this was just as much a test for you as it was for us. If you fuse it, what happens to your career?"

I remembered now, how Aerrem had said "When has the class ever not been a test?" when we faced the possible complications of our final. Maybe it applied to Tarnek too!

Tarnek put his head in his hands. "I can't—I can't have half of you quitting! You have no idea what pressure I've been under, although I suppose that's no excuse. You must understand, Shanden, I was ordered to put you through tests even I considered unfair. And I was the one who insisted you should have at least one friend recruited for the class, before we let you in!"

"Shandy did as well as any of us," Branem said. "After reviewing all our accomplishments on Shielvelle, I don't see how you could possibly flunk him."

"Don't forget that as our T.A., Shandy also had to learn everything we did, faster and better, so he could help all of us," Aerrem said. "Everyone in the class accepted him. Why can't you?"

Shandy and I said nothing. Instead we stood gazing steadily back at our teacher as we both sniffled and wiped our faces with our hands. Dizzy settled into a forlorn heap on my feet.

Tarnek scanned the blank comscreen on his desk. Shandy suddenly looked startled, and Tarnek sighed. "Yes," he said softly, "I actually envy this mysteriously unbreakable bond the four of you share, which has brought each of you so far."

Tarnek finally looked up at Shandy. "If I oppose my colleagues on this and pass you, Fehrokc, I don't want to hear about you quitting later on or failing."

"I won't," Shandy said, his hands now in tense fists at his sides, and there was a tone of anger and confidence in his voice that I had never heard before. I quit holding my breath.

"I've made some mistakes," Tarnek confessed. "Although I refuse to take all the blame. Oh well, it's over. You—all four of you—have your answers and nothing further to worry about, except more homework than ever.

"I'd wish you all luck, but I think I should reserve that for your future teachers. I'd also like to say it's been a real pleasure, serving as your primary instructor over the last year—"

"But it wouldn't be entirely true," I said ruefully.

"Oh yes, such a pleasure!" Branem mockingly agreed.

"But thanks anyway!" we all chorused as we escaped into the hallway. As soon as the office door slid shut we all screamed aloud our relief, although Tarnek must have heard us. We put our arms on each other's shoulders in one long row as we strode forward in search of a translift, Dizzy bouncing on ahead.

"There's got to be a snack bar somewhere aboard this tub where we can properly celebrate!" Aerrem said. She and Branem raced ahead to ask the next wall-com for a map.

"It may be a bit early for lunch, but I say a pan-galactic pizza is definitely in order!" Branem said, and he, Aerrem, and Dizzy took off again. "Space, it's been so long since I've eaten a truly civilized feast!"

"With tofu!" I exchanged fond looks with Shandy. "And don't forget my krazzle claws!"

"Ugh! How could we?" Aerrem said, and then she noticed how far Shandy and I had fallen behind. She called to Dizzy and slowed Branem down so we could catch up with them. Instead we halted in our tracks and scanned each other's faces.

"You called for me again, Taje!" Shandy said softly, for my ears only.

"And you came for me again, Shandy!" I said, in wonder, just to him.

We hugged each other for the first time in our lives. Then we marched arm-in-arm after Aerrem, Branem, and Dizzy, in search of our victory feast.

If you liked this book, tell your friends!
It can be ordered online,
Make it a gift! Liz

ACKNOWLEDGEMENTS

First, I must thank my Mom for the early access she gave me to the library she collected, earning her master's degree in English at Stanford University. My Dad's Danish immigrant father, who earned his doctorate and became an English professor, probably also contributed to my writing genes.

I thank my private art teacher, Mrs. Sherman, and many teachers and professors at Terman Junior High, Henry M. Gunn High School, and U.C. Davis for my art and science education.

Andre Norton's *Catseye* set me on this path, and Alexei Panshin's *Rite of Passage*, introduced to me by my wonderful high school English teacher, Mr.Warner, opened my eyes further. Tangerine Dream provided my early musical sustenance, and Lennon-McCarthy's "Paperback Writer" was my theme song.

I must also thank Tom-Who-Waits-By-The-Door for his unwavering support, and for the title of this novel; and Andre Norton, for her support and advice so late in her life. I will always miss both of you.

I give many thanks to Brian J. Boudler, Erika Milo, Kelsey Shapira, and Jackie Melvin for their extensive editorial assistance. Any errors are my responsibility.

I also wish to thank Kathy Baron for her remarkable cover layout, and Terry Whittaker for his generosity. So many people helped this dream come alive. Thank you, everyone!

ABOUT THE AUTHOR

Liz J. Andersen grew up in Silicon Valley (Palo Alto, California), and wrote the first draft of this novel when she was about the same age as her main characters. Liz has red hair like Taje, but Liz is *not* Taje. The author just became tired of too many red-haired villains, and a scarcity of red-haired heroes.

In real life, a serious lack of mentors undoubtedly led to this book, and a solution aimed at the author and other kids floundering on their own. However, once done, Liz realized she needed more science for an accurate SF novel.

So she set her manuscript aside to earn a B.S. in Animal Physiology with Highest Honors at U.C. Davis, which required physics, chemistry, and calculus, as well as numerous physiology classes. It also allowed broad electives such as ecology, astronomy, and art. She proceeded from there immediately into veterinary school, and also earned her D.V.M. degree at U.C. Davis.

During summer breaks Liz backpacked, primarily in the Sierra Nevada with her friend Carla Salido, where they enjoyed their own adventures. Liz has also defied death at least four times to bring you this novel, so it must be important.

She now lives in Eugene, Oregon, with her husband, Brian, and has published several short stories about Dr. Tajen Jesmuhr in *Analog Science Fiction and Fact* magazine. Find her website LizJAndersen.com, and her husband's music at labbwerk.bandcamp.com.